KU-370-981

MONSTER FROM THE DEEP!

Huge yellow eyes loomed quickly before him. He glimpsed a fast onrushing head, dark green and covered with scales, mouth open and filled with thin blade-like teeth as long as swords.

He thrust down hard with his spear. Its sharp bronze tip struck the creature's scales and thick skin midway between the eyes—then shattered. He didn't let up, but ground down with all his strength. A sharp piece of the metal, still attached, slid along the scales and then under one.

This is my chance! he thought. He twisted the spear with both hands, driving it farther under that scale and into the monster's flesh . . .

ALSO BY JOHN GREGORY BETANCOURT

The Wrath of Poseidon
The Vengeance of Hera

THE
GATES
OF
HADES

John Gregory Betancourt

TOR®
fantasy

A TOM DOHERTY ASSOCIATES BOOK
NEW YORK

NOTE: If you purchased this book without a cover you should be aware that this book is stolen property. It was reported as "unsold and destroyed" to the publisher, and neither the author nor the publisher has received any payment for this "stripped book."

This is a work of fiction. All the characters and events portrayed in this book are either products of the author's imagination or are used fictitiously.

THE GATES OF HADES

Copyright © 2001 by John Gregory Betancourt

All rights reserved, including the right to reproduce this book, or portions thereof, in any form.

A Tor Book
Published by Tom Doherty Associates, LLC
175 Fifth Avenue
New York, NY 10010

www.tor.com

Tor® is a registered trademark of Tom Doherty Associates, LLC.

ISBN: 0-812-53912-5

First edition: March 2001

Printed in the United States of America

0   9   8   7   6   5   4   3   2   1

For my editor, Greg Cox,
without whose faith and patience
these books would not have been possible.

CHAPTER ONE

The drumbeat paused, and Hercules paused with it, holding his oar just above the water. Had something happened? He half turned on the rower's bench, craning his neck to see Jason and Theseus in the *Argo*'s bow. Both men were staring intently across the low waves, but neither seemed particularly alarmed. Another ship? Or a town? Hercules couldn't tell from where he sat.

On the benches around him, men began to sigh and lean back, enjoying the break. Even Hercules had to admit it felt good to stop and catch his breath. He might be stronger than any ten mortal men, but the constant rowing made even his powerful shoulders ache.

He brushed sweat from his forehead with the tail of the lion skin he wore. Over the last week, as their ship approached the Black Sea, the weather had gradually turned against them. First a hot, sticky wind began to gust the wrong way, and then slate-colored skies slowly darkened, threatening rain. He tilted his head and studied the swollen clouds far above. Had Jason felt the first raindrop? If so, the *Argo* would have to take shelter in a cove or inlet until the storm passed. They might have the greatest ship ever built, but it was always wise to protect her from the sea's fury. This far from home, it would be difficult if not impossible to repair her if she crashed upon rocks.

"I wish the wind would turn in our favor again," Atalanta said loudly from behind Hercules. "I signed on to help win the Golden Fleece, not row a ship!"

Hercules laughed as he glanced over his shoulder at her. "First we have to get *to* the Golden Fleece," he said. "You know how impatient Jason can be. Why wait for favorable winds when he has fifty followers willing to row?"

"Make that forty-nine!" Atalanta pulled a sour face, pushing a strand of limp black hair out of her eyes. "I'll row, but not willingly!"

Hercules laughed again. She had pitched in with the rest of the Argonauts when the winds turned the day before yesterday, and they had spent the last two days rowing the *Argo* toward the Black Sea. The work had taken its toll on her, too, Hercules saw; the legendary female athlete looked exhausted. For that matter, almost everybody around them looked exhausted. He probably would have felt the same way, he supposed, had he been a mortal instead of a demigod. But with Zeus as his father, he could row all day and only begin to feel the strain.

"Ship oars!" Jason called from the bow. "Rest for five minutes!"

Powerful muscles rippling beneath his lion skin, Hercules slid his oar up onto the *Argo*'s deck, then stood and began to twist left and right, stretching the kinks from his muscles. Around him, the other Argonauts did the same. He heard half a dozen quiet discussions starting, mostly speculation as to why Jason had called a halt. Nobody seemed to have any idea what their leader had in mind.

"Something must have happened," Atalanta said softly. Hercules found her peering toward Jason. "We still have plenty of daylight . . . and it's far too soon to take a break. Not that I'm complaining, of course!"

"They must have seen something," Hercules said. "Look how they're staring ahead."

"Pirates? Or maybe some kind of sea serpent?" Atalanta suggested hopefully.

Hercules laughed. Atalanta had an obsession with killing monsters—not that he objected; in this part of the world, you could still find many savage creatures.

He said, "If it's a monster, Jason doesn't seem very concerned. You know how careful he is—he would raise an alarm at the first sign of danger."

Atalanta sighed. "I suppose. It's probably nothing."

"Probably."

And yet Hercules wondered. He knew their leader's greatest fear involved damage to the *Argo*. Sometimes it seemed as though Jason cared more for his ship than his crew, but Hercules knew better. Jason had quite a lot of problems back home in Thessaly . . . most of all his uncle, who had refused to yield the throne to its rightful heir, Prince Jason. A civil war would have been devastating to the kingdom, so Jason had set out to find the Golden Fleece. Winning it would prove him a champion worthy of his throne, and then his uncle would have to step aside. Jason's obsession with the Golden Fleece drove him ever onward, sometimes almost recklessly.

Atalanta was nodding. "True," she said, "he *would* call us if he saw danger. After all, he's got the greatest heroes of Greece on board. He would have to be crazy not to ask for advice in dealing with *any* monster."

"And Jason isn't crazy."

Atalanta frowned. "Perhaps it's a whale," she said, "or sharks."

"There's only one way to find out. I'll ask!" Hercules rose and strode briskly toward the front of the ship. Behind him, he heard quick, light footsteps following, and he had to smile to himself. Atalanta refused to be left out of any adventure, no matter how exhausted she might feel.

He joined Jason and Theseus in the *Argo*'s bow. From here, he could see a small island just ahead. Both men seemed to be watching it intently.

Hercules stared at it silently for a moment, then frowned. What had they seen? Savages? He saw no sign of boats or rafts . . . and no smoke from cooking fires, for that matter. A monster? He saw no sign of one. Had Jason and Theseus spotted something else?

Then he felt a drop of water hit his arm and he blinked. Rain—that had to be it. Jason was searching for a place to put ashore to wait out the storm.

"We passed a cove about twenty minutes ago," Hercules said. "Shall we head back?"

"Shh! Wait!" Jason said, holding up one hand. "Watch the channel!"

Hercules heard Theseus counting under his breath: ". . . three . . . four . . ."

Squinting, Hercules studied the narrow stretch of water between the island and the coast. What had they seen? This shore offered rocky beaches fronting a lush green tangle of trees and underbrush. He had assumed they would sail through the channel to save time.

Theseus continued to count: ". . . five . . . six . . . seven—"

And on seven, in the exact center of the channel, a plume of water shot twenty yards into the air, hung for a moment, then fell back with a tremendous splash.

Hercules blinked. "What is it?" he asked. Some natural phenomenon? Or had a god or a monster of some kind caused it?

"I don't know. I've never seen anything like it before," Jason said.

"Nor have I," Theseus added. "Whales and dolphins breathe that way, but it would take a hundred of them to make a waterspout that big."

"It's a monster," Hercules said. He had a sudden premonition of danger from ahead and felt a prickle of excitement. "It has to be!"

"Don't get any ideas about fighting it," Jason said with a sharp warning glance. "We're not here to kill monsters. We're out to win the Golden Fleece."

"I know that," Hercules said. He felt a little hurt by Jason's tone, but shrugged it off. After all, Jason had his own problems. Since winning the Golden Fleece might well solve them, Hercules understood the rush to get on with it.

Quickly, Theseus said, "Hercules doesn't go around slaughtering monsters for the pleasure of it, but to help people. He refuses to let a single injustice go unpunished."

Jason sighed, then gave an apologetic nod. "I know. It's just that we keep getting sidetracked! We've taken an extra two months to get this far!"

"You need to relax more," Hercules said. "The Golden Fleece isn't going anywhere. You'll live longer if you enjoy yourself. After all, this is supposed to be an adventure, and adventures are supposed to be fun!"

A new water plume erupted before them. Like the previous one, it fell back into the sea with a tremendous splash. Hercules stared. Had it moved? Wasn't it closer to the *Argo* than the last time?

Theseus began to count again. "One . . . two . . ."

"Besides, we don't even know it's a monster yet," Hercules said. "Maybe it's something else."

"Poseidon?" Atalanta asked. "Could it be your uncle, Hercules?"

Hercules hesitated. "I don't *think* so."

"Whatever it is, we won't provoke it," Jason announced. He turned to the rowers. "Oars to the water, Argonauts! Prepare to turn the ship! We'll go around the island!"

There were a few grumbles of disappointment—it would add several hours to the day's rowing, Hercules realized—but everyone seemed resigned to the task. They had all sworn to follow Jason, after all, and follow him they would . . . right around the island, if that's what he wanted. Besides, Hercules told himself, as long as the monster left them alone, they had no quarrel with it.

Theseus said, ". . . five . . . six—"

This time, the spout came a second earlier.

Hercules hesitated, staring out across the waves. Clearly the creature was heading toward them. Should he return to his bench to help the others row? Or should he prepare for a fight?

"I don't think we will have a chance to go around the island," Theseus said to Jason.

"What!" Jason said. "Why?"

"It's heading this way faster than we can row!"

Biting his lip in frustration, Jason stared out across the water. His knuckles grew white, Hercules noticed, from the strength of his grip on the railing. What looked to Hercules like an expression of supreme annoyance crossed Jason's face.

In happier circumstances, Hercules might have

laughed. Instead, he felt the hairs on the back of his neck start to prickle in alarm once more. When monsters approached, he knew from long years of experience, men often died.

Theseus began counting again: "One . . . two . . ."

Leaning on the forward railing, Hercules stared down at the water. Although still two hundred yards away, he glimpsed something like a shadow beneath the waves, something huge and dark that sent a sudden shiver through him. This was no mortal creature, he realized, but a monster from the earliest days of the world, when the Titans had ruled. You could still find such things in remote corners of the world . . . like this one.

"What *is* it?" Jason whispered beside him. "What does it *want*?"

Theseus said urgently, "Give the order to break out weapons, Jason. We're going to have to fight!"

"If we must . . ." Jason muttered. He turned to the crew again, cupped his hands to his mouth, and called, "Break out swords and spears! Prepare to defend the ship from a sea monster!"

Half a dozen men scurried to open the deck's main hatch. Orestes and Philoran disappeared into the hold for a moment, then began handing up weapons—spears, swords, bows and arrows. Spears would probably be best, Hercules thought . . . although edged weapons like swords might prove more useful if the creature had tentacles like a giant squid or octopus.

Another plume of water rose and fell only thirty yards ahead now. A cold, salty spray settled over Hercules, and he wiped his face dry on one of his lion skin's paws.

"There's its head!" Atalanta cried, pointing.

Hercules leaned forward, peering deep into the water. At the front of that inky patch of darkness he spotted a pair of yellow disks, glowing faintly with a cold, weirdly flickering light . . . *eyes*. Hercules felt an unpleasant prickling along the back of his neck. This was no mere beast, something told him, but a creature with a cunning and deadly intelligence.

"Look at the size of that thing," Atalanta whispered. "It's larger than a whale."

Hercules nodded. "Ten times larger than any whale I've ever seen," he said.

Twenty yards out, the eyes veered to the left, the creature circling the *Argo*. Hercules turned slowly, following its course. If only it would surface, he thought. Suddenly he wanted a closer look at it. Was it more fish or squid? Or something else entirely? *At least it seems slow-moving*, he thought. It seemed to be circling them at an almost leisurely pace, as though it had all the time in the world.

Armed men began crowding up against the port railing, trying to see the monster. When it sent another gush of water into the air, everyone began shouting eagerly, pointing and waving their weapons. Several men began calling, "Here, monster! Here, monster!" and whistling as though for a dog.

"Just what we need!" Jason said with snort. "Another epic battle!"

Atalanta shot him a mischievous look. "You *did* want songs sung of your voyage, didn't you? Well, we could use a few more epic battles!"

Hercules tried to hide his own smile. Sometimes Jason didn't have much of a sense of humor. "At least it keeps the voyage from getting dull," Hercules added. "I certainly needed a break from all that rowing."

"I would have rather put ashore early," Jason grumbled. "If I wanted epic battles, I would have fought my uncle for Thessaly's throne. Besides, I think we've already had more than enough excitement for one voyage."

Hercules knew Jason had a point. Every time they set

sail for the Kingdom of Colchis and the Golden Fleece, something seemed to get in the way. First they had found bandits and a sea monster near Troy. Then a fierce storm blew them off course to the island of Thorna, with its resident cyclops, who devours six boys and six girls each year as tribute. And finally the goddess Athena had diverted them to the island of Sattis to destroy a colony of flesh-eating birds called the myserae. All told, the last month had been full of more adventures than Hercules normally saw in an entire year.

"Well, the monster's here, and it's not going away, so you might as well make the best of it," Theseus suggested to Jason. "Why not lead the attack yourself? Have some fun, for once! You might never have another adventure like this again!"

Jason looked at the older man, then gave a nod. "You're right, of course," he said. He took a deep breath—then grinned happily, and Hercules realized his young captain had been holding his natural enthusiasm in check. It was almost as if he needed Theseus's permission to loose the tight reins he kept on himself. Hercules nodded to himself. This was a good time to do it, too. Everyone aboard needed a break from the last week's monotony and backbreaking labor.

"Ready your weapons!" Jason called, striding back along the deck. "Wait until it attacks! We don't know that it's hostile!"

"Have you ever met a monster that *wasn't* hostile?" Atalanta asked Hercules.

He thought back for a moment, then shook his head. "No. They all wanted to eat me."

"I was afraid of that!"

He shrugged. "That's why they're monsters, after all."

"I don't suppose you'd let me have this one all to myself?" Atalanta asked, still grinning. They'd had a friendly competition on the islands of Sattis and Thorna, Hercules recalled. More by accident than design, he kept slaying the monsters she fought. Through it all, he kept promising the *next* one would be hers.

"Not a chance!" he said. "I think this one belongs to the whole ship!"

Hercules glanced back at the channel again. The monster continued to circle. "I think," he said slowly, "I better get a couple of spears. And you need your bow."

From behind him, a low voice said, "I already have them, Hercules. Catch!"

Hercules turned and found Hylas behind him. The youth held a pair of spears, which he offered to Hercules with a quick grin.

"Still want to be my spear-carrier?" Hercules said.

"Well . . . you *do* need one," Hylas said. Next he pulled Atalanta's bow from his shoulder and passed it to her, along with a quiver of arrows. "Here, I brought your weapons, too."

"Thank you." Atalanta strung her bow in one swift motion, then notched an arrow.

"Don't mention it." Turning, Hylas jogged back toward the open hatch. "I'll get you more spears!" he called over his shoulder. "I know you'll need them!"

To Hercules, Atalanta said, "He worships you, you know. And you could use a spear-carrier."

Hercules sighed. "Ever since his brother died, I've been trying to watch out for him. Now he wants to be just like me. It's hero-worship, that's all."

"I can't fault him for that. He couldn't find a better hero to worship, after all. Well? Are you going to do it?"

"Do what?"

"Make him your shield-bearer?"

Hercules hesitated. "He's a little old . . ."

"True. But he wants it very badly."

Slowly Hercules nodded. Yes, he knew Hylas wanted very badly to learn the arts of war at his side. But at sixteen, Hylas was already a man and a proven warrior. Most spear-carriers began at half his age . . . some even younger.

"Truly," he said, frowning, "I don't know what to do."

"Do you want some advice?"

"From you?" He squinted as he studied the creature in the water. Those cunning eyes glowed with intelligence, he thought. The creature swam toward the *Argo*'s bow, coming within a few yards, before suddenly veering to the right. "All right."

She paused a long second. "Don't do it."

"Why?" The monster rose to within a foot of the surface. From end to end it seemed about half as long as the *Argo*, Hercules estimated, with huge fins and a powerful tail. Could Atalanta have been right? Was it a whale of some kind?

Suddenly it blew another geyser into the air. The water rose before them, hung for a second, then began to descend. A second later, Hercules realized it was falling toward him. He barely had time to cover his head with one arm before gallons of icy seawater sluiced over him. He gasped in shock.

"Because he doesn't need you!" Atalanta said behind him. "Watch out for the water, by the way."

"Argh!" Hercules said, shaking his head like a dog and trying to blink the salt from his eyes. His vision blurred. "Now you tell me!"

He heard Atalanta laughing and peered back at her. She was completely dry. She must have danced nimbly out of the way just in time to avoid getting soaking, he realized.

"It's not funny!" he said, glowering a little. "Do you know how long this lion skin takes to dry?"

"Yes, it *is* funny! I wish you could see yourself. Even better, I wish I had a bard here to compose a verse about 'The Drenching of Hercules.' That would certainly add some spice to the tale of our adventures!"

He took a deep breath, then suddenly laughed. He couldn't help it; it was funny. If he hadn't been leaning over too far, trying to see the monster, he wouldn't have gotten wet. He'd done it to himself. He gave a mental snort. Good thing they *didn't* have a bard along, or he never would hear the last of it.

But what of the monster? Hercules leaned over the rail again, gazing deep into the water. It circled below him. It seemed to be gazing up almost mockingly. Slowly one of its glowing eyes closed. *A wink!* It had *winked* at him!

Rage surged through him. "I know you!" he bellowed down at the water. The creature really *had* been mocking him, he knew. Poseidon must have sent it . . . a little lesson in humility from the god of the seas. "I know who sent you!" he cried. "Rise and face me, beast—if you dare!"

In reply, it gave a powerful twitch of its tail and sped around the *Argo*'s port side. It circled the ship twice, then paused at the bow, blowing another spume. This time Hercules leaped back a safe distance. *You won't catch me twice with the same trick*, he thought triumphantly.

Raising his spear, he took careful aim. Now it was his turn, he thought. He wouldn't let anyone mock him, neither man nor beast nor god. And especially not a monster sent by his uncle, Poseidon!

"Hold there, Hercules!" Jason called, running to join him. The leader of the Argonauts had already sheathed his sword. "It hasn't done us any harm. Maybe it doesn't mean to attack after all . . . it seems more playful than angry."

Grumbling a little, Hercules lowered his spear. "Playful? Malicious, more like it!"

"It could have attacked the *Argo* a dozen times over," Jason said. "Let it be. We'll continue on our way."

Hercules took in a breath through his teeth, but gave a nod. "Very well." He might not like the orders, but he would follow them.

Jason gave a nod. "Good. It's for the best."

Leaning forward, Hercules shouted down to the monster, "Off with you, then! Tell your master I won't play his games any more!"

As if in reply, the creature glided forward, rolling over on its pale green belly and staring up at him with those odd yellow eyes. A moment later, it gave a powerful kick with its tail, turned, and swam rapidly out to sea.

Jason clasped him on the shoulder. "You did it!" he cried. "Now *that's* a story for the bards to tell!"

Everyone began to cheer. Hercules gave a rueful grin. Might as well put a good face on things, he thought.

But something tickled at the back of his mind. It had been too easy, a little voice inside him said. He lingered at the railing a moment, staring off after the sea monster. He had the strangest feeling they hadn't seen the last of it. He would keep watch in case it returned, he promised himself. And next time *he* would have the upper hand.

"Back to the benches!" Jason called. "Round up those weapons and stow them away! We'll row through the channel after all, and tonight we'll have a feast to celebrate Hercules's triumph!"

"It wasn't that much of a triumph," Hercules mumbled half to himself.

"Any excuse for a party!" Atalanta said, slapping his back. His lion skin made a squishing sound under her hand. "Though you might want to change first."

"Feh! And people wonder why I hate monsters . . ." He

stomped off toward the hatch. It only took a minute to find a spare white tunic and change into it. When he returned to the deck, he spread out the lion skin to dry. It would probably take a good two days, he thought, since the sun was setting rapidly to the west now.

He joined Atalanta at their rowing bench. "I can't believe it!" Atalanta was grumbling. She had already put her arrow back in its quiver and unstrung her bow. Hylas took them from her. "We have to find a monster that minds its own business! That's no fun."

"At least Jason will be happy," Hercules said. Hylas moved to take his spears, but Hercules shook his head. "I'll hold onto these for now."

"Oh?" Atalanta narrowed her eyes. "You're up to something!"

"Me?" He smiled charmingly.

"Don't give me that innocent look. Come on, tell!"

Hylas looked from one to the other, then sighed and handed Atalanta her bow and arrows again without being asked. She didn't restring the bow yet, but Hercules could tell she was thinking about it.

The youth said, "It's coming back, isn't it?"

Hercules shrugged. "I don't know. Probably not. But I don't want to be caught unprepared if it does."

Everyone else continued passing their weapons to Orestes and Philomon, who were stowing them away belowdecks. Hercules tucked his spears under his bench and Atalanta did the same with her bow and quiver of arrows.

Jason joined them. "Keeping your weapons?" he asked, eyebrows raised.

"For now," Atalanta said. "Can't hurt to be prepared."

"I have a strange feeling we'll see that monster again before this day is through," Hercules added. "I don't know why. It's just a feeling I have."

Jason looked troubled. "I thought I'd be glad the monster didn't attack," he said, gazing in the direction the creature had gone. "But now, I'm not so sure. I trust your instincts, Hercules. Maybe all the men should keep their weapons."

"Why?" Atalanta asked. "Did I miss something? It soaked Hercules, then ran!"

Jason said, "The first time I saw those eyes, when it looked up at us . . . I would have sworn it meant to destroy us all."

"I had that same feeling," Hercules said, nodding. He knew exactly what Jason meant. "It gave up *too* easily. It may well return later, when it can catch us off guard. Perhaps we should post a lookout."

"Theseus already suggested that," Jason said. "As soon as the weapons are stowed, I'll have Hylas climb the mast and keep watch. It won't sneak up on us again."

"*Jason!*" Orpheus called suddenly. He was pointing toward the horizon. "*Look! It's coming back!*"

Hercules leaped to the railing and stared out across the waves. "Where?" he called.

"Arm yourselves!" Jason cried, running toward the hatch. "Get those weapons back up here!"

A moment later, Hercules spotted the monster. It swam just below the surface of the sea, leaving a broad rippled wake in its trail. Using its powerful tail and fins, it was swimming toward the *Argo* as fast as it could, gathering speed.

Instantly Hercules realized what it meant to do, and he seized the railing with both hands.

"Brace yourselves!" he called. "It's going to ram us!"

CHAPTER TWO

Fifty miles away, a battle-scarred centaur known as Koremos the Black forced his way between two gnarled old pine trees. Overhead, gulls wheeled and called to one another, and he could smell salty brine on the air. He knew the Black Sea couldn't be much farther now.

Suddenly the last branches parted and he found himself gazing down a steep sixty-foot drop. Below, small waves lapped against a sandy white beach in a small, sheltered cove. He narrowed his eyes, studying the stream trickling from a cleft in the rocks to the left. That would be a good source of water, he knew, for anyone who made camp here. And the tall, chalky cliffs offered plenty of shelter from the wind.

Yes, he thought, *the Argonauts will almost certainly stop here for the night. And this time, I will be ready for them.*

They had shattered his outlaw band and driven him

from his home two months before, when he tried to steal their magnificent ship, the *Argo*. He could never forgive them for the humiliation he had suffered.

After his defeat, he had gathered the remains of his forces and marched his men across land, risking everything to beat the Argonauts to the Black Sea. According to every Oracle and two-bit fortune-teller they had encountered over the last month, his plan had worked. Hera had driven the *Argo* far off course, and it would be some days yet before Hercules, Jason, and the rest of them reached the Black Sea. His timing couldn't have been more perfect.

"Do you see their ship?" a low voice growled from behind him.

Koremos stamped his two front hooves. "No," he said for the third time in the last hour. He let a faint note of annoyance creep into his voice. "It's still much too soon, Lorron. You know they won't be here for another week, maybe longer."

"But what if—"

"Quiet!" Tail twitching with annoyance, Koremos glanced back across his flanks. "You talk too much. Listen, learn, and do as you are told. That's all I require from you today, Lorron."

Lorron hunched his shoulders and made a pouting face, showing crooked yellow teeth through his scraggly black beard. Slowly he turned his brutish eyes toward the ground in submission.

Koremos gave a mental snort. A better man would have challenged him over such a remark, but not Lorron the Strangler. Despite his lieutenant's broad, deeply muscled chest and huge, powerful hands, Koremos knew Lorron would never confront him. Lorron had the brains and ambitions of a trained monkey. He would follow orders without argument, and he would serve faithfully the rest of his life. But he would continue to ask dumb questions.

Only a month ago, the Strangler had been a minor robber on a minor road two hundred miles to the west of here, Koremos recalled. Lorron had guarded a small pass through the mountains, demanding tribute from everyone who went through. He strangled anyone who failed to satisfy him, and that was how he got his nickname.

Their meeting had been anything but memorable. Koremos, leading sixty-two men and a line of ten heavily laden mules, had trotted up to the crude blockade—really little more than half a dozen fallen trees that Lorron had dragged across the winding mountain path.

As Koremos paused to consider the blockade, Lorron leaped from cover, growling deep in his throat like a wild animal. He was dressed in the filthiest tunic Koremos had ever seen, and he reeked of sweat and grease and human waste. In one hand, he held a massive club. None of that surprised Koremos; peasants had been warning him about the Strangler for miles. From their description he had expected a large man, but even so, the height and width of this fellow astounded him. Lorron had to be seven feet tall, if not taller. Beneath the dirt and grime, muscles like iron bands rippled across his broad chest and shoulders.

"By the gods!" Koremos said, taking a half-step back. The Strangler towered half a head over him. "You're even bigger than I expected!"

Lorron grinned, showing chipped yellow teeth. "Toll!" he thundered. "I demand tribute!"

"What kind of tribute would you like?" Koremos asked calmly.

Lorron blinked at him. Then he frowned, eyes taking in Koremos's hooves, horselike body, and manlike upper torso and head as if noticing them for the first time.

"Are you man or horse?" the Strangler demanded.

At that moment, Koremos realized how stupid this man had to be. And he knew that the Strangler's life was his for the taking. And just as quickly he vowed to have this man as part of his outlaw band. He could certainly put that muscle to good use.

"Not a horse, no," Koremos said. He folded his arms and raised his head proudly. "I am a centaur."

"Centaur." Slowly Lorron the Strangler nodded. He seemed almost awed. "Yes. I have heard of them."

"What is *your* name?" Koremos asked.

"My . . . name?" Lorron lowered his club, frowning. "All know my name!"

"I don't," Koremos lied. "What do they call you?"

"Lorron the Strangler. All men fear me!"

"Yes, of course they do. And I can see why—you're quite fearsome looking."

"Fearsome." Lorron puffed out his chest in pride. "Yes, Lorron is fearsome!" He seemed to find the thought delightful, as though it were a revelation sent from Olympus.

Koremos chuckled inwardly. This would be even easier than he had thought.

He flicked his tale twice, a signal for his forces to close in. He heard the soft, almost childlike sigh of swords leaving scabbards. From the corners of his eyes, he watched a dozen of his men drifting to either side, slowly surrounding Lorron.

"Now, Lorron the Strangler," the centaur went on without pause, shifting from foot to foot and making little clopping noises on the road with his hooves. The Strangler's gaze never left his face. "What sort of toll did you want?"

"Food!"

"Food? Is that all?"

"Have you women?" Lorron licked his lips, eyes drifting toward the mules. "And mules. They're good eating!"

Koremos took a half-step backward, like a nervous stallion shying from danger, and Lorron's attention snapped back instantly.

"No," the centaur said. "No women."

"Then your food and your mules! *All* of them!"

Koremos saw that his men had surrounded Lorron with drawn swords. And Lorron hadn't even noticed yet. It seemed almost *too* easy, he thought.

Behind Lorron's back, Old Tybos made "Shall we?" gestures with his sword.

"Not yet," Koremos replied almost casually.

"Huh?" Lorron slapped his club against the palm of his hand. "Lorron wants your food!" he thundered. "Or you will not pass!"

"Of course. Take what you want." Koremos turned at his waist, indicating their supply train. All ten mules carried heavy bundles. Some contained food, but others held bedrolls and extra weapons, and even some gold and silver. They had looted two villages on their trek thus far and had equipped themselves more than adequately from the loot.

Grinning like an idiot, Lorron started forward. Then, without warning, Koremos reared on his hind legs and lashed out with his front hooves. One hoof struck the club from Lorron's hand, sending it spinning away. The other struck the man's forehead dead center.

With a faint grunt, Lorron the Strangler toppled backward like a falling tree. He sprawled there, eyes glassy, staring up at the heavens. A half-circular, hoof-shaped bruise slowly purpled on his forehead.

"Tie him up," Koremos said. He gave an impatient flick of his tail as his men leaped forward eagerly. Two placed blades to Lorron's throat in case he recovered enough to resist. The others quickly bound the huge man's hands and feet with leather thongs, knotting them securely. Hercules would have had a tough time freeing himself from those knots, Koremos thought with satisfaction. Lorron didn't have a chance.

"Phew, he stinks!" Goran said, stepping back.

"Shall we kill him?" Old Tybos asked eagerly, turning to look up at the mountains around them. "He must have a hoard of treasure hidden around here somewhere!"

"Idiot," Koremos said. Didn't anyone else have a shred of common sense? "He wasn't interested in gold, he wanted food. Would you kill for ancient salted meats and age-rotted fish?"

"I've killed for less," Tybos admitted.

"Not with me, you haven't," Koremos said, a note of scorn creeping into his voice. He didn't like arguing with his men. "He's much more valuable to us alive."

"What?" everyone began to demand at once. "How?"

"I will tell you when the time comes," he said. "For now, Jason may have his Hercules . . . but we have one of our own, too!"

Everyone began to nod as if he'd said the wisest thing in the world. Koremos trotted up to Lorron the Strangler, leaned forward, and peered down at his captive. Again he marveled at the man's size, at the bulging muscles in his arms and neck, at the breadth of his chest. This man more than matched Hercules in height and weight, he realized. Could Lorron be another demigod? Some stray child of Zeus who had never amounted to anything?

No, Koremos decided, this fellow had to be human. No demigod could possibly be as stupid as Lorron. No one could ever have captured Hercules with such a simple trick. Clearly, Lorron had been relying on his muscles for so long, he no longer worried about anyone outsmarting him. If he ever had.

Groaning, Lorron stirred and tried to rub his head. Two men knelt on each of his arms. Four more sat on his legs. They all made faces at the smell, and Koremos found he agreed. They would have to get Lorron cleaned up if he was going to accompany them.

"I still say we should kill him," Old Tybos said again, pressing his knife to Lorron's throat. A trickle of blood appeared under the sharp bronze blade. "Say the word and he'll feed the crows!"

"Get up, all of you," Koremos said. "Tend to the mules. Pitch camp. We'll spend the night here."

"But—" Tybos began.

"Do it!" Koremos snapped. He took a step toward Tybos, glaring fiercely. "Or would you rather I have *your* throat slit instead?"

Tybos paled, but rose and quickly sheathed his sword. Without another word, he stalked toward the mules. In silence, the rest of the band followed. They began unloading their packs and setting up camp. Several times, Old Tybos cast angry glances at Koremos.

I'll have to watch that one, Koremos told himself, narrowing his eyes. Tybos had been becoming increasingly difficult of late. *He thinks he knows more than I do. It will only lead to trouble.*

Lorron groaned. The centaur glanced down at him, noticing that his eyes had become slits. Koremos read bewilderment there. And . . . could it be shock?

"You have never been beaten before, have you?" Koremos asked softly.

"No," Lorron said quietly.

"Listen to me well, Lorron the Strangler," Koremos said. He leaned forward, looming over the bound man. "I am called Koremos the Black, and I command the greatest army of thieves, brigands, and cutthroats the world has ever seen. Few men survive my wrath."

"How could you beat Lorron?" the Strangler said. He bit his lip and seemed almost close to tears. "No one has ever beaten Lorron!"

"I did, Lorron, because I'm stronger, faster, and smarter than you are. I'm not human, Lorron. No *man* can beat you. It took a centaur . . . and that's nothing to be ashamed of."

"A centaur . . . that is right . . . that is why you beat Lorron!"

"I need a man like you, Lorron. Someone strong, someone brave, someone fearless."

"Why?" He asked it with such childlike simplicity that Koremos almost laughed. Oh, yes, he would do well to have Lorron join his band. This man would follow him to the end of the Earth, if he asked.

"Because, Strangler, I intend to rule all of Greece—and I can't do it alone!"

"Oh." Lorron frowned, heavy brow furling in thought, and Koremos could see him slowly working his way through the possibilities. At last he nodded. "Very well. Lorron agrees. Lorron will join you."

Koremos untied him, and on that very spot Lorron knelt and swore to serve Koremos for the rest of his life. It was, the centaur thought, one of the most touching oaths ever sworn to him, primarily because he knew the Strangler meant every word. He didn't have the guile to deceive.

Then, when it was done, Koremos turned and vaulted the roadblock in one great jump. It couldn't be much farther to the Black Sea, he thought, studying the pass ahead. Then he could begin laying a trap for Hercules, Jason, and the rest of the Argonauts. This time he would see them *all* dead, and this time he *would* take their ship for his own.

Somehow, he knew Lorron would prove useful in his plans. He didn't quite know how yet, but the answer would come to him in time. It always did.

In the days that followed, Lorron proved himself useful several times. Since he had prowled this countryside for years, he steered Koremos to two small, nearly defenseless villages on the other side of the pass. They looted both, taking a few more weapons, a handful of silver coins, and plenty of fresh provisions.

In the evenings, Koremos watched in silence as the rest of his band tested Lorron—dicing with him and cheating him out of his share of the loot, playing stupid tricks on him, and making jokes at the big man's expense. Through it all, Lorron remained strangely calm and unbothered. He seemed happy with his lot in life, Koremos thought, with no ambitions beyond eating his next meal.

Then, nearly a week after Lorron had joined the band, jeers and catcalls awakened Koremos from a sound sleep. The centaur rested little—no more than an hour or two each night—and he found himself groggy and a little disoriented at the sudden disturbance. Nevertheless he leaped to his feet, unfolding his four long horselike legs, and whirled around to see what had happened.

His men surrounded him, but they had no weapons out. They were all watching two men rolling on the ground to his left. A fight? Koremos frowned. He didn't allow brawling in the ranks, but some instinct made him hesitate here. It was Lorron and Old Tybos, an unlikely match.

"Bring a torch," he commanded.

Balorion lit one from the campfire and brought it over.

By its flickering yellow glow, Koremos watched the Strangler give a jerk of his powerful arms, throw Tybos down, and sit on his chest.

"Lorron kill you!" the Strangler snarled. His thick fingers closed around the old man's throat, and he began choking the life out of the little man.

Old Tybos let out a pained wheeze. His eyes bulged from their sockets.

"Stop that! Release him!" Koremos demanded, striding forward. He meant to pull them apart.

"Old Tybos tried to kill you," Lorron said intently. He nodded toward the ground at Koremos's feet. The centaur stepped back and spotted the small, slightly curved bronze knife that Old Tybos used to slit the throats of his enemies. "Lorron told him no. He would not listen, so . . . now Lorron will kill him for you!"

Koremos took a deep breath. Although he slept little, he knew it left him vulnerable. Tybos might easily have killed him. He might be a centaur, but he bled just the same as a human.

"Is this true?" he asked the rest of his men.

They muttered and looked at the ground. None had the courage to face him. Clearly they had known about the plan . . . and clearly most of them had hoped Tybos would succeed. After all, it would mean an end to their march across country in search of Jason and the *Argo*. They could settle down here as robber barons, terrorizing the countryside until some local king—or squabbling among themselves—killed them off.

"I see," Koremos said. His tail flicked in anger, and he stomped his front hooves on the ground half a dozen times, tearing up clods of earth and grass. "Get from my sight!—all but you, Lorron. When you're done."

"Yes!" Lorron tightened his grip. Koremos heard a

dry snap, like a branch breaking, and Old Tybos went limp.

Slowly dusting off his hands, the Strangler climbed to his feet. "Dead," he announced proudly.

Koremos nodded. It seemed Lorron had saved his life. Old Tybos had been increasingly vocal in his complaints over the last month, but the centaur hadn't believed the old man daring enough to act on them.

With one hoof, he nudged the curved bronze knife on the ground. "Pick it up," he said. "It's yours. As well as Old Tybos's possessions. You've more than earned them."

"Thank you!" the Strangler said. He seemed genuinely surprised and pleased.

"I always reward loyalty," Koremos said loudly. "This night, you have earned a better place in my band. I name you as my first lieutenant. You will be my hands and my eyes and my voice in all things, and everyone here will obey you as they would me."

There came grumbles from around the campfire, but Koremos glared and the men there grew silent. "Any of you could have warned me and received the same reward," he said. Let them consider that as they take orders from Lorron!

Wheeling around, Koremos strode away from the campfire and into the darkness. He wanted to be alone now. The unexpected betrayal had given him an idea for dealing with Jason, and his plan had only just begun to form in the back of his mind. He needed to work through the details.

Now, a week after the death of Old Tybos, on the cliff overlooking the Black Sea, Lorron's string of dumb questions began to get to him again. Sighing, Koremos longed for his old lieutenant, Bix. Bix had known when to shut up. Bix had known how to take orders. Bix had been the closest thing to a friend he had ever known.

The centaur pressed his eyes shut for a second. No, that was not entirely true. Long before he came to this part of the world, when he lived in Africa, he had befriended the giant Antaeus, the son of Terra, who was a mighty wrestler. They had been the closest of friends—the first true friend Koremos had ever had—until Hercules showed up.

The thought of the demigod sent a new jolt of rage through Koremos. Except for Hercules, he would still be living in the palace of Antaeus, enjoying a life of decadent leisure, full of hunting and gambling, wine and sport and good song.

Antaeus, whose strength was invincible so long as he remained in contact with the mother Earth, liked to force all strangers who came to his country to wrestle with him, on condition that if conquered (as they all were) they should be put to death. It became a game to the two of them, each betting on how long the next opponent would last.

"This one looks strong," Koremos whispered in Antaeus's ear when guards escorted Hercules into the giant's court. They did not know Hercules was a demigod; indeed, at that point Hercules had only begun to make a name for himself in the world. He wore only a simple white tunic, since he had yet to slay the Nemean Lion, and he carried no weapon but a spear slung over one shoulder. "Look at those muscles! I say he lasts a good twenty minutes against you."

Antaeus gave a snort of derision. "If he lasts five minutes, I'll be surprised."

Hercules bowed to the throne. "Your highness," he said to Antaeus after introducing himself. "I am a traveler newly come to your land. Why have I been arrested and brought here?"

"You are not under arrest, Hercules," Antaeus said, leaning forward. "I have all strangers brought before me so I may meet them and ask for news of the world. Will you dine with me this evening? And afterwards we shall take our sport."

"Gladly, sir," Hercules said. He still looked a little suspicious, though. Several times he glanced at Koremos, but he said nothing about the black centaur. At the time, Koremos thought him too awed by being in the presence of both a giant and a centaur to worry about it.

The king rose and descended from his throne. He towered a good three feet over Hercules. Taking the smaller man by the shoulder, he steered him into the banquet hall, where servants had already begun to lay out the evening meal: wild boar basted in rare herbs and honey, roasted peacocks, delicate cakes, bread, and plates of apples and figs artfully arranged around honeycombs fresh from the hive. Meanwhile, the court musicians began to play their Pan's pipes and lyres.

As the honored victim—though he did not know it yet—Hercules sat to the giant's right, while Koremos sat to his left. Antaeus watched while Hercules ate ravenously, as though he had never tasted such excellent fare. The centaur's opinion of Hercules continued to decline as wine loosened the man's tongue, and he chattered on and on about his travels through Greece and Africa.

At last the meal ended. The tumbling acrobats who had been the final entertainment took their bows, received an appreciative handful of coins from Antaeus and the rest of the court, and vanished.

Only then did the giant stretch and rise. "It is time," he said, "for our evening's sport."

"Gladly," Hercules said with a grin. "What did you have in mind?"

"A wrestling match . . . between the two of us!"

"Oh?" Hercules raised his eyebrows. He did not seem as surprised as he should have, Koremos thought uneasily. "That sounds like fun," he said. "But to make it interesting, surely we should have stakes."

Antaeus slowly smiled, like a python unwinding from a tree, and he said: "Stakes? Why now. Life for the victor, death for the loser."

"Agreed!"

They rushed together without a second's hesitation. At once Hercules threw his opponent, but it seemed to have no effect. Every time Hercules grappled with him, Antaeus rose with renewed strength and rushed back to continue the match. Twice Antaeus threw Hercules, but the Greek just shook it off and returned for more.

"It's been five minutes," Koremos called.

"I know," Antaeus said. "But I can't seem to hurt him!"

"Nor he you," Koremos added dryly.

"It's the ground!" Hercules said suddenly. "Every time you touch it, you're healed!"

"There *are* advantages to being the son of a god!" Antaeus said with a laugh.

Grim faced, Hercules seized him as if to throw him again. But this time, as he lifted the giant from the ground, he shifted one hand to Antaeus's neck and began to squeeze. And slowly, painfully, over the next five minutes, he held the giant above the ground and strangled him in the air.

Koremos watched his best friend die with a numb sort of shock. Had he thought about it, he might well have tried to save Antaeus. But it happened so unexpectedly that he could not think fast enough to act.

Suddenly Hercules threw down the body. This time not even the Earth could save Antaeus. A tremor ran through the ground underfoot, like a mother's distant sob. The giant was dead.

"Thus are tyrants vanquished!" Hercules said, putting one foot on the giant's chest. Throwing back his head, he roared to the heavens: "*Thus will it always be! Are you listening, stepmother?*"

Koremos swallowed and forced his attention back to the beach and the present day. Even now, twenty years later, thinking about Hercules made a rope of anger tighten in his stomach.

He had two grudges to settle. Hercules may have killed his first friend, Antaeus, but Prince Jason had killed his second friend, Bix, during the daring but ultimately unsuccessful attack on the *Argo*.

Since that defeat, Koremos had marched steadily across land, gathering men willing to join him, heading east to the Black Sea. All the while he dreamed of revenge. Now, with sixty-two seasoned fighters under his command, he knew he outnumbered Jason's Argonauts. His men had sufficient swords and spears and shields. And they had surprise on their side, plus enough time to lay a deadly trap. He began to smile. They could not help but succeed.

"Yes," Koremos said. He glanced down at the cove again, musing through his plans. Archers and spear-throwers would take the Argonauts by surprise when night fell, he thought. Then his men would storm their camp, overrunning their defenses, killing all who would not surrender.

But what of Hercules? One demigod could turn the tide of battle. *He must be lured away.* But how? He would have to think on it. He knew the answer would come to him, in time.

He nodded. "This is the spot, Lorron. Tell the others. We will lay our ambush here."

A slight whine crept into Lorron's voice "But what about Hercules? You said—"

"Silence!" Koremos said sharply. "I will tell you what you need to know when you need to know it."

Lorron gulped. "Yes, sir."

Backing out from between the trees, Koremos turned. Hercules *would* be a problem, he thought. Most of the men he'd gathered knew at least a few tales of the demigod's prowess: the famous Twelve Labors, or the adventures he'd had, or the battles he'd fought. They feared Hercules almost as much as they feared Lorron. Well, he would simply have to get rid of Hercules first. But how?

"I have a plan to get rid of Hercules," he told Lorron.

"I knew it!" His lieutenant grinned like a puppy about to be rewarded by his master. "What are you going to do to him, sir?"

"Lure him away. I know just the bait to do it, too . . . we shall send a message from a friend in trouble. Hercules will go to him at once. He cannot help it. That is his nature."

"But *how*? Who does Hercules know *here*?"

Koremos sighed. *I need Lorron's strong back, not his brains,* he reminded himself. On the battlefield, Lorron would prove his worth a dozen times over. He had better. These constant interruptions were becoming very annoying.

"Let me take care of the details," the centaur said. "For now, fetch the rest of the men. We will make camp two miles back, in the clearing where Huron speared that deer this morning. After that, it's just a matter of waiting for the right moment . . . and then we strike!"

"Yes, sir!" Still grinning, Lorron turned and jogged off

through the trees, heading for the meadow where the rest of their band waited.

Koremos began to smile cruelly. Already his mind had turned toward the coming battle. Jason, who had cost the life of his oldest and dearest friend, would suffer most horribly of all.

CHAPTER THREE

Hercules leaped onto the ship's railing and raised his first spear for a throw. The creature still swam toward them, gathering speed, leaving a broad choppy wake behind it. *It really is going to ram the* Argo, he thought. Realizing it intended to stave in the ship's hull, then snatch them one by one from the water as the ship began to sink, Hercules thought of the cold, calculating intelligence in those glowing yellow eyes and shuddered involuntarily. The monster knew their weakest points, he thought, and it planned on exploiting them. In the water, they would all be helpless.

He couldn't let it succeed.

"Not today, fish," he said through clenched teeth. "Not while I have a spear in my hands to fight!"

Forty yards away, thirty—

Around him, men scrambled to retrieve their weapons

from the hold. Then they took defensive positions to his left and right. Beside him, Atalanta notched an arrow and began to take careful aim.

Hercules shut them out. Against a monster like this, he would be their only chance. He couldn't let himself become distracted.

"Hold!" Jason cried. "Wait until you know your shot will hit! Don't rush or you'll miss!"

I know that, Hercules thought. *I've been killing monsters since before you were born, Jason!*

Still it rushed at them. He could see the gleam of its yellow eyes, the iridescent blue-green sheen of its scales beneath the surging water. Tensing, he drew back his spear, taking careful aim.

Twenty yards away, fifteen—

The rest of the Argonauts let loose their shots. Spears and arrows flew, striking the water with hissing sounds. Hercules heard Atalanta curse when her shots seemed not to do any good. A few arrows struck the creature's head and body, but that didn't even slow it down. Perhaps its hide couldn't be penetrated by mortal weapons, he thought with a sudden jolt of fear. The Nemean Lion, whose skin he usually wore, had been like that—no blade could pierce its hide. He ended up having to strangle it with his bare hands.

Twelve yards—

Swallowing, he tightened his grip on his spear. Suddenly he knew what he had to do. They wouldn't be able to stop the creature from crushing the *Argo*'s hull if he didn't act immediately.

Ten yards—eight yards—

More arrows bounced off its hide. It was too big, too strong for them, he realized. Clearly no weapon aboard the *Argo* could stop it in time. If he didn't act fast, it would be too late; the ship would be sinking and they would all be at the monster's mercy.

"Hold your fire!" he shouted to the archers. In one swift move, he shrugged off his tunic and let it fall to the deck.

"What do you think you're doing?" Atalanta shouted. "Hercules—you'll be killed—!"

Sorry, I don't have time to argue right now, Hercules thought. Without another word, he dove off the side of the ship, spear held tightly before him. He would have to force the monster down, under the Argo, to keep the ship from being destroyed. And the only way to do it would be to turn its charge.

He hit waves at an angle, sliding smoothly into the cool embrace of the sea and right over the monster's head. He kept his eyes open; the seawater began to sting, but it didn't matter—he needed to see his target.

Huge yellow eyes loomed quickly before him. He glimpsed a fast onrushing head, dark green and covered with scales, mouth open and filled with thin bladelike teeth as long as swords.

He thrust down hard with his spear. Its sharp bronze tip struck the creature's scales and thick skin midway between the eyes—then shattered. He didn't let up, but ground down with all his strength. A sharp piece of the metal, still attached, slid along the scales and then under one.

This is my chance! he thought. He twisted the spear with both hands, driving it farther under that scale and into the monster's flesh.

A weird keening sound filled the water. A dark, oily fluid that could only be blood gushed out from the wound. Hercules bore down on his weapon again, and felt the spear hit bone.

The monster dove to escape its pain, its powerful tail

and flippers driving it deep into the sea. Holding his breath, Hercules clung to the spear. Water tore at him, and he saw a dark shadow pass directly overhead.

I did it! he thought triumphantly. *We went under the* Argo! A brief surge of elation swept through him.

Only he didn't have time for rejoicing just yet, he reminded himself. Clinging to a monster, underwater and unable to breathe, wasn't exactly the best position he'd ever been in. Now he just had to get himself safely free . . . and make sure the monster didn't return to finish off its work. But how?

The water grew black and cold as they went deeper, and his lungs began to burn with an urgent need for air. He couldn't stay down much longer, he realized as the edges of his vision began to darken. But then neither could the monster—it had a blowhole, which meant it had to have air, too, just like him. How long could it hold its breath? *Longer than me*, he thought with mounting panic.

At last its crazed flight began to slow. The water around Hercules grew bright, and when he looked up, he saw the shimmering of sunlight on the underside of waves. He clung to his spear with a grim determination. *Just a few seconds more*, he told himself. *Then I'll be able to breathe.*

They broke through to the surface. The creature sucked in huge mouthfuls of air, and Hercules did the same. They both seemed to need a rest, Hercules thought. He watched the creature warily, and one of its eyes rolled toward him and it seemed to do the same. *Truce . . . for now*, he thought. The battle would begin anew soon enough.

"If you surrender and leave," he told it, "I'll let you go in peace. Depart our ship and let us pass."

He hadn't expected a reply, and sure enough he didn't get one. But he had been speaking as much for Poseidon's benefit as for the monster's. He had hoped his uncle might call off this creature's attack.

After another moment, the monster began to move, slowly shaking its head as if trying to knock him off. He held on tightly. His spear, still stuck under that scale, was wedged tightly in place.

"You won't get rid of me that easily," he told it.

It paused and seemed to be considering. Hercules took the opportunity to stand on its snout. Huge muscles straining, he gripped the spear firmly, set his feet, and drove the point still deeper into the creature's flesh. The bronze tip bit through bone and lodged more firmly in place.

That must have really hurt, he realized. With a whistling shriek, the creature rolled onto its side, almost throwing him off, and suddenly they were underwater again, rushing forward with the speed of a runaway horse. Hercules struggled to hold onto the spear and barely managed to keep from being swept away.

Then, from the corner of his eye, he glimpsed a shadow rushing at them. He ducked instinctively, and something huge and dark passed a hand's breadth over his head. Only then did he realize they had just swept under the *Argo* for a second time. The creature had tried to scrape him off against the ship's hull.

Rage filled him. *Not so easily!* he thought again with determination.

Twisting the spear, he ground it into the wound. That must have caused true agony—the creature began to shriek again, and its whole body quivered from snout to tail.

It surfaced, flipped onto its side, and rolled like a snake shedding its skin, over and over again. Hercules felt himself being whipped through the air and water, a child's doll caught in a maelstrom. Still he clung to his spear.

The creature slowed. Had he exhausted it? He hoped so. He didn't think he could last through much more of its acrobatics.

Still holding the spear with one hand, he reached down with the other and caught the edge of the scale he'd pried loose. Setting his feet, he began to pull, huge muscles straining, and a moment later the scale ripped free.

Shrieking, the creature rolled again, and water closed over Hercules's head. He clung to his spear. He had ridden it out before; he could do it again, he thought.

This time the creature's struggles were halfhearted at best and lasted only a minute or two. At last it turned and broke into the open air, its head whipping around. Hercules skidded across its tough, scaled green hide and came to a stop before its left eye.

It paused a heartbeat, staring at him, and he had the distinct impression it was glaring with rage and pain. He swallowed.

"I don't suppose we can talk about this?" he said. "I'm willing to let you go free—"

As if in reply, it raised its head from the waves, five feet up, ten feet up. Water slid from its hide in sheets. Hercules scrambled across its broad snout, keeping one hand firmly attached to the spear that was still lodged between its eyes. He had a feeling he hadn't seen the worst of the creature's tricks yet.

Suddenly it snapped its neck violently from side to side, throwing him off his feet. If not for the spear, he would have been flung into the water. As he slid across its broad face, it snapped at him. He pulled his legs away from its bladelike teeth, never loosening his grip on the spear. As long as the spear was lodged in place, he knew the creature couldn't get to him.

He heard the monster make that weird keening sound again, and this time, above the waves, it sounded even more like the cry of a beast in agony. *It's the saltwater in its wound*, he realized. The salt must have made the stinging ten times worse.

Without warning, a single arrow thudded into the creature's left eye, two feet from where he stood, burying itself up to the fletching. A clear liquid splattered across him. He gaped. *That was a brilliant shot*, he thought, awed. It had to be Atalanta's work. She was the finest archer he had ever seen.

The creature paused. A tremor ran through it, and then it began to spasm. Its fins flailed. Its head twisted and shook. Its back arched out of the water like a bucking horse.

Hercules felt his grip slipping, though he tried to cling in place. This time not even his immense strength could save him. He felt his spear wrench loose, and a second later he followed it, flying across the water and out of control.

CHAPTER FOUR

Arms flailing, trying to catch his balance, Hercules came down fifty feet away from the creature. He hit the sea feet first with a huge splash.

The water around him churned with the monster's death throes. Knowing he couldn't do much else but get out of the way, he held his breath and struck out in what he hoped was the right direction—away from the beast and toward the *Argo*. The shot to the eye must have penetrated to the brain, he realized. It had been an amazing, perfect shot, and one that had almost certainly saved his life. He didn't think he could have stood against the creature's wrath much longer.

When his lungs couldn't stand the pain of not breathing, he struggled to the surface. He began to tread water and turned to look back at the monster.

It still twitched repeatedly, but the force lessened. At

last it stopped moving and slowly slid into the deep, vanishing from sight. Poseidon had reclaimed his own.

As the water around him calmed, Hercules realized distant voices were shouting his name. Still treading water, he turned until he spotted the *Argo* to his left and two hundred yards away. With slow, tired strokes, he swam until he reached the ship. Everyone began to cheer.

"Here you go, Hercules!" Atalanta threw a rope down to him. "Well done!"

"Thanks." He slowly pulled himself toward the deck, panting heavily. His limbs felt like stone and the breath rasped in his throat. He couldn't remember ever being this exhausted before.

A dozen hands reached down and helped him over the railing. Everyone crowded around and began to pound his back and compliment him. Hylas fetched his white tunic, and Hercules pulled it on.

"Incredible!" Theseus told him over and over. "I have never seen such a battle before! I thought it would kill even you!"

"It was close," Hercules said with a modest grin. "Luckily I'm hard to kill." He accepted a bowl of warm, spiced wine from Iolaus and drained it in a single swallow. "I thought it had me when it went under the ship the second time. It nearly knocked my head off against the *Argo*'s hull. I'm lucky to be here."

Rising, he crossed the deck and looked out at the last place he had seen the monster. He saw not a trace of it now.

Everyone followed him. "On our next quest," Jason said, "we'll travel by land."

Hercules laughed. "We *have* had our share of bad luck, but if the Fleece is worth having, it's worth fighting for. At least the end is nearly in sight."

"And about time, too," Atalanta said a trifle crossly. "If

only the wind would turn, we could get on with it!"

He remembered the arrow that had killed the monster. Although he had probably saved the ship, he couldn't take all the credit—a lot of it belonged to Atalanta.

"That was a magnificent shot," he told her. "One of the best I've ever seen."

"It *was* amazing," she said. "One of the best I've ever seen, too. I'm quite envious."

He blinked. "It wasn't yours?"

"No—I couldn't bring myself to shoot," she admitted. "We were so far away, and you were moving so fast, I was afraid of hitting you."

He frowned. "Then who killed it?" He glanced at Jason, who shook his head, then at Theseus, who smiled faintly then indicated someone behind Hercules with a nod of his chin.

"It was me," a small voice said almost meekly.

Hercules turned. Hylas shifted from foot to foot, looking at the deck apologetically.

"You?" Hercules asked. He couldn't believe it.

The youth gulped. "I—I thought it was going to eat you. I couldn't stand here and watch!"

"When did you become such a marksman?" Hercules said with a puzzled frown. He couldn't recall seeing Hylas so much as pick up a bow for practice. "Why haven't you spoken of this great skill before?"

"I . . . uh . . ." Hylas blushed and looked down, and everyone on deck burst into laughter. Hercules looked from face to face with increasing confusion. Had he missed something funny?

"He was aiming for the monster's throat," Atalanta finally explained. "He *missed*."

"Oh." Hercules paused a moment, then threw back his head and laughed long and hard. "Then I should thank whichever god steered your arrow to its proper target!"

Hylas breathed a sigh with obvious relief. "Then you're not mad?"

Atalanta folded her arms. "He thought you'd skin him alive when you found out. After all, he might have shot you in the eye!"

Hercules shook his head. "I wouldn't want you shooting at me every day. But just this once, I'm grateful. You should be proud . . . your first monster!"

"Thanks, Hercules."

Hercules said to Jason, "I don't particularly feel like waiting around for anything else to show up. Shall we get out of here?"

Jason nodded. "Still no breeze for our sails. Are you up to rowing?"

Hercules sighed, but forced a nod. Exhausted as he felt, he wouldn't shirk his duty. They needed every available Argonaut at the oars.

The rest of the day passed uneventfully. Without a monster blocking their path, they navigated the narrow channel between island and mainland without mishap and continued to skirt the coast. As the afternoon wore on, they passed a poor-looking fishing village.

"Ship oars!" Jason called. "Take a rest."

Hercules stood at his bench and gazed across at the villagers. Dozens of them had turned out to stare at the *Argo*, and many of the women and children waved almost invitingly. Half the crew waved back.

Their small fishing boats had all been pulled ashore for the day, but a couple of men slid one back into the water and began to paddle out.

Rising, Hercules hurried to the railing to see better. The rest of the crew followed.

The two men were dressed rather strangely, even to Hercules's eye, and he had seen hundreds of different peoples in his travels. Instead of tunics, both wore short leather skirts. The sandals laced up their legs almost to the knee. Except for dozens of white necklaces, their deeply muscled, sun-bronzed chests were bare.

"Ho there!" Jason shouted down to them. "I am Prince Jason of Thessaly, and these are my comrades-in-arms, the Argonauts! What village is this?"

"Baobis!" the elder of the two called in halting Greek. "I be head man! Stop you and trading?"

Beside Hercules, Atalanta whispered, "Look at those necklaces!"

Hercules squinted. Tiny white pieces, carved of bone or perhaps ivory and then strung together, didn't exactly appeal to him. But perhaps around a more delicate neck . . .

"Want me to try to trade with them?" he asked. "I could probably get you one—"

"No, you idiot!" she snapped. "*Look* at them! They're made of human bones!"

"Huh?" That made him really stare. As the two drew closer to the *Argo*, he could make out individual teeth and finger bones. And some of them had what looked like teeth marks.

He swallowed, abruptly feeling sick. "Cannibals!" he said.

Those around him who had overheard began whispering to others, and soon the word reached Jason. He frowned, but said nothing to the headman of the village about it. Instead, he said, "No—we have leagues yet to sail this day."

"Stop you and trading with us?" the villager called. "Stop you and trading!"

"Another time," Jason said. "Perhaps on our return."

That seemed to satisfy the villager, for he made a quick gesture and spoke in some harsh, guttural language to the other man, and they began to paddle back toward their village.

"Back to your benches!" Jason called. "Let's put a safe distance between us for the night!"

This time not one person—not even Atalanta—complained about the rowing, Hercules noticed with amusement. Better to row than be someone's dinner.

Sure enough, they found a small, sandy beach three hours and thirty miles later. As the sun began to touch the west with fingers of pink and gold, they anchored the *Argo* and began ferrying people and equipment ashore. Hercules found himself with rowing duty and spent the next half hour helping to load and unload his boat.

Meanwhile, on the beach, Theseus organized camp, posting sentries and sending Hylas and several others off to gather wood for a fire.

When everyone was ashore, Jason drew Atalanta and Hercules to one side. It looked like he wanted a private conference, Hercules thought. It was the first time Jason had ever consulted him without Theseus being present, though, which struck him as odd. Something had to be bothering their captain, he thought.

"Let's take a walk up the beach," Jason said. "Bring your weapons in case we spot game. We'll make it a private hunt, too."

"I'm ready now." Hercules hefted his spear with a grin. A little side trip would be fun, he thought. As Atalanta ran to fetch her bow and a quiver of arrows, he took the opportunity to ask, "What's this about? Do you really want a friendly walk, or do you have something else in mind?"

Jason hesitated. "I've been thinking about what you said earlier," he replied slowly. "I *have* been pushing everyone too hard, including myself. We're almost to the

Black Sea, after all, and it won't be much longer before we reach the Kingdom of Colchis. We need to be fresh when we get there. I know I need a little time to relax and regain my strength. We all do . . . and that includes you."

"Me?" Hercules laughed. "I've had my fun for the week!"

"Wrestling sea monsters?"

"That's right. What I'm in the mood for now is a nice, quiet tavern and several large jars of wine."

"Well, I can help with the wine part." Jason drew a wineskin from his belt and passed it over.

Hercules unstoppered it, tilted it back, and took a deep swallow. Cool and dry, with a slightly fruity aftertaste—it could only be one of the excellent summer wines from the island of Sattis. He had thought the ship's supply had been exhausted long ago, but it seemed Jason had been holding a little back for special occasions. Smacking his lips in satisfaction, Hercules passed the skin back.

Jason took a swallow. "Now *this* is a wine!" he said.

Atalanta rejoined them. "Is that what I think it is?" she asked, eyeing the skin.

"Yes." Jason passed it to her, and she drank, too.

"So what's this meeting about?" she asked.

"It seems Jason wants to have a little fun."

"Oh?" She raised her eyebrows. "More fun than fighting sea monsters?"

"He doesn't seem to think that was fun at all!"

She laughed, and Hercules joined in.

Jason asked her, "Is that so hard to believe?"

"Coming from you? Yes!"

"I'm just careful!"

"I'm all for being careful," Hercules said, "but there is such a thing as being *too* careful. You have to enjoy yourself or life isn't worth living."

"There's a difference between fun and recklessness."

Atalanta said, "That's the Jason I know!"

Hercules just shrugged. "Give me fun any day."

"This is the day for it." Jason picked up his spear. "Let's see what we can find," he said as he started up the beach at a brisk pace without looking back.

Hercules and Atalanta exchanged a quick look, then followed. Jason definitely *had* experienced a change of heart, Hercules thought. Well, knowing Jason, it wouldn't last long . . . they would be back to business in the morning. But for now, he intended to take full advantage of the chance for sport and adventure.

At first none of them talked much, and Hercules contented himself with watching the wheeling gulls and listening to the soft *shush-shush* sounds of the low waves. Now and then Jason or Atalanta would pause to examine shells, seaweed, or bits of driftwood that had washed ashore during storms.

As time wore on and Jason made no real effort to find game, Hercules began to suspect their young leader had something else on his mind . . . something that he was reluctant to discuss. Hercules sighed to himself and kept quiet. Sometimes you just had to wait for the words to come, he thought. Jason would find voice for them soon enough.

Finally Jason shaded his eyes and looked out to sea. "It's pleasant enough here, I think," he said. "We're far enough from the cannibals that we should be able to spend a couple of days, have a hunt, maybe hold a few games. I don't know about you, but I'm getting a little tired of dried meat and salted fish."

Atalanta smiled. "So the grumbling finally reached your ears, too, eh?"

"We all eat the same food," Hercules pointed out. "I'm sure Jason's stomach complains as loudly as yours."

"Shh!" Atalanta raised one hand, turning her head and frowning. "Do you hear that?"

Hercules strained to listen. From somewhere to their right, over a grass-topped sand dune, came a low snuffling, grunting sound. A wild pig? He felt his mouth begin to water at the thought of roast pork for dinner. For once, it seemed luck was with them.

Jason hefted his spear, grinning. "Shall we?" he whispered.

Hercules and Atalanta nodded. Jason motioned Atalanta to the left of the dune and Hercules straight over the top. He headed to the right. They would surround their prey, Hercules knew from long experience, and finish it quickly.

Kicking off his sandals, Hercules padded up the low hill as softly as a mouse. The sand felt scorchingly hot against his bare feet, and the weeds, small burrs, and thistles scratched at his legs and snagged on his tunic. He would be spending hours picking them out, he thought with some annoyance, but a belly full of roast pig would be worth it.

Nearing the top, he dropped to his hands and knees, inching forward cautiously. A small grassy plain lay on the other side of the dune, he now saw. Here thick, yellowish grass rose chest high, dotted here and there with small green bushes and gnarled trees.

The sounds of snuffling grew louder. He lay still, watching and waiting, and soon he glimpsed movement about forty feet ahead. Something large but low to the ground was foraging in the grass.

Then it raised its long, serpentlike head . . . and a second head . . . and a third. Hercules swallowed as he stared into slitted red eyes that shifted constantly with the wariness of a predator. Something yellow glistened on two of its mouths . . . *egg*, he realized suddenly. It had found a nest.

Two of the heads lowered and began to feed again, making those strange snuffling sounds. So much for a pig, he thought. He made it a habit never to eat monsters; too often they were cursed or unclean. And since it didn't seem to be bothering anybody, he thought Jason would want to leave it alone. That's what Jason always did with monsters, after all.

But suddenly he heard a man's voice raise a war cry, and Jason came bounding through the grass toward the creature, spear in hand. Hercules gaped. Jason attacking a monster? It didn't seem possible!

Instantly the creature whipped its raised head around and hissed at Jason. Hercules glimpsed needlelike teeth and a long forked tongue in its mouth.

Atalanta had been stalking it more quietly. With the creature distracted, she burst into action and took two quick shots with her bow. A second later, the creature's upraised head sprouted two arrows from its neck. Giving a fierce war cry of her own, Atalanta charged in from the opposite direction, bow in hand.

Hercules grinned. Battle it was! Shouting his own war cry, he leaped forward, spear raised high.

CHAPTER FIVE

As they closed on the creature, its other two heads snapped upright, hissing like angry serpents. The injured head flopped back limply, and to Hercules it looked dead. One down, he thought.

Instead of fighting, though, the creature turned and slithered across the grassland faster than a horse could gallop. Now that it moved, Hercules saw that it had the body of a gigantic snake.

Halfway to the nest, Hercules drew up short. They would never be able to catch it, he realized.

Even so, Jason followed it twenty yards farther into the grass, whooping and brandishing his weapon like a madman. Atalanta managed two more shots, nicking the creature once on its third head, but doing no real damage. Then it was gone, vanished into a thick copse of trees on the other side of the plain.

Hercules pushed through the grass until he reached the nest, then stopped and stared in amazement. It was *huge*, easily ten feet across. He had been expecting to find the half-eaten remains of three or four bird eggs. Instead, it held only one . . . but he had never heard tell of such an egg in all his travels. Before the creature had smashed it and begun to feed, it had been easily five or six feet long.

The serpent-creature had apparently been feeding for some time, smearing the yolk and scattering bits of leathery brown eggshell around the nest.

"What do you think laid it?" Atalanta asked wonderingly as she joined him. She reached down and picked up a small piece of the shell, turning it over in her hands. It was as thick as her wrist, Hercules saw, but it seemed supple and leathery—more like a turtle's egg than a bird's.

"I don't know," Hercules said, "but think of the omelet we missed!"

"I thought you didn't eat monsters."

"Maybe a big chicken laid it!" he said with a laugh. "I haven't had one of those in weeks!"

"We had best get back to camp," Jason said, joining them and suddenly looking somber as he considered the nest. "When the mother returns, we don't want to be here."

"As it is, she's going to be plenty mad," Hercules said. He glanced up at the sky warily. "It has to be something *big*. Maybe two or three times as big as the myserae."

The myserae were huge predatory birdlike creatures that had plagued the island of Sattis, until the Argonauts had tracked them back to their home and destroyed them. Killing those monsters—and the priest of Hera who controlled them—had been one of the hardest tasks of Hercules's life. None of them would be alive now if not for the goddess Athena's assistance. But then, he thought, she had pulled them into the whole mess to begin with by diverting their ship from the quest for the Golden Fleece . . .

"Come on," Jason said. He jogged back toward the beach. Atalanta and Hercules followed close behind. Hercules kept a wary eye on the sky all the while, but only gulls and a few stray songbirds circled above, their cries suddenly shrill and lonely.

"Say nothing to the rest of the crew about that nest," Jason told Hercules and Atalanta. "I don't want to panic them. We'll leave at dawn tomorrow."

"Agreed," Hercules said. "But what about the fun you promised? The crew *is* tired."

"We'll find another spot farther up the coast tomorrow night. Someplace a little safer."

"Maybe a town?" Atalanta asked.

"Maybe a town *with a tavern*?" Hercules added.

Jason snorted. "You two are single-minded when it comes to wine! All right, if we see a town that *isn't* inhabited by cannibals and *doesn't* have monsters or *anything else* that's going to try to kill us, we'll stop!"

Hercules grinned. "We're going to hold you to that!"

The trek back to camp seemed to take forever. Afternoon deepened to dusk, and still they trudged up the beach. A silence fell over the little party. Neither Jason nor Atalanta seemed interested in talking, Hercules found. They both looked a little depressed . . . but monsters could do that, he knew. He had faced enough of them over the years. They had to be wondering what sort of creature laid that egg and whether it might return tonight to try to eat them.

Sighing inwardly, Hercules contented himself with watching the sky and listening to the crunch of their feet on sand. Slowly he found his own thoughts turning darkly inward, toward other monsters he had faced and epic battles he had fought. *But it wasn't enough*, he told himself. *Despite all I have done, when it really mattered, I could not save my family.* He felt a pit open up in his stomach. A lump the size of an apple choked his throat.

He shook his head, trying to clear it. *I promised never to think of those days again,* he told himself. *I must look to the future, not to the past.* He had lived by that philosophy since the death of his wife and sons. At times, it had been the only thing to keep him going.

Fortunately they had almost reached their campsite. When they finally rounded the last spit of land and the *Argo* came into view, Hercules felt his heart quicken at the sight. Even now, with the sails furled and the oars stowed away, she looked magnificent. Indeed, she was like no other in all the world. The gods had surely inspired the shipbuilder Argos when he created her.

As the ship rocked lightly in the low swells, the two men standing watch on board spotted them and waved. Hercules waved back.

Jason cupped his hands to his mouth. "Is all well?" he shouted.

"Yes!" came the distant reply.

"See?" Atalanta said. "I told you Theseus could set up camp without you. It's not like everyone hasn't done it dozens of times before."

"Mmm," Jason said.

"And if we hadn't gone out," Hercules added, "we never would have known about whatever made that nest. It could have attacked us without warning."

"We're far enough away, we may be safe."

"We may have walked for thirty minutes," Hercules said, "but a monster with wings could fly here in a tenth of that time."

"Still," Jason said, "it has not shown itself. It may have abandoned the nest days or even weeks ago."

"True." Hercules shrugged. "But I would rather be prepared for whatever may happen."

Jason suddenly grinned. "Now you sound like me!"

Hercules laughed, but he had to admit he felt more than a little concern. *Perhaps Jason is right and it isn't going to appear*, he thought. He knew some animals laid their eggs, then abandoned the nests, trusting in the Fates to keep their offspring alive. *Let's hope that is the case here.*

They continued to walk, quickening their steps, and the camp soon came into view. All the other Argonauts seemed in high spirits. The foraging parties had met with success: a huge bonfire burned near the water's edge, and a couple of deer turned on spits just above the flames. As grease sizzled and hissed, a mouthwatering smell filled the air, carrying even to Hercules a hundred yards away. On the sand around the fire, he saw men wrestling, drinking, gambling, and lounging about, enjoying their respite from ship's routine.

"Theseus seems to have things well in hand," Hercules said as they all paused to survey the scene. "You should take side trips more often and trust him to keep things in order for you here."

"I may well do that," Jason said. Somehow, Hercules didn't believe him, though. Jason had never been one to surrender any responsibility. But then, perhaps that was what made him a great leader . . . and would one day make him a great king.

"Care to take part in the evening games?" Atalanta asked Hercules, dropping back to join him as they headed for the bonfire. "It looks like fun!"

Hercules sighed. "These days, I can never seem to find anyone willing to wrestle me!"

"I'll do it," Jason said, glancing over his shoulder. "I've never tried my skills against yours, after all, and I've known you all my life."

"What!" Hercules said. He stopped and rubbed a finger in one ear dramatically. "Did I hear right? You want to wrestle me?"

"I'll wager a dozen horses that you can't pin me in the first minute of our match."

"A challenge? Done! Those will be the easiest horses I've won in my life."

The rest of the Argonauts had spotted them by then, and most had overheard the challenge. Cries of, "A match!" began to echo up and down the beach. Everyone immediately dropped whatever he was doing and formed a large circle to the left of the bonfire. Jason entered the circle and Hercules followed.

Slowly, Jason handed his spear to Theseus. Then he passed over his knife and pulled off his tunic. The firelight gleamed redly on his smooth, well-muscled chest.

"Come on, old man," he said to Hercules, motioning him forward. "I want my horses!"

"Old man!" Hercules said with a snort. "At least I can grow a beard, boy!"

"Ignore his comments," Atalanta whispered in Hercules's ear. "He's trying to get you mad. I think he's up to something. Watch yourself or you *will* be out twelve horses!"

"What kind of trick do you suspect?" Hercules whispered back. He had seen Jason wrestle half a dozen times, but though strong and quick, their leader hadn't impressed him as a great wrestler . . . especially in this company of heroes. Half the men here probably could have beaten Jason in a fair match.

Atalanta bit her lip thoughtfully. "I don't know. But doesn't he always have one?"

"Hmmm . . . I think you may be right." He nodded slowly, then handed his spear to Atalanta and shrugged. "I'll be careful."

"First the rules!" Jason said loudly, so all could hear. "We must both stay within the circle of men. I don't want you running off in fear!"

A light laughter ran through the men around them.

"Agreed," Hercules said cautiously. That seemed straightforward enough, he thought. "There is little chance of me running off, though—and certainly not in fear of you!"

"And you must pin me before one minute passes—that was our bargain. Theseus will count the time."

"Also agreed," Hercules said. That, too, seemed entirely acceptable. Few of his wrestling matches against mortals had ever lasted more than a few seconds. He narrowed his eyes, studying his opponent. What sort of trick did Jason have in mind? It would have to be something crafty, something to catch him off his guard. Throwing sand in his eyes? No—that wouldn't be fair, and Jason always bided by the rules. Then what?

Theseus raised one hand and said, "Wrestlers—begin!"

Hercules dropped into a cautious stance and advanced toward Jason warily. If the young prince had a trick in mind, he wouldn't fall for it, he vowed. Jason crouched, too, making a low growling noise deep in his throat, like a dog guarding some meaty bone.

Slowly they circled one another. Jason feinted left, and Hercules countered, trying to grab his arm and throw him to the ground. As quick as a cat, though, Jason danced back, laughing.

"You'll have to be faster, Graybeard!" he cried. "You're getting slow!"

"Graybeard," Hercules snarled. "Stop your dancing around, pup, and I'll show you the match of your life!"

"Fifteen seconds!" Atalanta called.

Hercules hesitated. With only a minute to pin Jason,

he told himself, direct attack seemed the easiest way to get it over.

Lowering his head, he charged.

Jason danced out of the way nimbly, and Hercules wheeled around and rushed at him again. This time, Jason darted to the left, and again Hercules found himself clutching air.

The rest of the Argonauts began to laugh. Hercules felt his ears start to burn.

The next time, he approached Jason more carefully, and he managed to snag Jason's arm for an instant only to have it slide through his grasp like an eel. Stumbling, clutching at air, he barely caught himself before he fell face first into the sand.

Jason laughed with delight. "Come on, Hercules," he said. "You'll have to do better than that!"

Snarling in frustration, Hercules wheeled and charged again. "I have you!" he cried, when Jason seemed to freeze in panic.

Then Jason doubled back at the last second, and Hercules crashed headlong into Odysseus, knocking him through the circle. They both ended up sprawled headlong in the sand.

"Get off me!" Odysseus growled.

"Sorry about that," Hercules said. He climbed to his feet and gave Odysseus an arm up. Grumbling, his friend began to brush the sand from his tunic.

"I believe I win," Jason said from the ring of men around the fire.

"What!" Hercules cried. "You never touched me!"

"He didn't have to," Atalanta said. She was shaking her head in mock disappointment. "You did it yourself, Hercules—remember the rules?"

Hercules groaned and slowly shook his head. Not only had he left the circle around the fire, more than a minute had passed . . . and he hadn't managed to grab hold of Jason, let alone pin him.

"I'll give you a chance to get even," Odysseus said to Hercules. "I'll bet you a dozen horses that you can't pin *me* in a minute, either!"

"I don't know . . ." Hercules said slowly, trying to keep his inner smile from showing. Even though he'd lost, he still enjoyed the sport. And for the first time in years, people were clambering to wrestle with him!

"What are a few horses!" Odysseus said.

"A lot to a poor man like me," Hercules said. "We'd best make it three this time. I'm not rich like Jason here! And he's already won the cream of my stables back home."

"Done!" Odysseus cried. He strode forward into the ring, and Hercules trailed him.

Odysseus would be easy to beat, Hercules thought. Although he was just as tough and fearless in battle as Jason, he was also older and slower moving.

They circled each other warily for a few seconds, and then Hercules charged forward, arms swinging. On the second try, he snagged Odysseus's left arm, whirled him around, and threw him to the ground. In a second, he had him pinned.

Odysseus laughed. "You got me!" he said. "It's a good thing we only bet three horses!"

"Three down, nine to go!" Hercules replied. Other heroes were crying out to wrestle with them. His gaze fell on the closest, Orestes, and he gave the man a nod.

"Two horses," Orestes said.

"Agreed!"

And the fight was on.

CHAPTER SIX

They spent the rest of the evening wrestling. Hercules managed to win back his original twelve horses, but only after losing half a dozen more. All thoughts of the giant egg and the nest left him, and he found he was truly enjoying himself, lost in the fun of the moment.

After everyone who wanted to wrestle him had gotten a chance—winning or losing horses in the process—the venison was finally cooked enough to eat. Everyone helped themselves and began to settle down around the fire to enjoy the evening meal.

Only Jason and Theseus took their plates and went off to talk in private. Doubtless Jason wanted to tell him what they had found, Hercules thought. He glanced at the sky, but saw only stars. Few birds flew at night, anyway, he knew. They wouldn't have any worries until tomorrow.

He and Atalanta found a quiet spot to the side to eat

and talk. Hercules sank back on the sand, took a sip from his bowl of wine, and took a big bite of meat. It tasted as good as it smelled, rich and greasy, just the way he liked it.

"You know," Atalanta said between bites. "I may have been wrong about Hylas."

"Oh?" Still chewing, Hercules raised his eyebrows. This was the first time he'd ever heard her admit to being wrong about *anything*.

"Seeing him on deck while you were in the water made me realize how much he needs better training. He handles a sword and a spear well enough—and a bow passably well—but he doesn't have the discipline of a real warrior. It's going to get him killed in battle."

Hercules hid his smile by taking a sip of wine. "You're saying he shouldn't have shot that arrow. A *disciplined* warrior wouldn't have done it."

"Yes—no! I mean, I don't know what I mean! Just that he needs someone good to train him. Why not you?"

Hercules paused for a second. "I can think of a dozen reasons. First, he's already been trained—"

"But you can do a better job."

"—and most of all, I don't *want* any family or followers. In case you haven't noticed, anyone who gets too close to me ends up dead. Hera sees to that. If I accepted him as my shield-bearer, she might well have him killed."

That's the real reason, he told himself. *That's why I can't let myself get close to anyone . . . even you. I've lost too many people I cared for over the years.*

"I find it hard to believe that Hera would be so petty."

"You don't know her like I do . . . you're not the bastard offspring of her husband. She has wanted me dead from my birth. Did you know she sent two pythons to strangle me in my crib?"

"No, I haven't heard that story." She sipped her own

wine, brow furrowing. "But Hera doesn't interfere in your work, does she?"

"Not openly," he said. "She's more concerned with my personal life . . . in trying to make me as miserable and as uncomfortable as possible."

"Then I'll make a deal with you. This will be a simple job, like your Twelve Labors. Well, maybe a little bit easier. Don't make Hylas your shield-bearer, but train him in the arts of war . . . like a paid tutor."

"Hmm . . . my Thirteenth Labor? Perhaps." Hercules took another bite as he considered her proposal. Hera's attacks had always been personal . . . perhaps she wouldn't interfere if he trained Hylas. It offered some interesting possibilities for the future, if it worked.

"Well?" she prompted.

"What sort of payment are you offering?"

"Payment?"

"This *is* a job, remember." He grinned at her suddenly nonplussed expression. "I'm famous. I don't work cheaply."

"In that case, you can have the next monster we find."

"Only *one*? That's hardly a bargain. How do I know I'd get a good monster?"

"All right, how about the next *big* monster?"

"Like the sea monster we found this morning?"

"Yes!"

He shook his head. The fine art of negotiating required him to turn down her first offer, almost as a matter of principle.

"I don't know," he finally said. "What else can you throw in?"

"How about the rest of the summer wine from Sattis?"

"You've been holding out on me!"

"I put a little aside for a special occasion."

"Then—done!" he cried. They shook hands. Hercules

smacked his lips over the thought of that wine. "So, where is it?"

"On the ship. I have a small jar stashed in the hold. I'll get it for you tomorrow. Now, when do you start Hylas's training?"

"No time like the present." Cupping one hand to his mouth, he called, "*Hylas!*"

A second later, the youth sprinted to his side. "Yes, Hercules?" he asked, almost breathless.

"Atalanta tells me you want someone to train you."

Hylas licked his lips and looked at Atalanta, who nodded encouragingly.

"That's right," the youth said. "I know I can improve my skills with sword and spear."

"Very well, I'll train you. If you agree, that is."

"Really?" Hercules heard a note of excitement creep into Hylas's voice.

"Yes. And now the first lesson . . ."

"Anything!"

"Get me some more venison."

Hylas blinked. "Venison?" he asked slowly.

"That's what I said. Do you have a problem with my order?"

"No, sir!" Hylas grabbed Hercules's plate, turned, and sprinted toward the bonfire and the roasting deer. Hercules heard him shouting his news to the other Argonauts with near glee. Eonos cut him a piece of venison while other men clasped him on the shoulders and congratulated him. If their words were to be believed, it seemed many of them actually *envied* him having Hercules as a tutor.

Hercules gave a snort. *Let's just hope I don't come to regret it*, he thought. Casting a dark look toward the heavens and the queen of the gods, he mentally added, *If anything happens to Hylas, I'll never forgive you, Hera . . . or myself.*

Atalanta was glaring at him. "More venison?" she de-manded suspiciously. "What kind of lesson is that?"

Hercules gave her his most innocent look. "Why, the first and most important one, of course . . . to take orders from your commander without question." Unfortunately, his stomach chose that moment to rumble with hunger. "And I'm starving. He'd better hurry if he's going to pass!"

Atalanta groaned and shook her head. "Maybe this wasn't such a good idea after all!"

"We're off to a very promising start," Hercules went on, getting into the spirit of things. "It looks like he's going to pass his first lesson admirably. But I'm going to have to test him on this subject quite a lot, you know—"

"—especially around dinner time!" Atalanta finished. "What have I done to that poor boy!" she added in mock horror.

Hylas returned with a plate laden with thinly sliced venison. "Here you are!" he said.

Hercules began to eat ravenously. "Thanks," he man-aged to say between bites. "Don't forget to get some more for yourself. A hero always has a big appetite. He never knows when he'll get his next meal."

"Oh! Right!" Hylas turned and ran back to the bonfire for a second helping.

"I'm *definitely* going to regret this," Atalanta said.

"You should eat more, too," Hercules told her. "If you want, I'll have Hylas fill your plate again."

"If you don't mind, I'll get my own!"

"And tell Hylas to bring us both more wine!" Hercules called after her. "I'm thirsty, too!"

"*Rise and pack your gear!*"

Jason's voice broke into Hercules's pleasant dreams of life with his wife and children. Groaning, he pulled one of his lion skin's paws over his face and clung to the shreds of sleep. His wife . . . his children . . . those days, so long ago, had been the happiest of his life.

"*Rise, Argonauts! We sail at dawn!*"

Around him, he heard grumbles and the crunch of feet on sand as the rest of the Argonauts began to roll up their blankets, gather their weapons, and head for the boats.

"I saved you some venison, Father," the voice of his dead son said.

Hercules sat bolt upright, the lion's paw falling away. In the dim morning twilight, his son stared back at him, a plate in his hands. Then the figure stepped forward and Hercules saw it was only Hylas.

He sank back on his elbows, trembling, almost overcome with emotion. Rocks filled his stomach. *Only a dream. It was only a dream.* He almost wept. His wife and children were long dead, he knew. His boy wouldn't be coming back to serve him breakfast, not now, not anytime.

"Are you all right, Hercules?" Hylas asked. "You look strange . . ."

"Yes," Hercules said gruffly. Swallowing, he forced himself to his feet. To cover his sudden confusion, he said gruffly, "Many thanks, Hylas. There's no need to wait on me, though—leave that for shield-bearers and spear-carriers. You're a pupil."

"But you don't have any shield-bearers—"

"And I like it that way," he said sharply, trying to sound severe. He was going to take his job seriously, he told himself, and Hylas needed to know that. "I will tutor you in weapons until I'm satisfied you won't get yourself killed in battle through ignorance or poor skills. But I'm not here to be your friend, and I'm not here to be your father! Do you understand?"

Hylas gulped. "Yes, sir."

"Good." Hercules gave a curt nod. He seemed to have put a proper amount of fear into the lad, he thought. And his son . . . his dead son . . . was pushed to the back of his thoughts again.

Gone, but never forgotten, a small voice whispered in the back of his mind. *Never forgotten*.

Around them, the Argonauts began to pick up camp. Hercules glanced up at the graying sky again. Maybe half an hour till dawn, he thought, maybe a little less. Insects sang in the grass and trees surrounding the cove; a few morning birds gave their first tentative cries and began to stretch their wings. Remembering the nest and the giant egg, he began to stretch the kinks from his back and shoulders, getting ready for the day's action—be it rowing or fighting monsters. They shouldn't stay here any longer than necessary, he thought. No wonder Jason had gotten everyone up so early.

"What do you want me to do?" Hylas asked, still holding the plate.

He thought for a moment. "Eat that yourself. You'll need your strength today. After that, don't miss the boat when we row out to the *Argo*. Make sure you sit next to me."

"Yes, Hercules." Sitting cross-legged, Hylas began to eat ravenously.

Picking up the spear that had lain beside him all night, Hercules climbed to his feet and shook the sand from his lion skin. There were advantages to traveling lightly, he knew; he was now packed and ready to go.

Then he scooped up his wine bowl, poured out the few remaining dregs, and headed for the boats without a backward glance. He set the bowl inside one of the boats, with the rest of the dirty dishes. Hylas would scrub them out later—as the youngest, his duties aboard ship included keeping the galley and eating utensils clean.

Nobody else was ready to row out to the ship yet. Glancing around, he spotted a few dark shapes beside last night's fire pit. A steady rasping noise came from there, like metal on stone. He headed over.

A few coals still glowed orange, and by their ruddy light he saw Atalanta, Xerxes, and Pallon. They had found whetstones and had begun to sharpen their spear-tips and arrowheads.

"How's it going with your kid?" Atalanta asked. She began to whet another bronze arrowhead. "I thought I heard yelling."

"Oh?" Hercules glanced back at Hylas, who still hunkered down to eat. "Not yelling. Establishing the proper teacher-pupil relationship. I may have gone too far last night . . . he brought me breakfast."

"Mmm." She finished and tucked her last arrow back into its quiver and offered him the whetstone. "Don't tell me you're having regrets."

"Not yet." He accepted the stone and began to sharpen his spear's broad, flat blade. "Just trying to curb his enthusiasm. This is work, not a game."

"Mmm," she said again. "You don't sound very convinced of that yourself."

"You know me too well." He paused, then lowered his voice so Xerxes and Pallon wouldn't overhear. "He woke me from a dream. For a moment, I thought he was my son returned from the dead."

She paused a second and then squeezed his arm gently. "I'm sorry," she whispered. "If there's anything I can do . . ."

"It's not your fault, it's mine." He tested his spear's blade with his thumb and found it sharp as a razor. "I've always had a hard time dealing with death. It doesn't always seem real to me, you know?"

"Yes," she said softly, her gaze growing distant. "I lost

my older brother, Iolanos, when I was six. For years I pretended he was still alive, still living with us."

"What happened?" Hercules asked.

"My father finally sat me down and told me it had to stop. I was upsetting Mother horribly. I cried for days after that, but I never spoke his name again. Until now, that is. Sometimes I wonder if that's why I became who I became . . . a woman warrior in a man's world."

"You tried to take your brother's place," Hercules said, nodding.

"I . . . suppose. I don't really know anymore. It all seems such a long time ago."

"Time to go!" Theseus shouted from the beach by the boats. "Argonauts to the boats!"

"That's my cue," Hercules said, climbing to his feet. "I'm rowing, you know . . ."

Hercules spent the next half hour ferrying people over to the *Argo*. It seemed to him like the gods had chosen to send a perfect day for their journey: the sun rose in a cloudless blue sky, a nice breeze gusted from the west, and everyone's spirits seemed higher than they had been in weeks—both from the games of the night before and from the prospect of sailing instead of rowing.

As soon as everyone had boarded and the boats had been safely lashed down on deck, Jason shouted for sails to be raised.

Instantly, the wind died.

"Typical for this trip," Atalanta grumbled beside Hercules. "Just when it looks like things might start going our way . . ."

"If the gods are against us," Hercules said, "there is nothing we can do."

"Nothing but row," Atalanta said.

Hercules headed for the rowing benches. Everyone followed him.

The morning wore on without event. Hercules kept a lookout for a promising village in which to spend the night, but no new settlements of any kind appeared along the desolate shore. It seemed this land was sparsely inhabited. Which might well explain the monsters they had run into over the last two days, he reminded himself: they tended to avoid more populous lands, after all.

Just after lunch break, as they resumed rowing, a shadow fell across the ship's deck for a second. Hercules stiffened, a sudden sick feeling in his stomach. There weren't any clouds in the sky to cast shadows that large, he thought. Without missing a beat on his oar, he glanced up and soon spotted a tiny dark shape circling high above. It was hard to gauge its size from this distance, but he had a feeling it was huge . . . as large as the *Argo* or perhaps even larger.

"Do you think that's our bird?" Atalanta asked him in a whisper.

Slowly he nodded. "I think so," he said just as softly. "Can there be many of them so close together? It's seen us. And it's going to attack."

CHAPTER SEVEN

W hat bird?" Hylas asked from beside them. He had taken the seat to the other side of Hercules, as instructed. "What are you talking about?"

Keeping his voice low, Hercules explained about the nest they had discovered the day before. Hylas grew pale at the thought of such a monster, but he kept rowing without missing a stroke.

"You don't think it will attack, do you?" he asked, staring at the sky.

"Don't look up so much, you'll attract everyone's attention," Hercules said.

"Sorry." He stared at his oar again.

Atalanta said, "The way our luck has been running of late, it will not only attack, but wreck the *Argo*, leaving us stranded here."

"Unless I kill it first," Hercules said cheerfully.

"Unless *you* kill it—!"

"Shh! Have you forgotten our bargain? The next big monster is supposed to be mine!"

She grimaced. "Oh, all right, if you intend to hold me to that."

"I do!"

The bird circled lower. Hercules glanced at the bow, where Jason and Theseus were locked in frantic discussion. He couldn't hear what they said, but he knew they had to be deciding which course of action to take: try to fight, take cover aboard ship and hope it leaves, or row toward shore and try to make a stand on land. Unfortunately, at the rate the bird was descending, he knew they wouldn't have long before decisive action of some kind would be required.

"Rowers—rest!" Jason finally called. "Ship oars!"

Finally! Hercules thought.

Everyone began to pull their oars up onto the deck, laying them at their feet. The bird's shadow fell across the *Argo* a second time, and more people spotted it. Instantly speculation began.

"It has to be a roc," Odysseus said loudly as he shaded his eyes and peered upward. "I heard tell of them once. They say they lay gigantic eggs, which are prized in the East above all other foods."

Everyone began to nod sagely. "It must be!" Hercules heard several of them saying.

"A roc . . ." Hercules murmured. Yes, now that he thought of it, he *had* heard that same story long ago. Why hadn't he remembered it before?

He glanced up. The roc was no longer a spec in the sky; now he could make out its mottled brown color, not terribly attractive, and its long hooked beak, which reminded him of a vulture's. It flew in an almost leisurely style, with its taloned feet tucked up close to its body.

Now and again its wings flapped, but mostly it seemed content to glide on high-above winds.

It had definitely spotted the *Argo*. At its current rate of descent, Hercules estimated, it would reach them in a couple of minutes.

"What should we do?" Hylas asked softly. "Will it attack?"

"If it thinks we destroyed its egg and is hunting us," Atalanta said, "I know it will attack. Any mother would."

"Then what's Jason waiting for?"

Hercules glanced at their leader again. Arms folded, Jason stared calmly upward, deep in thought. Clearly he hadn't decided on a course of action yet. The roc's almost leisurely descent must have lulled him into a false sense of safety. It didn't *seem* bent on destroying them; therefore it wasn't a threat yet. However, Hercules had run into too many monsters over the years to fall for that ploy. It would be on them faster than they realized, and when it attacked, he knew they had best be prepared.

Yet he didn't want to panic the rest of the crew. Jason was their commander, and Jason would have to give the order for everyone to get their weapons. But surely no one could object if he and Atalanta prepared themselves ahead of time . . . that wouldn't undermine Jason's authority.

To Hylas, he said, "He's planning his strategy."

"Oh."

"But perhaps we should anticipate his orders. Fetch our weapons. Do it quietly and calmly. Do nothing to excite the rest of the crew or to attract attention."

"Right," Hylas said. "I can do that."

Standing and stretching, he headed for the one small open hatch leading into the hold, as though he were going to fetch a drink or dried fig from ship's stores below. In a second he vanished, and not one eye had given him more than a passing glance. Hercules grinned inwardly. Perhaps having followers *wasn't* so horrible after all, if Hera didn't know it.

Still the giant roc descended, a hundred feet above them now. It seemed more and more immense. At first Hercules had estimated it at fifty feet from wingtip to wingtip, but as it neared he had to keep revising his estimate upward.

"Orestes—Ionus—bring bows for the archers!" Jason finally called. "Everyone else, get belowdecks now! It's going to attack!"

Orestes and Ionus sprang to the large central hatch and opened it. It led to the storage compartment where the weapons were kept. Ionus climbed down first, then Orestes followed. Those among the Argonauts who used bows began to gather around, waiting impatiently. The rest flooded into the various other hatches, watching from cover.

"Archers—that's me!" Atalanta said with what seemed to Hercules to be exceptional smugness. "See you later, Hercules. *After* I kill it! Orders are orders."

Then Jason finished, "And Hercules—you stay, too!"

"Ha!" Hercules grinned triumphantly at her. "I knew Jason wouldn't leave me out of the excitement."

Atalanta pretended to sulk a bit. "Can't blame me for trying, can you? I've never killed a roc before."

"Neither have I!" he said. He glanced at the smaller hatch. What had happened to Hylas? The roc was nearly upon them—they needed their weapons.

At the large hatch, Orestes's head popped into view. He began passing out bows.

As if on cue, Hylas emerged from the small hatch with their weapons. He dashed over and handed Hercules two spears, then gave Atalanta her bow and a quiver of arrows. She strung her bow with casual speed, then notched an arrow, turned, and took careful aim.

The roc was only fifty feet above the *Argo* now. Slowly, flapping its huge wings, it began to turn its head one way then another, examining them and their ship with huge black eyes. It was enormous, even larger than Hercules had first thought, and the wind from its flapping wings felt like a storm's gale.

Around them, the other archers began to string their bows. Orestes passed quivers of arrows up through the hatch.

"First throw is yours!" Atalanta said. "Better hurry, if you want to beat the others!"

"It's a little high yet . . ." Hercules said. He knew his throw would lose a lot of momentum.

"You have two spears."

Hercules nodded. Backing up, he took two steps, then flung his first spear with all his might. It sailed up, straight for the monster's head—a perfect throw until the roc moved at the last second. His spear struck a glancing blow along its beak and opened a shallow cut under its left eye. A faint mist of blood spattered the deck around them.

The roc screamed in rage. Its shrill, unearthly voice cut through Hercules like fingernails scratching on slate, raising the hairs on the back of his neck.

"Argh!" Hercules growled. A couple of inches to the side and he would have taken out its eye.

"Close," Atalanta said.

"Fire!" Jason shouted. "Archers!"

Atalanta fired her first shot along with the other archers. Their arrows hissed through the air and struck the roc—several to the neck, more to the wings, but mostly to the chest and body. Although at least half the arrows buried themselves to the fletching, and the creature's blood flowed freely from the wounds, dripping down on the *Argo* and its crew like a red rain, the wounds only seemed to enrage the beast further.

Screaming again, it flapped its wings twice more, stretched out its legs, and descended toward the mast. Its claws closed around the wooden pole and twisted, and the mast shattered like kindling. Bits of wood showered the deck. Then it grabbed the mast again, breaking off more.

"Archers—fire!" Jason called.

Another round of arrows struck the creature. Screaming, it attacked the mast with renewed fury.

Hylas said, "Uh, Hercules . . ."

"What?" he demanded, taking aim with his last spear. The time for talk was over; Hylas should have taken cover with the others.

"What happens to the roc's body if you kill it in the air?"

Hercules blinked. *It falls. On us!*

He looked up, horrified at the thought. Not only would it crush everyone now fighting it, he thought, it would almost certainly destroy the *Argo*!

"Stop firing!" he bellowed. "Archers—take cover!"

In the bow, Jason turned to gape at him. "*What!*" he cried.

Hercules shouted, "Do it! Do it or we're all dead! I'll explain later!"

Jason hesitated only a fraction of a second, then gave a nod. "Do it!" he called. "Everyone get below! On the double!"

"You, too!" Hercules told Hylas and Atalanta.

Hylas gulped but nodded. Joining the throng of archers running to the open hatches, he was soon safely below-decks. That just left Jason, Atalanta, and Hercules on deck. And the roc, which was still destroying the mast a foot at a time.

"You need someone to cover your back," Atalanta told him.

He didn't have time to argue; he merely nodded. "Take the stern. Cover it, but don't fire unless it's over water."

"Right." Turning, she jogged to the rear of the ship, taking up a defensive position.

Then Jason joined Hercules, a brace of spears cradled in his arms. "Tell me how to kill it," he said simply. "We're in your hands."

"Thanks for trusting me," he said. "Cover me—I'm going to try to lure it away from the mast."

Bending over, running low to the deck, Hercules headed for the bow. As soon as he reached it, he turned and shouted, "Hey—you! Bird! *Hey!*" Waving his arms and his spear, making as much noise as he could, he tried to attract its attention.

It finally spotted him. Abandoning its attacks on the mast, the roc veered toward him, reaching with its powerful talons.

Hercules ducked under it, sprinting back to the middle of the ship. He had to get it over the water, he knew, or he couldn't risk attacking it.

Instead of flying over the *Argo*, though, the roc landed on the deck. One heavy foot crushed the bow's railing into splinters; the other staved in the decking ten feet away. The *Argo* shuddered under its weight, then slowly the bow began to sink into the water. Hercules realized the roc weighed too much—it was going to capsize the ship if it didn't move.

"The ship is sinking!" someone began to shout from the hold. Hercules thought it was Xerxes. Cries of panic followed from the rest of the crew belowdecks.

"Quiet there!" Jason shouted. "Don't distract Hercules or the roc!"

Those words did it though, Hercules saw. The roc began to shift around to face Jason, who gulped audibly and dropped all his spears except one.

From the other side of the deck, Hercules began to wave his arms, shouting, "Hey! Hey! It's me you want!" Hefting his spear, he lunged forward, jabbing the roc in the side.

Instantly the roc lunged at him, beak snapping. He ducked just in time; a half second later and it would have taken a large chunk out of his neck and shoulder, he realized.

As it shifted from foot to foot and tried to turn to face him, more railing splintered. The *Argo*'s bow, already tilted sharply, dipped low enough for a wash of sea water to sweep across the deck.

Hissing, the roc began to dance from side to side, shaking water from first one foot, then the other. Apparently it didn't like getting wet. But it wasn't smart enough to pull both feet out of the water at the same time. It kept putting one then the other back in.

As the deck continued to tilt lower, Hercules felt himself starting to slide forward. He grabbed onto the nearest railing. *Only one spear left*, he reminded himself. *I have to make this shot count.*

Suddenly Xerxes rushed from the hatch nearest the roc, a sword in his hands. Screaming a battle cry, he rushed straight at the roc.

In one swift move, the monster hopped forward and seized Xerxes in its beak like a sparrow holding an insect. Xerxes screamed, hacking at its face and drawing blood, but the creature merely threw back its head and began to swallow. Hercules stared in horror as Xerxes's legs, then chest, then head and arms vanished down its maw in the space of a heartbeat.

"*Aaaaghhhh!*" Hercules screamed.

The creature flapped its powerful wings and hopped toward him. Extending its neck, it seemed to peer at Hercules with its cold black eyes. Slowly it extended its neck, making a faint snuffling sound.

It was smelling him, he realized. It was sniffing the air almost like a dog—*a dog following its prey*, he thought. His heart lunged suddenly. He knew the creature had made the nest they found last evening. And he knew why it had come.

"Get over the side!" he shouted to Jason.

The roc whipped its head around, looking back toward him. Its eyes narrowed. It snuffled the air in his direction.

"It smelled us in its nest!" Hercules shouted. "It knows we were there! It thinks we killed its young! Quickly—over the side and into the water, Jason! That's your only hope."

Jason hesitated only a second. Vaulting the rail, he dropped into the water.

Atalanta joined him a moment later.

That just left Hercules on the deck. It had smelled him on the nest; it would come after him next, he thought.

He wielded his oar like a club, batting at the huge monster. Its wings beat slowly, creating a strong wind that threw him off balance. Then it grabbed the oar in its huge beak and gave a crushing bite. The oar shattered, leaving Hercules with little more than a sharp-pointed stick about as long as a spear.

The talons reached for him, but he ducked under them, and as the monster came to rest on the deck, he braced the oar against a hatch.

The monster slid cleanly onto the shattered oar like a giant chicken onto a skewer. It felt the pain and began to flail its wings, making the ship rock violently from side to side.

Hercules rushed it. Avoiding its thrashing legs, he came up against the solid mass of its body. Its feathers were hard, almost like rope. He dug his fingers into them, heaved with all his might, and suddenly the creature rolled backward.

Wood splintered as it crushed more of the deck's railing, and the *Argo* bobbed like a child's toy in a storm, but still he pushed until he felt it start to fall.

Still screaming, it tumbled overboard. A huge splash of water sloshed over the deck, drenching Hercules, and then it was gone.

He crept up to the railing and glanced over. It floated, head down, twitching all over, giant wings outspread. It couldn't right itself.

Slowly the other Argonauts joined him. They watched its death throes as it drowned.

CHAPTER EIGHT

The *Argo* had never looked worse, Hercules thought as he surveyed the damage. All the railings on the front of the ship had been destroyed by the roc's heavy feet. In several places the decking had been staved in. The top half of the mast had been sheered off. And Xerxes had died.

Hercules had buried many comrades over the years, but it made his heart ache. Brave but young, Xerxes had only begun to distinguish himself in battle. It was never easy to bury a comrade, but for someone like Xerxes—whose whole life and career still lay ahead of him—it was doubly hard.

Atalanta joined him, putting a soft hand on his shoulder. "It wasn't your fault," she said.

"Why did he do it?" Hercules asked. "If he had stayed below, with the others, he would still be alive."

"He couldn't swim," she said. "The water terrified him. More than the roc, it seems."

Slowly Hercules nodded. "Yes . . . I understand."

While Theseus made a sacrifice for Xerxes's soul, Hercules and the rest of the Argonauts busied themselves cleaning up the damage. Once more Hercules found his thoughts turning dark, back to the people he had lost, and no matter how hard he tried, images kept appearing in his mind. His wife, long dead, his sons . . .

He tried to bury himself in work. The railings were a complete loss—none of them could be saved. He ripped out the splintered pieces by hand. They would have to be careful on deck until they could get replacements fitted . . . though that might not be until they returned to civilized lands.

Finally they settled down to row again. This time Hercules heard no cheerful banter, no jokes or conversation. Only the ponderous beat of a drum, setting the rhythm that they all followed.

Hercules leaned hard into his task, helping to send the *Argo* gliding forward through the low waves. He breathed deeply and felt the warmth of the setting sun on his broad, deeply muscled back. It felt good, he thought, to relax and focus on his work, pulling to the rhythm of the drums and letting his mind go empty. After all the excitement of the last month, he told himself with an enthusiasm he no longer felt, they were finally heading for the Kingdom of Colchis once more. There would be new adventures and excitement there.

"Ship oars!" a loud voice called.

Hercules lifted his oar out of the water and pulled it back onto the *Argo*'s deck.

He turned. In the bow of the ship, Theseus and Jason

were talking animatedly, but he couldn't hear the words over the sudden babble of talk.

"Water?" a woman's voice asked beside him.

"Hmm?" He glanced over at Atalanta, who was holding out a goatskin. "I'd rather have wine!"

"Try it, you might develop a taste for it."

Grumbling good-naturedly, he pulled the stopper, put the skin's mouth to his lips, and tilted it back. A cool, pleasantly fruity red wine filled his mouth and throat, and he almost gagged in surprise. It was one of the excellent summer wines they had picked up on Sattis several weeks ago.

Of course, he realized, Jason didn't want them drinking while they rowed. So Atalanta had to call it water.

"Best I've ever tasted!" he said, wiping his mouth on the lion skin he wore.

"I think we're about to make camp for the night," Atalanta said.

Hercules studied the coast. Tall white cliffs, facing an inviting beach. Yes, it looked like a good spot, especially with that stream splashing down through a steep ravine. They could use fresh water.

"That looks like a good place."

"Port oars in the water!" Jason called. "On the count of three!"

"That's us," Hercules said to Atalanta.

"I know!" she said. "You're the one who keeps getting port and starboard mixed up!"

"Well . . . why can't Jason just say 'left' and 'right' like a normal person?"

"Would that be left as you face forward, or left as you face back?" she countered.

"Well . . ." he hesitated.

"See? It's much simpler this way."

"Port oars *pull!*" Jason called.

Hercules and Atalanta dipped their oars, then pulled with all their strength. Slowly their ship began to turn toward shore.

"Port oars *pull!*" Jason called a second time.

Hercules did as instructed.

"Ship oars!"

As Hercules pulled his oar up onto the deck, he glanced over his shoulder at the rapidly approaching shore. The small cove looked singularly inviting, he thought. With its white, sandy beach, twenty-foot-high cliffs, and a small stream trickling down from a cleft in the rocks to the left, it offered a safe haven for the night. Perhaps they could even find fresh game and have a cookout on the beach. He grinned at the thought. Yes, a nice place to spend the night indeed.

Jason and Theseus knelt in the bow, playing out a length of string tied to a stone. The string would tell them the water's depth. They didn't want to risk running the *Argo* aground and damaging her hull. They had already done that once, and it had taken Theseus quite a while to get it properly patched and seaworthy again.

"Drop anchor," Jason called back suddenly.

From behind came a tremendous splash as Orestes and Orpheus pushed the heavy stone weight overboard. The *Argo* slowed, then came to a halt.

Jason turned toward the rowers. "We'll set up camp for the night here!" he called. "We can start repairs on the ship tomorrow. For now, though . . . anyone care to join me for a hunt?"

"Aye!" Hercules shouted a half second ahead of everyone else . . . except Atalanta, whose voice matched his. But then, he thought, she was never one to be left behind for anything, especially not a hunt.

Jason laughed. "It looks like we're going to need several hunting parties!"

Atalanta folded her arms and looked at Hercules. "But only one of us can be the most successful."

Hercules burst out laughing. "You know what? I think you're the most competitive person I have ever met! What does it matter who finds the most game as long as we all eat well tonight?"

"Hmm," she said, "that's what you say now. But I know how hard it is to keep ahead of *you*!"

"*Ahead* of me?" He gave a mock grimace. "You're barely keeping up!"

"I believe," she said, "I'm exactly *two* sea monsters ahead in the tally."

"But—"

She folded her arms. "Admit it!"

Hercules sighed. "All right, but I'm ahead in myserae and rocs!"

She gave a dismissive gesture. "A few birds!"

"Birds!" he cried. "You call those monsters just a few birds!" He turned imploringly to Theseus, who had joined the circle of Argonauts watching them.

"I think you're going to end up betrothed," Theseus told them. "The way you two carry on, half the world thinks you are married already!"

Atalanta gaped at him. It was the first time Hercules had ever seen her speechless. He almost burst out laughing, but managed to hold it in.

"*Married!*" she finally cried.

As seriously as he could manage, Hercules told her, "Don't worry, you're not my idea of an ideal mate, either! If I ever marry again, it will be to a woman who can't out-fight me, out-shoot me, or drink me under the table!"

"Then you admit—" she began.

"I admit nothing!" Hercules said. "Nothing!"

Theseus shook his head sadly. "Just like a husband and wife," he commented.

Atalanta glared at him. "Feh!" she finally said, and she turned and stomped toward the hatch leading into the hold. Everyone burst out laughing.

Hercules watched her climb down the ladder and disappear from sight. Just before she vanished, he overheard her mutter, "Married! I can't believe it!" under her breath.

Hercules grinned at Theseus—a good joke, he thought, as long as Atalanta didn't take it too seriously. He'd have to try to cheer her up tonight.

They rowed to shore, and Jason sent runners up the beach in each direction, searching for signs of people. This cove seemed quite remote to Hercules, and he didn't think they would find any settlements nearby.

While they waited for the runners to return, Theseus set Hercules and the other Argonauts to setting up camp. Hercules dragged half a dozen huge driftwood logs into a circle of stones the other men were building. The rest of the party took turns rowing the large clay jars known as *pithoi* out from the ship; they would fill them with water from the spring.

At last the scouts returned. Hercules dropped a massive log on top of the huge pile he had assembled and hurried over to hear their report. Most of the other Argonauts soon joined him.

Hylas had gone east and was still panting. "I saw nothing of interest," he gasped out. "There are no signs of people anywhere!"

Orestes had gone the other direction. "I too saw no sign of villagers," he said. "The beach was deserted as far as I could see."

Jason nodded. "Then we won't be poaching on anyone's grounds if we hunt here," he said. "I think six parties of four men each ought to do nicely. I'll lead the first."

"And I'll lead another," said Hercules.

Orpheus said, "I'll follow Atalanta!"

Hercules looked at him in puzzlement. "She hasn't even volunteered yet!" he said.

"Oh, she will." Orpheus glanced across at her, and she gave him a quick nod.

"That's right, Hercules," she said. "And we'll bring back twice the meat of anyone else here!"

"A contest?" Hercules mused.

Jason laughed. "A good idea. An extra amphora of wine to the four who bring back the most game!"

All the Argonauts began to cheer, and Hercules studied Atalanta appraisingly. She seemed fiercely determined to win this contest. But then, she was fiercely determined to win *every* contest she entered. For a second, he wondered if he should join her team.

Then he forced that thought away. No, he'd already taken the lead of his own team—he would simply have to beat her with whichever men chose to join him. Who would it be?

Young Hylas looked at him eagerly. "If I may join you?" he asked.

"Of course," Hercules said. Hylas might be young, but he had sharp eyes and quick reflexes. He might well spot game that the rest of their party missed.

Then a distant voice reached them: "*Hello down there!*"

It seemed to be coming from behind and above them. Turning, Hercules studied the cliffs and quickly spotted a man waving to them. He wore a gray tunic with blue designs on the sleeves and hem, and even at this distance Hercules could tell that he was in his middle or late twenties. He carried a spear in one hand, but no other weapons.

Stepping forward, Jason called, "Ho there! Come down and be welcome, sir!"

"*Are you the Argonauts?*" the man called.

"Yes!" Jason shouted. "I am Prince Jason of Thessaly!"

Grinning broadly, the man began to scramble down the side of the cliff, following a trail that Hercules couldn't see. Apparently the man couldn't see it either, since he slid several times, creating small avalanches. But, catlike, he kept his balance and soon joined them.

"Welcome, stranger," Jason said to him. "We had thought these lands deserted. Meeting a civilized man here is a pleasant surprise. From which city do you hail? And how do you know of us?"

"Thank the gods I found you!" he gasped as he reached them. He flopped down on the sand, panting for breath. Evidently he had been running for quite some time, Hercules thought.

"Someone get him a drink," Jason said.

"I am from Arbora," the man said. "These are the king's lands, where he hunts for sport. No man may live here." His gaze swept across the circle of onlookers and settled on the lion skin that Hercules wore. "Are you the one?" he asked. "Are you the man called Hercules?"

"Yes," Hercules said. He didn't think he had ever seen this fellow before. "Do I know you?"

"No, we have never met. My name is Pthereon, and I serve the house of Laomon. Two months ago, a trader from Troy brought word that you were sailing with the Argonauts on a great quest. The head of our house sent me to find you."

"Laomon," Hercules mused. "Do you mean Laomon the Elder of Athens?"

"Formerly of Athens. You remember him, then. He inherited estates in Arbora—a small land about a day's journey from here—some two years ago, and he brought his family here to manage them."

Atalanta had found a flask of water and offered it to Pthereon. He drained it in several fast gulps. Then, settling back again, he wiped his mouth on his sleeve and nodded his thanks to her.

"Of course I remember Old Laomon," Hercules said. He hadn't seen his friend in—how many years? At least five, not since the last time he visited Athens. They had enjoyed some great times together, drinking, hunting, and most of all feasting. In his growing excitement, Hercules found his words bubbling out: "How is Laomon? What is he doing so far from Athens? And how is his son—"

Pthereon shook his head. "Laomon the Elder passed to the underworld some time ago," he said with a heavy sigh. "It is Laomon the Younger whom I now serve."

"Was it his heart?" Hercules asked. He remembered now that it had been giving Laomon trouble for some years.

Pthereon nodded. "It gave out one night. Now, there was a funeral feast to remember."

Hercules let his shoulders sag. "I can't believe he's gone!" he whispered. Laomon the Elder had been only a couple of years older than he was. "And his son?" he asked slowly. "How does Young Laomon fare?"

Pthereon's expression grew more somber. "That is why I came for you," he said. "Since he received word of your quest, he has looked forward to your visit. Unfortunately, two days ago, a wild boar gored him in a hunt. We thought he would recover, but the wounds festered quickly. There was nothing anyone could do . . . I'm sorry. Our healer claims he will be dead within the week."

Hercules swallowed. "My friend Theseus knows something of the healing arts," he began.

"That's right," Theseus said, stepping forward. "If I can help in any way—"

Pthereon shook his head gravely. "None of our local healers, including a priest of Apollo, has been able to help. Laomon is resigned to his fate. What he wants more than anything else is to see Hercules one last time before he dies. It is his last wish. Will you come?"

"Of course," Hercules said. He felt a lump in his throat. Losing two friends in one week—first Xerxes and now Laomon the Younger—disturbed him more than he liked to admit. *At least Xerxes died quickly*, he thought. Few deaths came as slowly or painfully as those from a festering boar wound.

Then he hesitated, looking to Jason. "Will you wait here for me?" he asked.

"Of course," Jason said quietly. "Take as long as you need. We should be here for at least a week, maybe two, with the repairs we need to make. If Arbora is but a day's walk from here, of course you must honor your friend with a visit."

"Very well," Hercules said to Pthereon. "I will go. Let me get my pack and we can set off. We can get a good start before nightfall."

Pthereon shook his head. "You must go ahead of me. I am also charged with the task of summoning his cousins, who live a day's run in the other direction."

"Cousins?"

"Second cousins, really—Plinos and Ioran. Do you know them as well?"

"No. But we will meet soon enough, I'm sure. Give me directions and I will set out at once."

"I'm sure Laomon would welcome any other friends," Pthereon said, looking around at the rest of the Argonauts. "Are there others here who knew him?"

"I did," Atalanta said, stepping forward. "With your permission, I will join Hercules."

Hercules looked at her in surprise. "When did you meet Laomon?"

"He feasted at my father's table a number of times," she said. "I will pay him my family's respects."

"I welcome your company, Atalanta. Mourning is easier when you share the grief with friends."

"Is there anyone else?" Pthereon asked.

A quiet murmur went up from the circle of men around them. Hercules scanned their faces, but no one else stepped forward. It seemed only he and Atalanta knew Laomon the Younger.

"Will you set out now or wait until morning?" Pthereon asked.

"Now, since his time is so short. How do we get to Laomon's estates?"

Pthereon stood, brushing sand from his tunic, then turned and pointed to the spot where he had descended to the beach. "From the top of the cliff you can see mountains. A road lies just beyond the first of the foothills. Follow it west through several small villages. Arbora sits in a small green valley, and if you stay to the road, you will pass through it. You cannot miss it. If you somehow become lost or confused, simply ask anyone you meet along the way. They will point you in the right direction. The house of Laomon is well known."

"It sounds easy enough," Hercules said. He looked at Atalanta, who nodded.

"It is," Pthereon said. "Now, I must be on my way. I have twenty miles yet to travel today."

"May Hermes lend wings to your feet," Jason told him. Then he looked at Hercules and Atalanta. "All of you."

*   *   *

Koremos the Black slowly parted the underbrush and peered down at the Argonauts on the beach below. He kept his movements carefully measured, moving only his eyes. He knew he risked being spotted, but as he expected, everyone had clustered around Pthereon. Not a single one of the Argonauts thought to keep lookout.

He chuckled. From the rapt expressions on their faces, it seemed they all believed his false messenger. Hercules and that warrior-woman had already busied themselves packing, he saw. He felt a brief pang of disappointment, but pushed it aside. He had mostly wanted Hercules to leave, and any others would simply be a pleasant surprise.

"And this time," he promised himself, "there will be no mistakes!"

Cautiously he eased back and let the branches close. Lorron the Strangler stood directly behind him, rubbing his large, gnarled hands together.

"Well, master? Did they believe him?"

"Of course." Koremos gestured grandly. He loved it when one of his plans came together so perfectly. "I knew they would. Now, back to our men, and quickly. We must prepare to strike! Tonight we take the *Argo*!"

CHAPTER NINE

Hercules and Atalanta struck out for Arbora within the hour. All thought of joining the hunt had been pushed from their minds: Hercules wanted to get this journey over as quickly as possible. If Laomon had but a few days left, he would try to give him whatever comfort he could.

From the top of the cliff he spotted the hills and distant mountains, exactly as Pthereon said. A small but well-traveled trail—perhaps for deer—led roughly in the direction they wanted to go, so they followed it. They still had two or three hours of daylight left, and Hercules planned to get as far along as they could before nightfall.

They alternated between walking and running, making good time. As they traveled, Hercules studied the wild growth of forest around them. Strange birds sang in the trees; insects *brrr*ed incessantly in the grass. Twice they startled deer in clearings.

This seemed to be quite a rich land, full of game, and he understood now why a king would make it his private hunting ground. And no wonder Laomon the Elder moved here—both father and son enjoyed the sport and spent as much time as they could hunting. An estate bordering lands such as these would offer them plenty of excitement.

Despite the gravity of their mission, Hercules had to admit it felt good to leave the ship and stretch his legs. He only wished a happier end lay at the close of the journey. Although he had seen much death in his long and often tragic life, losing a friend to an unexpected tragedy like a boar wound always hurt most deeply of all. If he could do anything to raise his friend's spirits in his last hours, to ease his passing to the underworld, he would do it. For all the countless hours he had spent in pursuit of pleasure with both Laomon the Elder and Laomon the Younger, he owed them both that much.

He breathed deeply, tasting the sharp, spicy smells of thyme, wildflowers, and forest loam. He wouldn't think of Laomon the Younger's death, he told himself. He would think of the good times they had had together, drinking, feasting, and bragging of their epic adventures.

He glanced at the sky and found the sun settling between two distant mountains. They had perhaps twenty minutes of daylight left; time to look for a place to camp. Although they carried ample provisions, he always preferred to stop at an inn or a tavern when the opportunity arose. Unfortunately, he saw no signs of either one appearing soon . . . no signs of so much as a hunting lodge. They would have to rough it outdoors. If not for Pthereon's directions, he would have thought these lands deserted.

"How about this for a camp?" Atalanta asked, slowing as the trail entered a small clearing.

Hercules glanced around but saw no signs of danger. He nodded; it would do.

"I'll get wood for a fire," he said. "Care to try your luck with dinner?"

"Two rabbits coming up!" she said, and she shrugged off her bow and pulled an arrow from her quiver.

That night they ate their fill of dove roasted over an open flame instead of rabbit, but Hercules didn't mind. Few dishes could have tasted better. And they washed it all down with a skin of wine Atalanta had brought. As he licked the last of the grease from his fingers and belched softly, Hercules leaned back and studied the stars overhead, feeling deeply contented.

Atalanta reclined on her elbow next to him. He realized she was staring at him and he shifted a bit uneasily. Had he done something to offend her?

"I have a confession," she said at last, "I really didn't know Laomon all that well."

He looked at her. "Oh?"

"We met several times, yes, but he had no time for me . . . I'm sure he viewed me as a silly little girl. I couldn't have been more than ten or eleven the last time he visited my father. I still had my hair in pigtails."

"Eleven is almost a woman."

She laughed. "Not if you're a tomboy more interested in hunting than husbands."

He shrugged. "You seem to have found an agreeable balance. Not only beautiful, but as skilled a warrior as anyone I've ever met."

"You flatter me."

"You keep me on my toes. Sometimes I think you're even tougher than I am."

She punched his arm. *Hard.*

"Hey!" Hercules said, rubbing his shoulder. It throbbed. She'd hit him as hard as she could.

"That's *not* what a woman wants to hear from a man!"

"I'm sorry! But you *did* bring it up, after all." He cleared his throat, deciding to change the subject, since he seemed to have unintentionally offended her. "So . . . if you didn't know Young Laomon that well, why did you come?"

"Stupid . . ." Her voice dropped to a whisper. "For a chance to be with you."

Then she leaned over and kissed him. It caught Hercules completely by surprise, but then he responded, throwing his arm around her and pulling her close. He had wanted to hold her, to kiss her, for as long as he could remember. Her hair smelled of wildflowers, and her lips tasted of honey, and he felt himself drowning in her passion.

This was what he wanted, he knew. Deep in his heart, he desired her more than he had ever desired anyone.

And yet some part of him resisted. When they came up for air, he gasped, "We mustn't—Hera—!"

"Let me worry about her," Atalanta whispered.

Hercules shuddered. *I can't do this. I can't love Atalanta.* It tore him up inside. *I can't bear the thought of her death.*

Tears filling his eyes, he leaped to his feet. "We mustn't!"

"What's wrong?" she asked, and he heard the words catch in her throat. "I thought—"

"Don't you understand?" he cried. "Everyone I love *dies.* It's happened all my life. My wife—my children—my closest friends—!"

He couldn't say any more. Turning, he fled into the darkness. Branches whipped at his face and arms and chest. He stumbled over rocks and roots. Finally he pitched headlong over a stream's embankment, landing face first in mud. Sobbing, he picked himself up.

It isn't fair. He sagged against a tree and began to pound a fist against its trunk. *It isn't fair.*

He loved Atalanta. He would have asked her to marry him in a second, if he thought it could work out well. But he knew it could only end in her death. *I must never love anyone again,* he told himself. *I must keep apart from the world. I must be pure to protect the innocent.*

He had been a fool to accept Hylas as a pupil. He had been a fool to join the Argonauts. He had been a fool his entire life. *If I want to protect people, I should stay away from them,* he told himself.

Only he couldn't live that way. He couldn't shut himself off from the world. His father had given him a great gift; he had to use it.

His hand ached where he had been pounding on the tree. He hugged it to his chest. Pity welled up inside him. *It isn't fair.* But there was nothing to do but go on. He would hold his head high, he told himself, and he would never love again, and Hera could never hurt him.

He heard a distant voice calling his name. It had to be Atalanta, of course.

He pressed his eyes shut for a second. *She must think I'm a prize fool,* he thought. *She must hate me.*

"*Hercules!*" he heard her call again, sounding farther off this time. She had to be going in the wrong direction.

"Here!" he shouted. He felt a lump in his throat the size of an apple. "Wait there, Atalanta! I'm coming!"

Rising, he brushed the worst of the mud from his face and lion skin, then tried to retrace his steps. Every now and then he had to call out, and each time she replied, she seemed a little closer.

Finally he spotted their campfire through the trees and stumbled into the clearing. She sat there, hugging her knees to her chest, staring silently into the flames.

"I . . . I'm sorry," he finally said.

"Don't apologize," she said with a faint and slightly regretful smile. "I understand. Really."

He nodded, then looked away. Relief flooded through him. *She understands.* Nothing would change . . . they could still be friends. She forgave him for running away from her.

She went on, "You're a mess. What have you been doing, wrestling in the mud?"

"Close. I tripped and fell into a stream."

She shook her head. "Well, I can tell you one thing, Hercules. You won't have any trouble keeping women away as long as you look like *that.*"

He glanced down sheepishly. Even by the flickering, uncertain light of their campfire, he could see how awful his lion skin looked, its fur matted with mud and tangled with dead leaves, bits of grass, and twigs. He started picking the debris out. His face and hair must be even worse, he thought.

"I think I need a bath," he finally admitted.

"First thing tomorrow, we'll find that stream again and you can wash up," she said matter-of-factly, as though nothing more serious than normal campfire conversation had passed between them.

"But . . ." He hesitated. How should he apologize? Where should he begin?

"You can't very well show up to see Laomon like *that.* If you're worried about your male dignity, I promise not to look. *Much.*"

He snorted. *That* sounded more like the Atalanta he knew.

"Very well," he told her. It seemed she had made the decision for both of them . . . they would pretend it never happened. "Let's get some sleep. We still have a long journey ahead of us."

She nodded, then curled up next to the fire without another word. In a few seconds, he heard low snores. She was asleep.

He took a deep breath and let it out slowly. Rebuffing her advances had not changed the way she treated him, he realized.

Slowly he lay down on the other side of the fire and stared through its flames at her beautiful, calm, unlined face. In sleep, she looked even more attractive, he thought. He had to resist the temptation to wake her, to tell her what a fool he had been . . . that he loved her with all of his heart.

Finally he rolled over, facing the night, and closed his eyes. Sleep took a long time to come.

Hercules awoke early the next day feeling stiff and out of sorts. Grumbling a bit to himself, he sat up and stretched. The mud on his lion skin had dried during the night, and it crackled a bit with his every movement. *I look even worse than I thought*, he told himself.

He glanced around the clearing in the gray morning twilight. Dew slicked the grass, and the morning birds had just begun to call to one another. Atalanta still slept beside the dim orange embers of their campfire.

Careful to make as little noise as possible, he rose, eased a few more logs onto the fire, then padded softly into the forest, heading toward the stream he had fallen into the night before. Perhaps he could find a place to wash himself up before she woke.

By day, the stream seemed much closer, perhaps fifty feet from their camp, and the water ran briskly over the mossy stones and clay lining its bed, though it was no more than ankle deep. He hesitated a second, then turned and walked upstream for another hundred yards before he came to a spot where it formed a little pond twenty feet across. Tall trees surrounded the pond, and a gently sloping embankment opposite him showed the footprints and hoofprints of animals that had come here to drink. It would do nicely.

He stripped and splashed out into the deepest part of the pond; ducking his head and using sand and pebbles from the bottom, he scoured his arms and legs and chest until the skin turned bright pink.

Suddenly he heard a soft titter of laughter behind him. Then came a splash as someone dived into the pool.

"I thought you promised not to look," he said.

"I promised you nothing," a soft, sultry, and completely unfamiliar voice said.

Hercules whirled, startled.

A woman with milky skin and tiny white flowers braided into her golden hair swam slowly around him. Her large lavender eyes met his gaze unblinkingly. When she smiled, it was as though the sun broke through a clouded sky. Hercules felt his breath catch in his throat.

"Who are you?" he whispered, caught up in her beauty.

"A child of the stream."

A neriad? He had met these water spirits more than once over the years. They inhabited secluded ponds, streams, and waterways. Usually they kept away from men, but sometimes they had been known to befriend them, as often as not for mischief.

"Do you have a name?" he asked.

"Nassa."

"I am called Hercules," he told her.

"I know," she said with a giggle, still swimming in a circle around him. "You are a son of Zeus. That makes us cousins."

"Cousins?"

"I am a daughter of Poseidon, after all . . ."

He smiled. *Cousins.* Clearly she meant him no harm. She seemed quite charming and innocent. Well, since she was here and didn't seem inclined to leave, he thought he might as well put her to good use. Somehow, he knew she wouldn't mind.

"Will you scrub my back?" he asked.

"If that is what you want," she said.

"I would appreciate it."

He turned his back to her, and he heard her scoop up a handful of sand and small stones from the bottom of the pool. A second later she began to scour his back with a touch that was delicate, but firm . . . and he found himself leaning into her hand, enjoying the sensation.

At last she finished, and then she began to gently massage his shoulders and neck.

"You're so strong," she whispered. "I have never felt muscles like these before."

"Ah . . ." he said, closing his eyes. At this moment, he felt more relaxed than he had in months. All his worries about Laomon and Atalanta began to melt away. He wished this moment could last forever.

"*Lean back,*" she said. "*I'll hold you, Hercules.*"

Her voice lulled him. He seemed to be drifting on a cloud. He lay back in the water, arms at his sides, legs free, and he felt himself begin to float, without a care or a concern in the world. Her soft hands touched his brow, caressed his cheeks, stroked the line of his lips. He leaned back, and her scent reached him, cool and wild and strange, like nothing he had ever smelled before.

"*Stay with me, Hercules . . .*" she whispered. "*I need a man like you . . .*"

"Yes . . ." he breathed. He hadn't a care in the world. He could spend all eternity here, in this pool, with Nassa.

He longed to bury himself in her scent, to wrap himself in her arms and never leave.

"*Stay with me . . .*"

"Always . . ." he whispered.

He floated, and he dreamed . . .

CHAPTER TEN

T**his is it!"** Koremos whispered as he peered down at the Argonauts on the beach. It was late, easily past midnight. Below him, more than half of Jason's men already slept, curled up like dogs around their campfires, dreaming away the hours until dawn. A few still nursed bowls of wine, telling stories to one another, or simply relaxed and enjoyed a respite from their travels. From what he could tell, only one man stood guard duty, and he seemed more interested in the stories than in watching the darkness around their camp. After all, Koremos thought with wry humor, what possible dangers could there be here, camped in such a remote cove as this one?

Koremos let his gaze drift to the edges of the camp, thankful for the exceptional eyesight that all centaurs possess. With only the light of stars and a half-moon, he could make out not only the entire camp below, but all his men now lined up along the cliffs. Every member of his band had taken his position; now Koremos had only to give the signal and the slaughter could begin.

He allowed himself a low chuckle. It would be even easier than he had anticipated.

His gaze drifted back to Prince Jason, still sleeping beside the largest campfire. Koremos narrowed his eyes. Jason would be their first target. Jason was a charismatic leader, an exceptional warrior, and an inspiration to all who followed him. If he died, it would shatter the Argonauts' fighting spirit. They would break and run.

He pulled back from the edge of the cliff, four hooves treading lightly on pine needles, then gave a nod to Lorron the Strangler. Koremos's lieutenant cupped one hand to his mouth and made a soft owl-call, "*Who-oo-oo.*" Others picked it up and carried it along their line.

"Take your place," Koremos said softly to his lieutenant. "Prepare yourself."

Lorron moved to the edge of the cliff, raising the first of his two spears as if to throw, and as he tensed Koremos could see the smooth ripple of muscles in his back and shoulders.

"Now!" Koremos said.

Lorron gave a piercing whistle, and the pines along the edge of the cliffs exploded with movement. All sixty-four of his men let spears or arrows fly. Even before their weapons hit their targets, they began scrambling down the cliffs, screaming bloodcurdling battle cries.

Around the campfires, men leaped to their feet in confusion and panic. Half a dozen Argonauts fell immediately as spears and arrows began to hit. *Yes! Exactly as I planned!* Koremos thought. He leaned forward, staring down at Jason, but the young prince seemed to be leading a charmed life. Every one of the two dozen spears aimed at him missed as he rolled to the side and leaped catlike to his feet.

Well, it couldn't be helped now. They would have to kill Jason the old-fashioned way, by hand. Already Koremos heard the ring of steel on steel as his fastest men locked swords with the closest Argonauts.

He picked up his own spear and started gingerly down the cliff. He wasn't built for this sort of descent, he told himself as his hooves skittered on loose sand and gravel, almost sending him tumbling. But he was determined to be part of the triumph, no matter the risk.

At last he reached the beach safely. Around him, the battle raged. He breathed deeply, and the scents of battle—the blood, the sweat—filled him with new energy. He tightened his grip on his sword and began to trot toward the fighters.

"Attack!" Koremos shouted. "Kill them! Let them feel the bite of your weapons!"

Dozens of new war cries filled the air as his men pressed their attack, taking full advantage of their surprise. He saw two more Argonauts fall, then a third, then a fourth. Koremos grinned. Everything was going exactly as planned.

Suddenly he found himself face to face with one of the Argonauts. The young man rushed at him, screaming, then stopped in his tracks.

"You!" he breathed, a shocked look on his face.

Then Koremos recognized him: it was Hylas, one of the two brothers who had betrayed him and joined Jason's band. The centaur felt his face twisting with rage. It seemed his revenge would be complete tonight.

Leaping forward, snarling in anger, he thrust savagely with his spear.

Hylas stumbled backward, parrying blindly, trying to escape. Closing, using his speed and size, Koremos cracked the butt of his spear across the young man's forehead. Hylas crumpled to the sand.

"I'll deal with you later," Koremos growled, "after I've taken care of your friends." A quick death on the battlefield was too easy for Hylas, he thought. A slow, painful execution would be much more satisfying.

He paused a second. Swords and spears sang around him. He picked a tall, blond-haired Argonaut and leaped forward, kicking with his hooves. The centaur felt a satisfying thud as his blows connected. The man stumbled, and another one of Koremos's band ran him through.

"*Ai-ai-ai-ai-ai—!*" dozens of voices cried from the darkness. Jason came awake with a start. "Ai-ai-ai-ai-ai—" the cry continued. A shiver of fear ran through him, and he rolled to the side and leaped to his feet.

An instant later two dozen spears buried themselves in the sand where he had been lying. It he hadn't reacted instantly, he realized, he would have been killed.

Men around him were rubbing the sleep from their eyes, milling about in sudden confusion.

"Argonauts—fall back to the boats!" he shouted.

He snatched up one of the spears that had been thrown at him, then turned and sprinted toward the boats. They had been pulled up onto the sand near the water's edge. "Get away from the campfires! Hurry!"

They had to get out of the light or they would never stand a chance against thrown weapons, he knew.

He ran a zigzag course toward the water. Another pair of spears bit into the sand near his feet, then an arrow zipped past his head. He ducked behind the nearest of their two boats. The hull offered ample protection for the moment. An arrow thudded into the other side of the wooden hull, and a spear passed overhead, slicing into the water behind him with a wet hiss.

Feet crunched in the sand, and then Theseus and half a dozen more men joined him. A few others followed—not all the Argonauts on shore by far. Hadn't they heard his order? What had happened to them?

He risked a glance over the boat's side. Most of his men had found their weapons and turned valiantly to make a stand. With the campfires at their backs, they made easy targets. *Fools*, he thought angrily. *They should have listened to me! We could have made our escape!*

"Back up, Argonauts!" he called to them. "Drop back and get out of the firelight! You're silhouetted! They will pick you off one at a time!"

Unfortunately, the order came too late. The chalky cliffs swarmed with dark figures, he saw as his eyes adjusted to the darkness, and a second later dozens of men dressed for war came leaping forward, brandishing swords and spears. More weird undulating battle cries filled the air. The Argonauts who had stayed behind to fight suddenly found themselves engaged in battle.

The men still with him began to shift anxiously. He knew they longed to join the others on the beach, even if it meant their deaths.

"Go," he told them. "All but Theseus, Menicles, and Aeros."

Giving battle cries of their own, the men charged into the battle, swords and spears held ready.

Jason began to push against the boat's hull. "Help me!" he said, and the others reached out to slide the boat into the water. They all splashed out waist deep with it.

"We're not going to abandon them, are we?" Theseus asked.

"Of course not. But have you forgotten? Our armor and war weapons are on the *Argo*. Menicles, you and Aeros row out to the ship and gather our weapons and armor. Get back here as fast as you can. We'll hold them off."

"Yes, Jason," they said, and they leaped into the boat and began to row quickly toward the *Argo*.

"Let's—" Jason began, turning toward shore.

A moment later, an arrow shot past, nicking his shoulder. He yelped in surprise, dropping his spear and pressing his hand to the wound.

Theseus pulled him over to the second boat, still on the beach. Two more arrows whizzed past. Then they crouched behind cover, safe for the moment.

"Let me see that—" Theseus began.

Jason shrugged the older man away. "It's only a scratch," he said. He had taken far worse than that in practice matches with his swordsmanship teachers. "Did you see who's shooting?" Jason demanded.

"No."

"Those arrows weren't meant to kill me. I think the archer has been told to shoot me first."

"Agreed." Theseus hesitated. "From the angle his arrows are striking, he must be atop the cliffs. I can kill him quickly if I go alone. It will be faster that way."

Jason nodded. "Do it."

"Give me three minutes." Theseus turned and, hunched over so as to present the smallest target possible, ran a zigzag pattern up the beach. He stayed on the firm wet sand close to the water's edge. Jason watched as long as he could, but Theseus disappeared from sight in a few seconds.

Then Jason peeked around the end of the boat in time to see a pair of spearmen take Orpheus in the stomach with a double jab. Jason gave a groan—he considered Orpheus one of his closest friends. With a muffled scream of pain, Orpheus collapsed.

A second later, Aneas fell, a backhanded slash from a

sword opening his throat. And then two more of his men fell, but Jason couldn't see who they were. He thought one might be Hylas.

That decided it. Archer or not, he couldn't hide and watch his people being slaughtered.

The archer must have seen him, since another arrow thudded into the sand a foot away.

Taking a deep breath, Jason darted out, heading toward a cache of weapons that lay just to the left of their campfire. Several arrows whizzed past his head, but he kept running. Luckily that archer didn't seem to be a very good shot. Another arrow ripped by, almost hitting him in the side, and a second shot whizzed within a inch of his right ear.

Pausing only long enough to scoop up a spear and a sheathed sword, he turned and dashed into the heart of the battle. By the flickering, ruddy light, he saw dozens of men engaging his people. The Argonauts seemed badly outnumbered—everywhere his men faced two or three opponents.

If only they had their armor and shields, he thought angrily. Unfortunately, he hadn't counted on fighting anyone here. They were lucky to have enough swords and spears.

Orestes killed one of his opponents with a slash, then did a quick turn and struck a second across the temple with the flat of his blade. Both fell side by side.

Jason leaped forward to join his friend.

Then Theseus's voice carried down to him from the clifftop, loud enough to be heard over the din of battle: "*Jason—I got him!*"

"The archer's dead," he told Orestes.

"Good news!"

"Back me up—we'll drive a wedge through them."

"Good idea," Orestes said, panting. "We can break

through them and get the cliff to our backs, then drive them into the sea!"

"Argonauts to my side!" Jason called. "Rally to victory!"

The men around him began to cheer. A second man joined him, then a third and a fourth.

"Form a wedge behind me," Jason said. "We'll charge into their fighters and try to rout them. Make as much noise as you can. To victory!"

"To victory!" all their voices cried as one.

He raised his sword. "Follow me!"

Taking a deep breath, he sprinted toward the thickest knot of fighters, screaming a battle cry and waving his spear.

The whole battle seemed to pause. All around him, his men took heart and attacked with renewed strength. Even before Jason and his wedge of fighters reached the heart of the battle, he saw three of their attackers fall.

And suddenly they were in the middle of the fighting. The wedge broke up, as everyone leaped for the nearest targets. Jason found himself facing a tall, scraggly bearded man with a wild look in his eyes.

Screaming a bloodcurdling battle cry, the man leaped at him, sword swinging viciously.

Jason blocked the blow with the side of his spear, then slammed the spear's butt into the man's forehead. He hadn't seen the blow coming and it hit him hard. His eyes went glassy and he slumped to the ground, dead or unconscious. Jason didn't wait to find out, but began to search for another opponent.

Most of the combat centered around the largest campfire. Raising his spear, he threw it at a pair of men trying to beat Orestes to the ground with clubs. The man on the left collapsed, clawing at his back, then his chest where the spear's bronze tip protruded. One less attacker to worry about, Jason thought with grim satisfaction.

Orestes took advantage of his one remaining opponent's startled pause. Running him through with a spear, he gave a loud cry of triumph, jerked his weapon free, and leaped to take on another attacker.

Fortunately there was a huge supply of lost or thrown weapons lying on the sand around him. Scooping up a new spear, Jason turned until he found a new target—a pair of men driving Nestor toward the sea. He threw his weapon at the taller of the two, but—curse his luck—he missed when the fellow moved at the wrong moment. He need not have bothered; Nestor gutted the first man, then wounded the other with a deft backhanded swing of his sword. Shrieking in pain, the wounded man turned and fled toward the cliffs.

"Sing out if you spot their leader!" Jason shouted. "I'll take him first!"

"Right!" Theseus called back, suddenly beside him. The older man, panting from his run down the cliffs, grinned madly. A long smear of red marred his tunic.

"It is not my blood," Theseus said, as if in answer.

"The archer?"

"He fought surprisingly well."

Jason nodded. He could respect a man who fought well.

Side by side, they leaped forward. The tip of Jason's spear moved like a bolt of lightning, slashing this way and that, thrusting, parrying, thrusting again. One man, then another, then a third fell, and still they attacked. He heard blood roaring in his ears, and everything became a crimson blur. Every way he turned, the battle raged on, and he raged with it, killing again and again and again.

Finally, as the flames leaped and danced, sending a flickering orange light over everyone and everything, Jason had a second to pause and catch his breath. For the moment, he was alone in an open space. Bodies littered the ground—eight of their opponents. He had slain at least seven of them himself.

He took the opportunity to study the two dozen or so attackers still fighting. They couldn't possibly be soldiers from some local kingdom, he realized as he saw their mismatched clothes and helms. A couple had small round shields with stars painted in red upon them; a few wore simple leather armor; one had the tattered remnants of a uniform. They could only be brigands, he realized, attracted to the *Argo* by the thought of easy loot.

Well, he thought grimly, they had certainly chosen the wrong victims this time! Instead of meek sailors, they were facing a team of seasoned warriors—professionals in the art of killing. It showed. At least two dozen of the attackers lay dead, their bodies strewn along the beach.

Screaming battle cries, two men charged him from the side. Thrown spears took both of them in the chest, and the pair collapsed at his feet, already dead.

Blankly, he looked around. Theseus and Ioron gave him a wave, found new weapons, and waded into the thick of the fighting. Jason gave them a quick wave of thanks as he picked a new opponent and charged.

The man might be a common brigand, Jason soon found, but he fought with a ferocious zeal. Jason parried, parried, and parried again; the man beat him back with blow after blow. Finally the man's strength began to wane and he lowered his guard for an instant.

Jason leaped forward, thrusting with his spear, and caught him under the chin, opening a jagged gash. Dropping his weapon, the man reeled back, gurgling and clutching his throat with both hands. A second later, he fell, twitching, and soon lay still.

The tide of the battle had definitely turned, Jason realized. Few Argonauts had fallen, and everywhere he turned, he saw the bodies of their attackers. Now his men engaged their foes with greater zeal, two-on-one, sometimes three-on-one. Sword rang on sword, spear on spear, and the air echoed with triumphant cries of victory.

Everyone around him was now engaged in combat, so Jason moved on, heading around the campfire as he looked for a new opponent or an Argonaut in trouble and in need of assistance.

From the corner of his eye he glimpsed Hylas staggering back, a huge cut over one eye spilling dark blood across his face. Unfortunately he could do nothing to help, as he found himself facing a giant of a man armed with a club the size of a small tree. He had to be larger than Hercules, Jason realized.

"Smash you!" the man snarled, and he brought the club down with such force that ducking away from its passage threw Jason off balance. Wheeling to the right, Jason jabbed with his spear and caught his opponent in the right foot.

Instead of shrieking in pain or trying to retreat, though, the huge man lunged, wrapping powerful arms around Jason's back and sides. Jason struggled to free himself, but the man's strength was incredible. Pain made him gasp as the air was slowly squeezed from his lungs. Lights danced before his eyes. Bones in his chest and back begin to grate together.

"Let—me—down—" he managed to wheeze. "Fight—like—a—man—"

"Do as our friend says," a low, powerful voice said behind Jason. "I will face him."

With a grunt, the giant released him. Jason staggered and nearly fell. He felt sick and dizzy. He could barely breathe, barely see. Somehow, he managed to draw himself up and turn to face whoever had spoken.

It was a black centaur. But how? A shiver of rage

passed through Jason. They had left Koremos—and his shattered band of brigands—hundreds of miles behind. How had he followed them this far?

Slowly the centaur smiled, and the flickering glow of the campfires gave his face an evil, sinister look. Slowly he raised his spear.

"I've waited a long time for my revenge, Prince Jason," the centaur said, voice like fingernails on slate. "You destroyed my band. You murdered my best friend. Now you must die!"

Jason raised his spear. "Not if I have anything to say about it!" he snarled.

Setting his feet, Jason braced himself for the centaur's charge. But with a smirk, Koremos wheeled around and galloped in the other direction. Then he whirled and threw his spear in a liquid motion.

Jason raised his spear to deflect the weapon, but the giant man behind him caught his arm. Off balance, Jason teetered—and suddenly a shock like nothing he had ever felt before ran through him. He couldn't breathe, couldn't move.

Gasping, Jason looked down and saw the spear protruding from his chest. It was buried a good eight inches into him.

He tried to draw a breath and heard a wet wheezing sound coming from his chest. Could that be him? Could Koremos really have hit him? It seemed so impossible—so crazy. How could he die here? How could this have happened?

He fell to his knees. He couldn't breathe, couldn't move. He tried to turn his head.

Koremos's laughter taunted him. Jason's vision began to grow dim. Somehow, he managed to raise his hands to the spear's haft, but they refused to close around the wood. He couldn't pull it free.

"Let me help you with that," a voice said, sounding almost kindly.

Hooves crunched on the sand, and Koremos suddenly stood before him. Large, gnarled centaur-hands reached down, grasped the spear, and jerked it free.

Jason felt the bronze tip grate on bones somewhere deep inside his chest, and a coldness touched his heart. He felt his spine become water. A tingling filled him. Slowly he began to sag forward.

"No," he breathed. This couldn't be happening. He wasn't meant to die here, on the Black Sea, on a strange shore. The great Oracle in Thessaly had prophesied that he would lead a long life full of adventure. He couldn't die here, could he? How could an Oracle be wrong?

Darkness rimmed his vision. He clutched at his chest, his fingers slick with new wetness. Then he fell to his side. Gasping, Jason couldn't move, couldn't breathe. Darkness closed in on his vision.

The black centaur gave a bark of laughter, turned, and waded into the thick of the battle, wielding his spear with deadly efficiency.

Then Jason knew nothing more.

CHAPTER ELEVEN

Atalanta came awake with a start, feeling hot and uncomfortable. She had rolled too close to their campfire, she saw, and she quickly moved back a safe distance. Hercules must have thrown several more logs on it. Where was he? Where was Hercules? She didn't see him anywhere. *Probably went off to get breakfast*, she thought.

She sat and hugged her knees for a minute, still a little groggy. Events of the night before flooded back, and she remembered how filthy he had been when he returned. *Or to get himself cleaned up.*

She remembered their kiss, how he had pushed her away, how wide and terrified his eyes had become. They reminded her of a deer, spooked by a hunter, and like a deer Hercules had run. She shook her head and pressed her fists to her eyes. How could she have been so stupid?

She *knew* he refused to start any lasting relationships with women out of fear of what Hera might do. He had told her so himself in Troy. The loss of his wife and sons had devastated him, and he wouldn't risk loving anyone ever again. Not even her. She had *known* that.

And she didn't even *want* a husband. Maybe someday, but not now, not yet . . . she had too many adventures still ahead to even *think* of settling down. So why had she kissed him? *Why?*

It had seemed like the right thing to do at the time.

It must have been the wine, she told herself, feeling embarrassed and guilty. *First I make a pass at him, and then I pass out. He must think I'm a prize fool.*

Sighing, she took a deep cleansing breath, then forced herself to her feet. They still had to find Arbora and Hercules's dying friend, Laomon. A long journey still lay ahead, even though they had made good time yesterday.

She banked the fire, then took her bow and arrows and went to find Hercules. Fortunately he had made no effort to conceal his passage. She followed a trail of freshly trampled grass, broken branches, and footprints straight to a little stream. From the looks of things, this had to be the spot he had fallen the night before—the mud still bore the outline of his body where he had sprawled. Today, though, his trail continued off to the right.

She followed the stream until it opened up into a small pond ringed with trees and lush marsh grass, and there she paused in shock.

Hercules, quite naked, lay half out the water, propped up against the far embankment, to all appearances asleep . . . and a pale-skinned woman—also naked—was bending over him. For a second Atalanta fought back a mixture of anger and embarrassment. Not only did he refuse her advances, but then he took off with the first comely stranger he found! Wasn't she good enough for him?

But then she realized things weren't *quite* what they seemed. As she watched, she discovered the woman was slowly and methodically covering Hercules in mud, from his waist to his head. Why? Was she trying to bury him alive? Why didn't Hercules do something? His chest rose and fell; clearly he hadn't been killed or injured.

Puzzled, Atalanta crept closer, trying to see exactly what the woman was up to. Burying a man in mud seemed bizarre, but in her travels she had seen more than a few strange customs. If Hercules *enjoyed* it, let him have his fun . . .

She pushed through the tall grass around the pond, moving as softly as a fox. She watched her steps, placing each foot with care.

Suddenly she jerked back in alarm. She had almost stepped on a face in the dirt. Cheeks . . . nose . . . eyes—a man had been buried alive so that only his face showed. *So that's what she's doing to Hercules.* The thought chilled her. *She's burying him alive!*

But why didn't he wake up? Had she drugged him . . . or worked some magic on him?

She studied the banks of the pool more closely. Wasn't that a human face to her left, among the reeds? And to the right, on the ground beside a tree's roots—another one! She turned slowly, spotting more and more of them. There had to be a dozen or more men trapped here.

Slowly and methodically, with practiced care, the woman began to plaster Hercules's arms with more mud and clay. If this kept up, Atalanta realized, her friend would be completely covered in a few minutes.

She swallowed. Hercules had been trapped by this woman—or whatever she was. He never would have willingly surrendered to her. Atlanta had to rescue him.

Luckily she had brought her bow. Silently notching an arrow, she took careful aim at the woman's back, then proclaimed in her loudest voice: "*Get away from Hercules!*"

The woman in the water whirled, hissing like a serpent. She had tiny needlelike fangs, Atalanta saw now that her face was turned, and her lavender eyes had slit pupils, also like a serpent's.

"He is mine!" the woman snarled. "Leave him to me!"

"Get away from him. *Now.*"

The woman-creature leaped forward, moving through the water with the speed of a crocodile. She crossed the pond in a heartbeat and launched herself at Atalanta, clawed hands outstretched.

Atalanta held her position, aimed, and fired. Her heart leaped as the arrow flew true. It pierced the creature's chest in a clean, perfect shot.

Screeching like a wounded pig, the serpent-woman fell face down in the water. She didn't move.

Atalanta notched a second arrow anyway. Monsters could fool you, she knew; this one might be faking its death so it could kill her when she let down her guard. Calmly she aimed, fired, fired, and fired again. Three more arrows hit the creature's back for good measure.

Pale green blood began to cloud the pond. Slowly the snake-woman drifted to the edge of the pond, slipped out into the stream, and floated away.

Atalanta didn't bother retrieving her arrows. For all she knew, the creature's blood might be poisonous. It certainly had an unhealthy color.

Circling the pond cautiously, being careful where she stepped, she soon reached Hercules. She crouched beside him and reached out hesitantly to touch his forehead. His skin felt chill as death. She gouged the mud and clay away from his head, arms, and sides, then seized his hand and pulled. He came free with a loud sucking sound and a moan.

"Wake up!" she said, shaking him by the shoulders.

He flopped like a dead fish. "Hercules! It's Atalanta—time to wake up!"

He began to stir and moan. His eyelids flickered.

"Wake up!" She slapped his face. *Hard.* "Hercules! Wake *up*!"

"Wha—" he said, eyes opening but not quite focusing. "Who—"

"It's me, Atalanta!"

He blinked bleary-eyed at her. "You hit me!"

"You were being buried alive by a monster. I just saved your life!"

He frowned in confusion, but managed to sit up. His strength seemed to be returning, if not his wits . . . but then, wits had never been his strong point. After all, he had passed up his chance to have her for a lover.

She reached into the pond and splashed clean water into his face. Sputtering, he began to rise, realized he wasn't clothed, and sank back down into the mud, looking faintly embarrassed.

"My lion skin—"

"You left it over there." She pointed to the other side of the pond, where it hung draped over a tree branch.

"And why am I covered in mud?"

"That's what I've been trying to tell you!" She sighed and shook her head. He really *wasn't* thinking. "I found you here with a monster that looked half woman and half snake. She was burying you alive. Just as she's buried quite a few other men."

"Nassa—" He looked around. "What have you done with Nassa?"

"She's dead. When I ordered her away from you, she attacked me."

He stared at her with horror in his eyes. "I can't believe it! She was so innocent, so beautiful—"

"*Beautiful?*" Atalanta cried. "She was a hag! If that's

your idea of beauty, no wonder I never stood a chance!"

"What do you mean, a hag? She was a neriad. They're always beautiful."

Atalanta folded her arms and glared. "So you've dallied with neriads before?"

He hesitated. "A few times."

"Trust me, Hercules, this was a monster, complete with fangs and claws and slitted snake eyes."

"That's not what I saw."

"Then she fooled you with her magic." That had to be the answer. Clearly this creature had bewitched him.

Hercules let out a deep breath, then abruptly changed the subject. "You said there were other men trapped by her?"

"Look around. They are buried everywhere around the pond." She pointed to the left, at the nearest face, then gestured to take in all the others.

Hercules turned slowly, and she could tell from the way his face grew pale that he had spotted the other faces and didn't like the idea of joining them.

"I didn't see them," he said. "I can't believe I didn't see them!"

"Blame her magic."

"Are they alive?" he asked, peering at the nearest face.

"I'll check while you wash yourself up. Then we'll get out of here. We still have to find Arbora, don't forget."

"Saving these men comes first—"

"Yes, yes, I know, I'll take care of all that. I rescued *you*, remember. Get yourself cleaned up while I investigate."

He nodded and, turning his back to her, slid into the pond. He waded out waist deep and began rinsing the mud and clay from his arms, chest, and head.

Turning, Atalanta crossed to the nearest face. It belonged to a man of about twenty, she thought, from the smoothness of his features. Slowly she reached out and touched his cheek, and as she did, his eyes sprang open. They stared up at her with a terror she had only seen in animals being led to the slaughter.

"Have no fear," she told him softly. "I will free you."

His eyes blinked twice. He understood, she thought.

Anxiously, she knelt beside him and began to dig at the soft earth and clay surrounding his face. It yielded easily under her fingers, but she did not feel his body underneath. She dug more deeply, pushing her hands in as far as they would go, and still she felt nothing but moist earth and the feathery ends of roots from the trees around her.

Suddenly she realized she didn't feel his flesh because there wasn't any. It was gone—absorbed by the ground or the pool or the trees or the monster, she didn't know which. Only his face remained, with those sad, terrified eyes.

She swallowed. "I'm sorry," she whispered to him. There didn't seem to be anything she could do. "I'm so sorry."

His face, loosened by her digging, began to slide down the embankment and into the water. Unblinking, the eyes stared up at her accusingly. Then, as that face entered the water, it began to dissolve like chalk. The eyes blinked frantically once, twice, and then they were gone, part of a dark muddy swirl slowly settling to the bottom.

Atalanta felt sick inside. She turned to find that Hercules, now clean again, had retrieved his lion skin while she worked on the face. He had put on his undergarment and had begun scrubbing the skin against a large flat rock, looking for all the world like an overmuscled washerwoman. In other circumstances, she knew the image would have struck her as humorous. But now, here, with all that she had seen, she just felt tired and sick at heart.

She hated being helpless to save these poor trapped souls.

For a second she considered telling Hercules what had happened to the face she tried to dig out, but then she thought better of it. No need to trouble him with the fate that had almost been his. She would leave the rest of the snake-woman's victims here, she decided, in case some greater magic could someday free them.

An hour later found them on the trail to Arbora again, traveling at a comfortable mile-eating jog. As they neared the hills, the forest gave way to grasslands with scattered clumps of trees. Now and then Hercules glimpsed ruins of long-abandoned farm houses. Clearly they were on the fringes of civilized lands, he realized.

He tried to think of Laomon and their grim task ahead, but his mind kept wandering back to Nassa. Everything around them brought back memories . . . scents on the wind, shadows beneath the trees, even the ripple of wind in the grass.

He couldn't believe she had tried to kill him. It all seemed so strange and distant, like a half-forgotten dream. *But it was real*, he reminded himself, *and Atalanta saved me*. It made him feel even worse about the night before.

They soon entered the hills, and there they came to the road Pthereon had mentioned. It looked ill-traveled, but certainly passable.

"I need a break," Atalanta announced, panting a bit. She sat on a rock beside the road and pulled off her left sandal. A small pebble fell out.

Hercules nodded and sat beside her. "Me too," he said, although he knew he could have kept jogging at this pace for hours. "It can't be much farther to the first town, though."

She made a face, crinkling up her nose. "Try to stand downwind, won't you? You smell like a wet dog."

"It's not me, it's my lion skin!"

"Then you smell like a wet lion!"

"Huh." He laughed, but moved a bit farther away. He had wrung as much of the water from his lion skin as he could, but it was still a little damp. From experience, he knew it would take the rest of the day for it to dry, and then its smell would be fine again. *Time to change the subject*, he thought. His throat felt a little dry, so he asked, "Is there any wine left?"

"A little."

She passed him her wineskin, and he took a long swallow before handing it back. Then he watched her upturn the skin and drain the rest, smacking her lips when she finished.

Then she rose, faced west, and said, "So, we have a dying man to see. We'd better get going if we're going to see him alive."

Another hour brought them to settled lands, with small olive and apple orchards, wheat fields, and vegetable gardens. Half a dozen small stone farmhouses dotted the hills around them. In the distance Hercules saw men and women working among their crops while children tended flocks of goats and sheep.

The farmers paused in their work to stare as though they had never seen strangers before. Hercules waved, and they had the courtesy to at least wave back. Though they returned to their work, he noticed they kept a careful watch on him and Atalanta.

When they crossed the next hill, they came to a small village, if a cluster of two dozen small, drab buildings could be called a village. Chickens wandered the streets, clawing and pecking at the dirt, and a pair of scruffy-looking dogs lounged in the meager shade. Hercules recognized a small tannery, a pottery, and several other shops, but nothing that looked like a tavern. He sighed and glanced at Atalanta.

"Maybe in the next town," she said, as if reading his thoughts. "And if not there, then Arbora will certainly have one."

He grinned. "All the more reason to hurry."

A couple of men in stained work tunics wandered out to stare at them from the tannery. Both had black hair, thin, pinched-looking faces, and dark brown eyes . . . father and son, Hercules guessed.

"Is this the way to Arbora?" Atalanta asked, pointing up the road.

"Aye," said the older of the two after a long moment's thought. "Straight on."

"Thanks."

Hercules led the way down the road, and as they left the little village behind, his strides lengthened to a run again. Atalanta matched his pace. Together, side by side, they jogged until the sun rose high.

They passed through the second village—even smaller than the first—without stopping. It didn't have a tavern, either. *Aren't the people here interested in drink and companionship?* Hercules wondered. *What kind of lands did my old friend retire to, where they have forgotten how to have fun?*

The hills rose; mountains loomed before them. The orchards grew larger and the fields closer together. At least the land seemed more prosperous here, Hercules thought.

"We must be getting close," Atalanta said, slowing. Sure enough, the smoke from dozens of cooking fires pillared the sky from beyond the next hill.

"Pthereon said Arbora would be the third town we came to," Hercules said. They passed through a last grove of olive trees, topped the hill, and the land suddenly fell away before them, revealing a lush valley. The road twisted and turned, working its way down to the valley floor.

Several hundred houses clustered around a bubbling spring, and the sun-bleached thatching of their roofs and the whitewashed walls made a pleasing contrast to the greenery around them. Hercules saw neat gardens, several temples, and plenty of shops around the square.

"This is more like it," Atalanta said. "Though I always thought Laomon the Younger had more of a taste for city life."

Hercules glanced at her. "He did love the theatre, didn't he? And all the court gossip."

"Well, let's find out where he lives."

They followed the road into the valley. Halfway to the village they came upon an old man herding three goats along with a stick. He wore a simple gray tunic and carried a small pack upon his shoulder—probably his lunch, Hercules thought. The old man peered up at them as they approached, smiling and nodding his head politely.

"Greetings, elder," Hercules said. "May the gods favor you and your goats."

"And ye," the old man said. Hercules guessed him to be at least seventy or eighty years old. "Ye're strangers here, ain't ye?"

"That's right," Atalanta said. "We are looking for Arbora. Is this the road?"

"Arbora!" He cackled with surprise. "Now, why would anyone *want* to come here? Especially noble-born people like you . . ."

"Then this *is* Arbora?" Hercules asked.

"Aye, 'tis so."

Hercules nodded gravely. "We seek the estates of Laomon the Younger. If—"

"Who? Who?" The old man frowned. "Laomon the Younger?"

"That's right."

"Never heard of 'im!"

"But he lives here," Hercules said. "This is the village of Arbora, isn't it?"

"Aye . . ." the old man said, drawing out his words. "But I reckon I know everyone 'ereabouts, and I've never 'eard tell of any Laomon the Younger."

"What about Laomon the Elder?" Atalanta asked. "I don't suppose you've heard of him, either."

"Well, can't say I've 'eard of him, either, because I ain't." The old man turned and pointed up the road with his walking stick. "Ye can ask at the Red Cow," he said. "If anyone's 'eard of Laomon, it'll be Old Tanos, the barkeep there."

"Thank you," Hercules told him. He exchanged a worried glance with Atalanta, then turned and hurried up the road.

At the center of the town they found a small square, and facing it was a small tavern. A fresco over the door showed a single red cow, so this had to be the place, Hercules thought.

When he stepped through the doorway, a sudden hush fell over the patrons. Hercules glanced around at a dozen or so men seated at rough-hewn tables and benches, then at the counter where a man in a gray tunic stood nervously wiping a red clay bowl.

"Are you Tanos?" Hercules asked.

"Aye," the man said, ducking his head once and eyeing their weapons. "That I am. Can I get ye bowls of wine?" He had the same accent as the old man with the goats.

"I'm looking for the estates of my friend, Laomon the Younger," Hercules announced. He looked around the room. Most of the people looked puzzled. "I was told to ask here. Does anyone know the way to Laomon's estates?"

"Who do ye want?" the barkeeper said, frowning.

"Laomon the Younger. Surely you know him!"

"Never heard of 'im," said the barkeeper. "We have Jerros the Younger, but 'e's got a couple of orchards, not an estate. Are you sure you're in the right place?"

"Is this Arbora? Then you must know Laomon. We were sent here to see him."

The man looked confused. "Perhaps it's another Arbora you want."

Hercules swallowed. He had a bad feeling inside.

"Is there another?"

"Not that I've 'eard."

Atalanta whispered to Hercules, "Pthereon *did* say west on the road, didn't he?"

"Yes. We followed his instructions exactly."

"Why would someone send a false message?"

"I can only think of one reason," Hercules said. "To get us away from the *Argo*." If someone planned to attack, the odds would improve greatly without a demigod fighting alongside the Argonauts, he realized. Twice before, attempts had been made to steal the *Argo*. Could this be a third?

He had a *very* bad feeling inside. He looked at Atalanta.

"I think we'd better get back," she said grimly.

CHAPTER TWELVE

N o!" Theseus shouted.

He felt a sick jolt run through him as he watched Jason fall. Jason couldn't die, he thought with shock, not here, not like this, not so close to the Kingdom of Colchis and the end of their quest for the Golden Fleece. It wasn't right. It wasn't meant to happen this way.

The flickering orange light gave the black centaur a sinister, evil look. Koremos jerked the spear from Jason's chest, turned, and waded deeper into the fighting, hacking and slashing at everyone around him. As Theseus watched, stunned, Pseron fell, then Moeton. The Argonauts were being cut down rapidly.

"*No!*" he screamed. He couldn't let it end this way. He couldn't let the greatest warriors in all Greece fall so far from home. "*No!*" He felt a rage building inside him that he had never felt before in all his life.

Suddenly a cry burst from his lips: "*For Jason! Rally for Jason!*"

He rushed into the heart of the battle, sword in hand, ready to fight to the death for what he believed. He slashed the legs out from under one of the attackers, clubbed another to unconsciousness, ran a third through—and screaming his war cry, he waded into the thick of the battle.

Everything became a blur as the sound of blood thundered in his ears. He stabbed, parried, slashed, and slashed again, cutting a broad path through everyone before him. Distantly he became aware of the rest of the Argonauts rallying around him, forming a wedge, and together they drove forward in an unstoppable assault.

"*For Jason!*" Theseus screamed. "*Argonauts! Rally to me for Jason!*"

As the surviving Argonauts began to rally together around him, his sword moved with the speed of one of Zeus's thunderbolts, stabbing, slashing, and stabbing again. Another, then another of their attackers fell, wheat to the scythe of his blade.

He moved like a man possessed, swinging his sword with the strength of a man half his age. He felt the savage pounding of his heart, the cold of sweat on his back and sides, and still he fought. His sword rained blow after blow, forcing his opponents backward. One swing bit deep into an attacker's forearm, and as the man reeled back, screaming in agony, Theseus's next blow took off his head.

Again Theseus roared, "*For Jason! Argonauts to me!*" as he charged the next attacker . . . the largest of all . . . the centaur.

"*Aaaiiieeeeee!*" he screamed.

With a flick of his tail, the black centaur turned and

bolted up the beach, hooves flicking up sand almost mockingly in Theseus's face. Still screaming, Theseus gave chase, but in seconds Koremos far outdistanced him.

The Argonauts began to cheer. Several found bows and arrows, and they fired shots at retreating backs, but no more of their attackers fell.

Gasping, Theseus stumbled, then sank to his knees, panting. He ached all over, and his chest burned for air. Slowly he turned. The rest of the battle—?

All of Koremos's thugs had fled, he saw with satisfaction. The fight had turned in their favor just in time.

No, not in time, he reminded himself, as Jason's death came back to him. *Not nearly in time.*

Climbing to his feet, Theseus returned to where Jason had fallen. Orestes already knelt there beside their leader's body. Slowly the other surviving Argonauts began to gather. By the flickering, uncertain light of the campfire, Orestes cradled Jason's head in his lap. Slowly Orestes began to rock back and forth, weeping softly.

"Is he . . ." Theseus began, voice hoarse, already knowing the answer.

"Yes," Orestes said. "Jason is dead."

Heavyhearted, Theseus stared down at Jason's pale, bloodless face. Jason's glassy eyes stared off into the darkness, fastened on the underworld.

Theseus felt his knees go weak. *It wasn't meant to end this way,* he thought. *You shouldn't have died here, Jason. The Oracle said you would succeed in your quest.*

He sat heavily beside Orestes. For the first time in many years, he did not know what to say or do. What of the quest? What of the *Argo*? What of his fellow Argonauts? Jason had been the one thread binding them all together. Without the captain and leader, they were like a ship at sea without a rudder.

"What should we do now?" Orestes asked.

Theseus blinked. They couldn't just sit here like sheep who had lost their shepherd, he realized. The centaur might attack again at any moment. Jason had always treated him like the *Argo*'s second in command. He would have to take the lead now. Everyone would be depending on him.

He forced himself to his feet. "Take Jason to the boat," he said, voice hoarse. "Find something in which to wrap him. I'll round up everyone else. We can't stay here."

"What about Hercules and Atalanta?" someone behind him asked.

Theseus hesitated. They couldn't leave yet, not without their two comrades. But they couldn't stay here, either. If they did, the black centaur might well make another attack. He had to get everyone safely away before then.

"We'll anchor offshore," Theseus said. "Tomorrow we'll decide what to do about Hercules and Atalanta. Perhaps they will have returned by then. Meanwhile, I pray they do not encounter Koremos!"

"Yes, sir," Orestes said in a strained voice. Rising, he picked up Jason and gently carried him toward the closest boat.

Theseus turned to the others. "Treat your wounds and gather the injured together. We will leave in twenty minutes."

"Yes, sir." Everyone began to move away, to find their packs and gather their weapons, to find their injured comrades and perform whatever battlefield medicine they could.

Theseus turned and walked up the beach. Bodies lay here and there, mostly bandits . . . seventeen of them, he counted. Two moaned and twitched when he nudged them with one sandal, and these he killed quickly and cleanly with thrusts from his knife. They could not live to prey on the innocent again, he thought.

Seventeen here. Perhaps forty or fifty attacked us. That means Koremos lost more than a third of his forces. And how many more would be too wounded to fight?

He turned back and gazed across the ruined camp. *We lost only a handful of men . . . and Jason.* It could have been much, much worse.

Argonauts now sat in dark clumps around the campfire. He heard low moans and the sudden hissed intake of breath as injuries were treated. They would be sewing wounds closed with catgut, bandaging gashes, and generally cleaning themselves up after the fight.

He shook his head. *Things were not meant to end this way,* he thought. Pushing all other thoughts from his mind, he hurried back to help get everyone up and into the boats. They still had a lot of work to do this night.

Koremos felt his fury boiling over. *We had them!* He told himself. *We had them, and they beat us!*

He hadn't counted on Jason's death rallying the Argonauts, he realized. That had been his mistake. Instead of breaking them, the hero's death had served to rally everyone to his cause.

He slowed, looking back. None of the Argonauts had given chase, but he knew it would only be a matter of time. Instead of destroying their spirit, he realized he had only served to kindle their fury. They *would* give chase, and he *would* have to fight them. And this time they would be attacking for a cause. He had made Jason a symbol. It may well have been the biggest mistake of his life.

"Gather around!" he called, and the survivors of his

band clustered before him. Quickly he counted. He had lost seventeen men. And how many had the Argonauts lost? Five or six at the most. The odds had definitely shifted against him.

CHAPTER THIRTEEN

They left Arbora at a run. Hercules took the lead, spear in his right hand, pausing only long enough to let Atalanta catch her breath whenever she grew too winded to continue. All the while, as she sat panting and sipping from her waterskin, he paced like a caged animal, frantic to get on.

She pushed herself to keep up with him, he had to give her that. Most other warriors would have fallen by the wayside after the first six grueling hours. But not Atalanta. She paced him as best she could.

Finally, as the sun settled into the west, they entered the forest close to where the Argonauts had made camp.

Hercules glanced back at Atalanta and frowned a bit. Should they rest again, or press on? Truly, she looked ready to drop from exhaustion: sweat ran in rivers down her face and neck, and he could see veins pulsing in her neck.

He slowed. No sense pressing her too far—nothing would change if they arrived five minutes sooner, but too exhausted to move.

"Don't—stop—" she gasped, drawing up beside him. "Almost there—"

"You need five minutes," he told her.

She hesitated, and he took her elbow and steered her gently into the shade of an ancient oak tree. Gratefully, it seemed to him, she gave in. He felt her trembling beneath his hand like a horse after a grueling race.

"Just for a minute," she said.

"Take as long as you need."

He seized the lowest branch and pulled himself up into the tree, climbing catlike into the upper branches. Finally, when the tree creaked and threatened to send him crashing down, he stopped and maneuvered around until he could see the path ahead.

"Well?" Atalanta called up.

Hercules frowned. The hills and the cliffs completely hid the little cove where they had left the *Argo*.

"I can't see anything," he said. "The cliffs are in the way."

"You should be able to see the *Argo*; it's out from shore."

That's right, he realized. He looked again, but their ship no longer lay at anchor in the cove. Had Jason brought it closer to shore . . . or had something else, something more sinister, happened to it?

He began to climb down.

Atalanta was already on her feet again. A little of the color had returned to her face, and she no longer breathed as hard, so he knew she would be ready to continue.

"Well?" she prompted.

"It's gone."

"Where?"

He shrugged uneasily. "Closer to shore, I hope."

He took the lead again, taking a mile-eating trot. She followed him silently.

At last the trail grew narrow and winding, and Hercules knew the cove lay just ahead.

They pushed through pines at the top of the cliff. Hercules found the breath catching in his throat. What would they find? Would Jason and the others still be there, making camp, laughing and feasting?

He felt a sudden pang as he wondered if maybe they had misunderstood the directions to Laomon's estates. No, they had made the right decision, he thought. Atalanta had heard exactly the same directions. They had gone to Arbora; only the people there had never heard of Laomon.

He pulled back a pine branch and found himself at the top of the cliff, gazing down into the cove. He blinked. He knew it was the right cove—ash, burnt wood, and circles of stone marked the campfires.

Only now it was deserted. The *Argo* had sailed without them.

CHAPTER FOURTEEN

Atalanta joined him. When she saw the empty beach, she sighed.

Hercules turned his attention to the Black Sea. A small island perhaps half a mile out caught his eye. A plume of smoke rose from it. Someone had made camp there, he realized with relief. It had to be Jason and the others.

Atalanta had spotted it, too. "Do you think it's them?" she asked.

"It has to be. They must have moved camp for some reason."

"The same reason someone lured us away—"

"That's right." Hercules nodded. "They must have driven off some attackers, then moved camp to wait for us."

"Perhaps they left a message for us on the beach," Atalanta said.

That made sense, Hercules thought. He nodded. "Let's take a look."

They made their way to a less steep part of the cliff and half slid, half climbed to the beach. As they crossed the sand, Hercules began to notice signs of battle. The sand had been trodden on by many, many feet, and he spotted two broken spears lying to one side, near the driftwood logs that the Argonauts had gathered for their campfires. And he found a few darker stains that had to be blood. He swallowed. Yes, a battle had certainly taken place here. If anyone had died, the bodies had been carried off.

"No messages," he said.

Atalanta poked through the nearest campfire. "The ashes are cold," she said. She rubbed her hands in the sand to clean them. "They have been gone for hours."

Hercules turned his attention toward the island again. "They must have left in a hurry."

"But who attacked them? And why?" Atalanta uneasily eyed the cliffs surrounding the little cove. Hercules found he shared her apprehension.

"There's only one way to find out," he said. "We'll have to go out to the island."

She studied the waves, frowning. "That's a long swim."

"I don't want to risk a signal fire. Do you?"

"No." She frowned. "But I don't think I'd make a swim that long."

Hercules nodded. "Then we'll make a raft. Come on, it won't take long." He started toward the pile of driftwood logs hauled up on the beach for firewood.

She joined him, and between them they laid out ten logs. Hercules found a stray coil of rope and bound the logs together, and using two long, flat pieces of driftwood for oars, they set off for the island.

They were about halfway there when Atalanta suddenly threw down her paddle and climbed unsteadily to her feet. The whole raft wobbled alarmingly, and Hercules's side dipped an inch deeper into the sea.

"Careful!" he cried. "You're going to capsize us!"

"It's Theseus!" she said. "Look!"

Hercules followed her pointing arm and saw a small boat just putting out from the island. He grinned. It seemed Jason had left a lookout for them after all—as he'd suspected, the Argonauts had merely withdrawn to a safer campsite on the island.

He put down his paddle and waited impatiently. Three figures sat in the boat, Theseus plus Hylas and Nestor. They looked unusually somber, Hercules thought. He had never seen Hylas sit so still for so long.

At last the boat pulled even with them. This close, Hercules saw his friends had all been wounded—Hylas bore a large gash across his forehead and a purple bruise to match, Theseus had sword cuts on his hands and left cheek, and Nestor had a black eye and wore a bandage around his left wrist. They looked like the survivors of an epic battle.

"What happened?" Atalanta asked, looking from one to another. Theseus stood, offered her his hand, and helped her into the boat. She sat beside him. "You're all a mess."

"We were attacked," Theseus said, "shortly after you left."

"The ship—?" Hercules asked.

"The *Argo* is fine. It's Jason who's dead."

"*What!*" Atalanta cried.

"Impossible!" Hercules said. He couldn't believe what he had just heard. "The Oracle in Thessaly prophesied that Jason would return victorious with the Golden Fleece! He *can't* be dead!"

"Impossible . . . but true." Theseus added softly, "Ten

others are now dead as well. We lost six in the battle and four more from their wounds. It is truly a black day for our company."

Hercules still gaped at him. "What—how—" He scarcely knew where to begin.

Bitterly, Hylas said, "It was Koremos, the black centaur. Somehow, he managed to follow us here."

"But you defeated him," Hercules said to Theseus, almost pleading. "You killed most of his men and chased him into the hills!"

"Apparently he was not as badly defeated as we believed," Theseus said. "Now we have paid the price."

Hylas added, "If not for Theseus, we would all be dead now."

"That was hardly my doing," Theseus said. "Everyone rallied when Jason fell. We couldn't let him die unavenged."

"What happened?" Hercules said. "I want to know everything—every detail."

"When we get ashore," Theseus promised. "We will have plenty of time for that later."

Feeling numb, Hercules climbed into the boat and sat heavily beside Nestor. He couldn't believe it. Jason dead . . . the quest for the Golden Fleece over before they had even reached the Kingdom of Colchis . . . it made his heart ache. He had never failed on a quest before. *Never*.

"How did it happen?" Atalanta asked quietly.

"They fell on us from the cliffs," Nestor said. "Spears first, and arrows. They charged us before we knew which way to turn."

"We fought as best we could," Hylas added. "We were outnumbered, caught by surprise and without proper weapons or armor. Koremos seemed to be everywhere at once. That creature is a demon!"

"He is no demon," Hercules said. "He is evil through and through, but he is mortal."

Theseus paused. "You know him, then?"

"Yes," Hercules said heavily. "I met him once, years ago, and there is no friendship between us. He knows nothing of honor and abhors the virtues all warriors seek to embrace."

"Evidently he holds a grudge, too," Atalanta said. "No sane creature would pursue Jason across half the world for revenge."

"Koremos would," Hercules said with a nod. "And he has two grudges to settle . . . he hates me as well as Jason. The last time we met, he swore he would take his revenge . . . and now I guess that day has come."

A lump filled his throat. He tried to swallow it away, but it wouldn't go. *Jason dead . . .* He felt like his soul had been torn. Jason had been like a brother to him.

But that is the way of things, he thought bitterly, narrowing his eyes to stare at Atalanta. She gazed out at the distant horizon. *I lose everyone and everything I care for. I must never allow myself to get close to her. Or to anyone, ever again.*

"It's my fault they're dead!" he said bitterly. "If I had been here—if I had fought alongside my comrades—"

"You can't blame yourself," Atalanta said angrily. "It's Koremos. No one could have guessed he would follow us this far. He must be mad!"

"Not mad . . . determined."

"At least he didn't get the ship."

"It is a small consolation," Theseus said, "considering the price. I would gladly trade the *Argo* to have Jason with us again." He motioned to Hylas and Nestor. "Get us back to camp."

As Nestor and Hylas began to row, Hercules sank back. His chest felt heavy. As he stared out across the sea, he could not help but brood on the trap into which he had walked. Of course, in retrospect, the idea of Laomon the Younger abandoning Athens for estates on the Black Sea seemed ridiculous. He had been a fool to fall for such a story. At this moment his friend was undoubtedly home where he belonged, or more likely reclining in some cozy little tavern, swapping stories, pinching the barmaids, and drinking the finest wines. *That* was the Laomon he remembered.

Hercules blinked and found their boat bumping against a rocky shore. He leaped out into calf-deep water and helped lift the craft onto a small beach.

"Where is the *Argo*?" he asked.

"On the other side of the island," Hylas said. "There's a little inlet."

"Just enough shelter to protect her from storms," Theseus said, "and to hide her from the mainland. I did not want Koremos seeing her and attempting to steal her again."

Hercules nodded. It seemed a sensible precaution. Never mind that the smoke from their cooking fires gave away their position.

"Our camp's over here," Hylas said, taking the lead and starting up a small trail.

Hercules followed him up over the island's pine-topped crest, and when the Argonauts' camp came into sight, a groan of despair burst from his lips.

Most of the company lay around a small smoky campfire, their arms, legs, heads, or chests covered in red-stained bandages. More than half had been badly wounded. He saw glazed eyes and knew many had begun to sink into shock and despair.

And it was his fault. All his fault.

"Ho, friends!" he called, forcing a smile, trying to raise their spirits. That was the least he could do. "I go away for a day and look what happens!"

A stir went through them, and he heard voices muttering his name. As he picked his way down the trail, men began sitting up and taking notice of his arrival.

"*Hercules will save us!*" he heard voices whisper. "*He will get us home!*"

He walked among them, stopping to pat old friends on the back, whisper a few words of encouragement, slap the shoulders of those who could still stand. He had never seen a more wretched company of men. And yet, as he walked among them, he saw the embers of defiance and anger begin to catch fire again. They *would* follow him, he knew. Just as he knew he could only lead them to their doom, as his friend Jason had been doomed.

"*Hercules will be our captain!*" they whispered. "*We are saved!*"

Yet he could not lead them. Hera would see to their destruction if he did, as she had seen to the destruction of everyone and everything he had. *Revenge.* That was the only option left to him.

For this, he swore silently, *I will see Koremos dead.*

CHAPTER FIFTEEN

As they walked among the survivors, Theseus watched Hercules carefully. The shock, the horror—yes, Hercules hid those well. But beneath the surface calm lay a bleak gray anger. He had seen this look on his friend's face only once before, when a madness sent by Hera, the queen of the gods, had made him murder his wife and sons . . . and that time it had almost cost Hercules his life. He knew what it meant: Hercules blamed himself for what had happened to Jason and his comrades.

Theseus knew he would have to do something, and fast, to turn that anger away before Hercules did something reckless.

"Sit with me," he said softly. "We will eat and talk and mourn the loss of our friend. Jason was a good man, and he deserved better. But if the Fates wove this end for him, who are we to deny it?"

"I deny it. The Fates be damned! I heard it from an Oracle of Apollo that we would finish this quest."

"Perhaps we were meant to finish it alone. Jason is dead; that cannot be changed."

As he spoke those words, Theseus realized they were a mistake. They would only fan the flames within Hercules's heart.

The great hero balled his hands into fists and pounded on his legs. "No!" he cried. "No no no! We make our own destiny! It *can't* end this way!"

Theseus drew out a wineskin, opened the mouth, and held it out to Hercules. "Here—we have wine. Drink, my friend. Drink and forget."

Hercules shook his head. There were tears in his eyes. "Neither wine nor words will soothe this loss," he said in a voice so full of pain that Theseus almost wept himself. "I will not eat or drink or rest until Jason is avenged."

The death of friends, of family, always leaves a hole inside. Then a plan—a daring plan, a plan so crazy that no sane man would ever voice it—came to Theseus.

Hercules visited the underworld before. He rescued me when I was captured and chained to a rock for trying to steal Hades's wife.

Why not a rescue mission? Why not bring back Jason?

Theseus hesitated. It was not a subject he could broach himself, not even with a friend like Hercules. Such a quest would be full of danger . . . not only to the body, but to the spirit. He could not ask it. This was something Hercules would have to think of himself, for only he could decide whether or not he would make the descent into Hades.

"Let me tell you a story," Theseus said softly. "Once, long ago, my best friend was a man named Pirithous. Do you remember him?"

"That name sounds familiar," Hercules said, frowning. He tried to conjure a face to go with it, but could not. "What does this Pirithous have to do with Jason?"

"I will get to that," Theseus said, and he let his gaze grow distant as he thought back to those days, so long ago, when he had been a brash young adventurer.

"My friendship with Pirithous began in the midst of battle," he finally said. "Pirithous led a daring raid into the plain of Marathon and carried off herds belonging to the king of Athens. Of course, I went to repel the plunderers, along with every other warrior in our city, and we fought an epic battle.

"Suffice to say, it came down to this: The moment Pirithous faced me and I him, we recognized kindred spirits, for we were as alike as two brothers. He stretched out his hand as a token of peace and cried, 'You must judge me—what satisfaction do you require to set aside our differences?'

'Your friendship,' I replied, 'and the return of the cattle you have stolen.'

'Done!' he cried, and we embraced as brothers.

"That night, we swore eternal friendship. We traveled together, fought wars together, drank and sang and whored together."

Hercules said softly, "I think I know where this is heading. I remember your friend now."

Nodding, Theseus went on, "Each of us aspired to marry a daughter of Zeus. I fixed my choice on Helen, then but a child, and with the aid of my friend I carried her off. Pirithous aspired to marry Hades's wife, Proserpine."

"A foolhardy stunt," Hercules said. "But not without its appeal. She *is* beautiful."

"We were young and foolish in those days," Theseus

said with a low chuckle. "We were both aware of the dangers, but nonetheless he determined to try for Proserpine, and like a true brother I accompanied him to the underworld."

"And there," Hercules said, "Hades seized you both and set you on an enchanted rock at his palace gate, where you remained until I arrived during my Twelve Labors, when I had to bring Cerberus to Earth."

"You left Pirithous behind," Theseus said. He gave a low chuckle. "He is probably still there to this day, moaning over his lot and cursing your name, unless Hades saw fit to release him from that awful punishment."

Hercules shrugged. "I could only take one of you, after all, and I didn't know him."

"Oh, make no mistake—I'm quite happy you chose to save me. The underworld is not a place I look forward to seeing again."

"Nor I . . ." Hercules frowned. "But as a demigod, it is only half as terrible as for a mortal."

"And yet we all must go in the end."

"Or in the beginning, for in the River Lethe souls find peace and rebirth."

Hercules blinked suddenly and focused his gaze on Theseus. "That wine . . ." he said.

"Here."

Hercules accepted the skin, tilted it back, and drank long and deep. Then he gave a deep sigh, eyes still fixed on distant shores.

"I must think," he said.

He rose, wineskin in hand, and Theseus watched him stride off, up the crest of the island, to be alone on the other side with his thoughts.

Atalanta hurried over, bow in one hand.

"Where is Hercules going?" she asked.

"To think."

She turned to go after him, but Theseus caught her arm.

"Let him be," he said.

"Why?" she demanded. "What's wrong? I've never seen him look that way before."

"He is considering what to do next."

Atalanta paused, then sighed deeply. "I'm for finishing the quest," she said. "And you?"

"What I do," he said softly, "will depend on Hercules."

She frowned. "You're up to something. What did you say to him?" she demanded.

"I reminded him of an adventure I had in my youth. I was a prisoner in the underworld, and he freed me and brought me safely back to Earth."

"Why–" she began, then she paused, horrified. "You can't be asking him to bring Jason back from the dead!"

"I did not ask him. It is a decision he must reach on his own."

Hercules sat on a rock, dangling his feet over the sea, and drank. The wine did little to lighten his heart, though.

He knew Theseus wanted him to descend into Hades and return with Jason. The more he considered it, the more it seemed the only possible choice. If he could bring Jason back to the land of the living, then the quest for the Golden Fleece would continue and his debt would be erased.

"I'll do it," he said. "*I'll do it.*"

That only left Koremos. He frowned as he thought of the black centaur. *But first, Koremos must die.*

Rising, he went to tell Theseus of his decision. He would undo what had been done, he thought. He would journey to Hades and win back Jason and his other friends, no matter what price the god of the underworld demanded.

He found Atalanta and Theseus together, and quickly he spilled out his plan. "I will get them all back," he said, "no matter what price Hades demands."

"It is a brave mission," Theseus said, nodding.

"And," Hercules went on, "I will hunt down and kill Koremos. It should have been done before we left Troy."

"I'll get my weapons," Atalanta said, rising. "Half the men are able-bodied enough to join us. We should be strong enough to destroy whatever remains of his band."

"No," he said, shaking his head. "You must wait here. I am the cause, so I must undo the damage alone."

"Why?" she demanded. "You can't just leave me here! I was tricked away from camp, too—I have just as much claim on his death as you do! And so does everyone else here!"

"Koremos must wait," he told her. "First I will find Jason in Hades and return with him." He looked to Theseus. "Burn his body on a funeral pyre. I will be back as soon as I can."

"Where will you begin?" Theseus said.

"At the beginning. I will seek out an Oracle."

Atalanta set her jaw stubbornly. "I'm coming with you," she said flatly. "You can't deny me."

"What about Koremos?" Hercules demanded. "If he returns and tries to take the *Argo* again, Theseus will need your help to defend our camp."

It seemed a logical enough argument, but Theseus knew Atalanta would never agree to it. He raised one hand before she could give an angry retort.

"Let her join you, Hercules," he said. "We are safe on the island, for now. You will need a friend on your journey . . . someone to guard your back, to keep you company, to counsel and assist you in all things."

"And bring back great songs of your heroics," Atalanta added.

"Very well," Hercules said. He pointed a finger and glared severely at her. "But no singing! I had quite enough of that on the way to Troy!"

She nodded. "Agreed. And what of Koremos?"

"We will kill him when we return," Hercules said grimly.

"No," Theseus said softly. "Leave him to us." One hand dropped to touch the sword at his side. "He had the advantage of surprise in his first two attacks. It won't happen again. This time, *I* shall hunt *him*."

CHAPTER SIXTEEN

Preparations for war started immediately.

As Atalanta, Hercules, and Theseus planned the expedition to the underworld, news of the mission spread quickly throughout camp. Honing the blade on a sword, Hylas listened intently as Orestes told tales of how Hercules had three times previously descended into the underworld.

The thought of Hades made a shiver run up Hylas's spine. Ghosts . . . monsters like Cerberus . . . Titans . . . it made for wonderful campfire stories, but to actually go there and see those awful wonders! The thought terrified him.

The alternative wasn't much better, though: if he stayed here, with the Argonauts, he would *have* to face Koremos, the master he had betrayed. Thoughts of the black centaur made him shiver, too, but with a much more real, much more immediate fear. Koremos would kill him as a traitor without a second's hesitation.

Three months ago, he had been part of Koremos's band. Koremos had sent him to spy on Jason and the rest of the Argonauts, and while he was among them, he had discovered what it truly meant to be a hero. They had welcomed him, albeit a little grudgingly at first, and had inspired him to abandon Koremos and join their quest for the Golden Fleece. Confessing his past life as one of Koremos's bandits had been the hardest thing he had ever done in his life. But he had done it, and he had lived down the shame. Now they accepted him as one of their own.

Only that past had caught up with him now . . . threatened to wipe away all that was good in his life. He couldn't let it happen. He *wouldn't* let it happen. He would never again be a killer and a robber.

And yet he didn't feel right about fighting Koremos, either. Despite being a bully and a thief, Koremos had taken him and his brother in when no one else would. He had taught them to use swords and spears and shields, to fight like men and hold their own. How could he help to kill Koremos?

Hylas hesitated, looking around as the older Argonauts busied themselves with getting ready to head off to war. Some sharpened spears and swords; others repaired shields and leather armor; still others worked on their bows and arrows. They were his family now, and he couldn't abandon them. But he didn't think he could fight Koremos, either.

He had only one alternative. He had to join Hercules. If he could help win Jason back from the dead, he knew he would be doing something good and useful.

Suddenly the tent flap opened and Hercules, Theseus,

and Atalanta ducked out. Rising, Hylas hurried over to stand before them.

"I want to help," he said. "What can I do?"

"Prepare packs of food," Theseus told him. "I will get Orestes and Nestor. They will row Hercules and Atalanta to the mainland."

"Yes, sir!" he said, and turning he ran to where the provisions were stored: huge bundles of smoked and salted fish and meats had been stacked at the far end of the camp, under a large piece of sailcloth. As he quickly assembled packs of food and extra water flasks for Hercules and Atalanta, he prepared a third set for himself.

Theseus hadn't actually told him he *couldn't* go, he thought. He nodded to himself. Yes, he would simply join them as if he had been invited. That was the best plan. Perhaps they wouldn't think to question his company.

Shouldering the packs, he ran for the boat to get them stored away.

Hercules rowed the boat toward shore with smooth, strong strokes, sending the little craft scuttling along over the low waves. With only Nestor, Orestes, Hylas, and Atalanta aboard as passengers, it weighed half as much as usual.

When they reached the mainland, he and Atalanta jumped out into knee-deep water, grabbed the packs that Hylas offered, and splashed up onto the beach.

When Hercules turned to wave to his friends, though, he found Hylas standing right behind him, grinning like an idiot and holding a pack in one hand.

"What are you doing here?" Hercules demanded.

"I'm joining you!" Hylas said.

"No, you're not!"

"I can't face Koremos—he was my old master. It isn't right. And besides, since you're tutoring me, I have to stay with you. How can I learn if I don't?"

"He's got a point," Atalanta said, smiling broadly.

Hercules gazed at her with dismay. "Don't you start it, too!"

This wasn't a pleasure trip—it was a mission to Hades, with Jason's life at stake. He didn't have time for nonsense like this.

"Besides, I have to come with you," Hylas said. "The boat's gone, and I can't swim."

Hercules gazed helplessly after Orestes and Nestor, who had each taken an oar and been rowing the boat steadily toward the island. They were fifty yards out and making good time. It would take them a little while to turn around and pick up Hylas . . . if they could be signaled at all. But he didn't want to waste a minute longer than necessary . . . and he didn't want to argue with Hylas and especially not Atalanta.

"Very well," he said a trifle gruffly. There didn't seem to be much he could do about it now. "But this isn't going to be fun—it's a long, hard, dangerous trip, and you'll do your share of the work along the way."

"When you put it that way, I'm not sure I want to go!" Atalanta said with a laugh.

Hercules frowned at her, but she turned and looked inland, refusing to meet his gaze. They really *weren't* taking the proper concern, he thought.

"Let's get going," Hylas said, shouldering his pack. "The sooner we find Jason, the sooner we can get back to the others." Without another word, he started forward, up the trail Hercules and Atalanta had taken three days earlier.

Hercules soon took the lead and spent the rest of the day charging across the land with the unstoppable force of a rhinoceros. Atalanta found herself struggling to keep up with him. He jogged with seemingly tireless strength, his long strides pushing through mile after mile. Hylas lagged behind several times, panting, but always managed to catch up when Hercules slowed for one of the infrequent breaks he allowed them. It wasn't that he didn't *want* them to rest, Atalanta thought; he simply didn't think of it. His thoughts were far away, on what lay ahead.

As darkness began to fall, Hercules stopped looking back altogether, and Atalanta realized that he had grown so obsessed with saving Jason that he no longer realized how fast he was running—or that she and Hylas still accompanied him. He seemed to be growing more and more moody, as if the thought of descending into Hades disturbed him more than he liked to admit. *He's already done it three times*, she thought. *He should be used to it by now.*

They kept to the trail well into the evening, through the forests, across the few grassy fields, to where civilization began. Rather than stopping at a farm or making camp in a clearing, however, still Hercules pressed on.

Atalanta's legs and back ached, but she kept silent. She would run all night, if she had to. At least Hercules had been forced to slow down with the coming darkness: he picked his way more carefully by moonlight.

They passed more forests and clearings, and then the two villages they had seen on the way to find Laomon the Younger. Finally, toward midnight, they reached the valley where Arbora lay.

Atalanta felt a surge of excitement. Surely they would stop here for the night. Glancing back, she spotted Hylas fifty yards behind. His face seemed a bloodless disk in the light of the moon. He looked even more exhausted than she felt.

"Hercules—" she called, as he started down the winding trail toward the valley floor. He didn't respond, so she called again, *"Hercules!"*

He drew up short. "Sorry," he said, panting lightly. "I did not hear you."

"We must rest. Hylas and I are mortals. We can't keep up this pace much longer, or we're going to collapse."

He hesitated, and she could tell the terrible anger driving him almost made him want to leave them behind. But despite his great strength, she knew he needed her . . . needed them both . . . to temper his impulsive nature.

With a low sigh, he turned and strolled back to join her. A moment later, Hylas reached them. His breath came in ragged gasps, and his arms and legs were shaking.

"Are you sorry you came?" Hercules asked him softly, without humor.

"*No!*" Hylas said.

"Sit," Atalanta told him.

Hylas sat, folding up his knees and putting down his head. In a few seconds, his breathing grew even, and then she heard low snores—he had fallen asleep.

She sprawled beside him, and felt her heart's pounding begin to slow. She had to force herself to stay awake. She could not recall ever being this exhausted, not even after a long day of rowing the *Argo*.

Hercules paced impatiently before her, almost like a caged animal, and he kept glancing at the moon then toward the town. He wanted to get on with the trip, she thought, but it wasn't going to happen tonight—not unless he wanted them so sick, he would have to carry them back to the *Argo*.

"I'm going ahead to Arbora," he suddenly announced. "I will be back for you and Hylas before dawn."

He couldn't be looking for a tavern, she thought—not after this trip. Then she remembered the temples they had spotted and realized he must be planning to visit one or all of them, looking for information about the nearest entrance to the underworld. A priest might well know, or be able to find out for him.

She nodded. "See if you can find breakfast, too. You have to keep up your strength."

"I'll see what I can do." Turning, he jogged off into the darkness and quickly vanished from sight.

Atalanta sighed, then forced herself to sit up long enough to pull a blanket from Hylas's pack. She draped it over his shoulders, then pulled one out for herself and lay down. In seconds, she fell dead to the world.

It was long past midnight when Hercules entered Arbora. He slowed to a walk, gazing at all the dark buildings around him. Gates had been locked, doors closed, shutters shut and latched. Not a soul moved in the streets.

And yet a bright light shone somewhere ahead. He headed for it and soon came to a small stone building surrounded by a chest-high stone wall. Over the wall he could see dozens of burning torches . . . and a clutter of sacrificial offerings—statues, huge jars probably filled with oil or wine, clay figures. It was a temple to Athena, he realized as he recognized the goddess's traditional garb: each statue showed her wearing her familiar helm and carrying both spear and shield.

The front gate stood open invitingly. He hesitated before it. Had the priest or priestess been expecting him? He didn't see anyone inside, but he had the strangest sensation of being watched. Then he relaxed. This was a temple to Athena, after all, and she had always aided them in the past. She must have told her servants of his coming, he decided. Of course she would help him in his quest to rescue Jason from the underworld. After all, she had diverted the Argonauts to the island of Sattis to aid her people; at great risk they had succeeded. She owed him this favor.

Nodding, suddenly resolved, he went through the gate walked up the path, and entered the temple. Inside, he found an old woman in gray robes standing before a small wooden altar covered with more sacrificial offerings—small statuettes, jars of spice, and rare incense. Small clay lamps surrounded her, and by their light her features took on an almost supernatural glow.

Her piercing gray eyes studied him. "You are the one She said would come."

"Yes," Hercules said, inclining his head slightly. "I am Hercules. My thanks to your goddess for aiding me."

"It is She who thanks you," the priestess said, pursing her lips. "She has not forgotten the service you and the other Argonauts rendered on the island of Sattis. Always remember that. Now, as to why you have come here . . ."

"My task is urgent. I must know of the nearest entry to the underworld."

"Come." Turning, she led him into the temple's next room. Here, more small oil lamps, designed to look like owls in flight, hung from the ceiling beams. They provided a clear yellow light by which Hercules carefully studied everything around him. This was the temple's sanctuary, where offerings were made. The main altar, a waist-high block of stone, sat in the exact middle of the floor. Bundles of dried herbs smoldered on top, filling the air with strange, spicy scents.

Leaning forward, over the altar stone, the old woman stirred the smoke with one hand. "By Athena's grace!" she croaked, "show us the knowledge that we seek!"

The smoke swirled twice, then came to rest. It had become a map of the land, Hercules saw, with hills and valleys and mountains and plains all in their proper places. He leaned forward to study it. Without warning, he felt himself falling forward—

—and abruptly he was flying across the land like a bird,

arms outstretched. Daylight burst around him; he could now see every tree and stream and village below with perfect clarity. Still he flew, along a rocky road, down a trail, toward the mountains. He went up a winding pass, out the other side, turned left, and still he flew. Finally a cavern halfway up a mountain yawned before him, and into its waiting mouth he flew . . . and fell into blackness.

Blinking, he found himself standing before the altar again. Smoke rose in meaningless lines from the herbs. The old woman had vanished.

"*Remember,*" a distant voice whispered, sounding like wind through pines. "*Beware the cold that burns . . . stay to the stones . . . and beware . . .*"

Shivering, he went outside. *Beware the cold that burns.* What did that mean? Slowly he shook his head; the answer would make itself apparent in time, he thought.

Dawn had already begun to finger the east with the palest of yellows and pinks, and roosters crowed the coming of morning. He spotted half a dozen people already up and about—a middle-aged woman sweeping her doorstep, an old man leading a small gray donkey with empty baskets across its back toward the fields, a couple of children darting about on errands.

I've been inside the temple for hours, he realized. It had seemed like only a few moments had passed. Atalanta and Hylas would be wondering what had happened to him, he knew.

Quickly he got his bearings, then headed for the tavern in the town square. The Red Cow hadn't opened yet, but he pounded on the door and soon a girl of six or seven opened it enough to peek out . . . probably the tavern-keeper's daughter.

"I want bread, cheese, and wine," he told her. "Enough

for three people. Pack it well and I will pay a fair price
in silver."

"Aye, sir," she said politely. "Please wait 'ere." She shut
the door.

A minute later, Tanos opened the door. Hercules
smiled and nodded to him.

"Come in, come in!" Tanos said jovially. "My daugh-
ters are preparing yer food and drink. It ain't often we
get customers 'ere at such an hour! Tell me, did ye find
that friend of yours—what was 'is name? Laomon the
Younger?"

"No," Hercules said. "I came back to visit the temple
of Athena."

"Temple of Athena?" Tanos frowned. "There ain't no
temple of Athena 'ere."

"But—" Hercules turned, gesturing toward the temple
. . . but it was gone. A large empty courtyard, paved with
broad flat stones, sat there now. He blinked. The temple
had been there. He couldn't have imagined it.

Magic. It has to be magic.

"My mistake," he said with a shrug and a smile, trying
to make light of it. He didn't think the tavernkeeper
would understand, nor did he care to go into great detail.

Frowning, no longer quite so friendly, Tanos regarded
Hercules through thoughtful eyes. *He must think I'm a madman*, Hercules thought. He opened his mouth to explain
about Jason, then thought better of it. *He really* will *think
I'm crazy.*

At the sound of light footsteps, Tanos turned and accepted a bundle from his daughter. She peered out at
Hercules from behind her father, but he pushed her back
gently with one hand.

" 'Ere are your provisions," he said. His cheerful tone
sounded forced to Hercules. "That'll be ten *denals*, sir."

"All I have is Athenian silver." Hercules gave him a

small coin from the pouch he carried. Tanos examined it closely, bit it to make sure the silver ran solid through, and nodded approvingly. Tucking the coin away, he handed over a small bundle wrapped in rough homespun cloth, then quickly shut the door. Hercules heard a bar drop into place on the other side.

With a snort, Hercules peeked into the bundle. Let them think him crazy. He knew he'd seen the temple, and that's what mattered. As he sniffed the warm bread, fresh from a baker's oven, he found his mouth watering. Yes, they would have a fine breakfast today . . . and then it would be back to the trail.

Turning, he started back toward the place he had left Hylas and Atalanta. All the time his thoughts drifted toward the lands he had seen through the smoke. Yes, it would certainly go much faster now that they had directions to follow. Athena wouldn't let him down—she owed Jason that much.

He soon found Hylas and Atalanta lying asleep at the side of the road. Neither one had moved an inch from the last time he'd seen them. They must have been exhausted, he realized.

"Time to wake up!" he said, nudging first one, then the other with the toe of his sandal. "Look! I've brought breakfast!"

Groaning and complaining, they finally sat up groggily and began rubbing the sleep from their eyes. Meanwhile, Hercules opened the bundle and spread the contents out on the cloth like a picnic: soft goat cheese, fresh warm bread, and two small skins of wine. He unsealed one skin and took a small sip, then made a face at the bitter, acidic taste. Clearly this wasn't a good area for vineyards . . . that, or the tavernkeeper had taken advantage of him and pawned off second-rate stock. *At least it's wet,* he thought.

"Did you find the temple?" Atalanta asked. She broke off a piece of bread and took a bite ravenously.

"Yes." He told her of his vision and what he had learned, then outlined their course ahead.

"That sounds easy," Hylas said. "So all we have to do is go through that mountain pass, find the cave, and we're there! We'll be back at the ship with Jason within a week."

"I hope so!" Hercules said. "But things never seem to go quite as well as planned."

"I think it sounds *too* easy," Atalanta said suspiciously as she began to work on the cheese. "You know what they say . . . the road to Hades is paved with good intentions."

Hercules shrugged. "For once I will travel the easy road." He took another deep swallow of the wine, then stoppered the skin. "Come, let's get going. You can eat while we walk."

They spent the rest of the morning on the road, heading toward the still-distant mountains. Atalanta had a slight limp, favoring her left leg, and Hylas seemed to be stepping a little too gingerly, as if he had blisters. Hercules slowed down to let them travel more easily, despite how the slowness of their pace gnawed at him. At this crawling speed, he thought with frustration, it would take two or three *weeks* to get to Hades. And they still had to find that pass through the mountains, then locate the cave itself . . . it might be *months* before they finished their quest.

As the day edged toward noon, Hercules found his attention wandering. The bright sunlight grew blinding and a strange burring noise filled the back of his head. His steps grew leaden. Every movement became an effort, as though he waded through chest-deep waves.

At last, as though in a dream, he came to a crossroads.

There a young man of perhaps twenty years sat on a rock, a walking stick across his knees. He wore a simple blue tunic and sandals that laced up his calves. As Hercules approached, the man turned, tilting his head and blinking blind white eyes.

"Have you forgotten me, Hercules?" the young man asked.

"I know you, Oracle," Hercules said. The blind man was a priest of Apollo in a temple outside of Troy.

"I told you we would meet three times," the blind priest said. He leaned back and smiled. "This is the second time."

"Tell me of my friend—" Hercules began.

Slowly the Oracle shook his head. "Let him go, Hercules. He will be reborn and lead future heroes on future voyages. Jason was not meant to win the Golden Fleece. Perhaps the gods intend for *you* to win it in his name."

Hercules frowned. "I seek no such glory."

"But glory has always sought you. Would you forsake it to save one friend?"

"Glory does not matter!" Hercules said. He gave an angry wave of one hand. "I would give all I am, all I can be, to have Jason returned! He was not meant to die here. I could have prevented it. I *should* have prevented it!"

The Oracle grew silent. "It may be possible to win him back. But the cost will be great. You yourself will not be able to finish this quest for the Golden Fleece."

"Why not?"

"Because it is the will of the gods. For everything there is a price. For Jason to finish the quest, you must give it up."

Hercules swallowed. In all his life, he had finished everything he had ever started. He did not like the idea of abandoning the quest for the Golden Fleece. But if it would get Jason back, so be it.

"Agreed," he said, nodding. There would be other adventures, other quests, and other battles to be fought.

The blind priest went on, "Since you avoid Olympus, you know little of the powers that struggle for and against you. Hera schemes to kill you. Poseidon—for now—is mad enough to do you harm. Only Athena aids you . . . and as you know, my master, Apollo, bears you no ill will. But neither will he aid you."

"Then why are you telling me this?"

"I'm not." The Oracle laughed, and the sound echoed in Hercules's head. "I am but a wisp, a fleeting daylight dream, come to set your feet on the path to Enlightenment."

"Enough games," Hercules growled. "What must I do to save Jason?"

"*That will be up to you.*"

"No more riddles!"

The Oracle regarded him with his white, sightless eyes. His appearance shifted ever so slightly, and a glow appeared beneath his skin, almost like a lamp masked by flesh. Hercules realized, then, that a god now spoke to him through the Oracle.

"There are many paths to the underworld," the god said in a high-pitched voice. "Kill yourself, then negotiate with Hades when you get there."

Hercules chuckled, but there was no humor in it. "I am not a fool. If I kill myself, I can never return to the land of the living . . . *Auntie Hera.*"

The glow passed from the Oracle. The blind man slumped as though exhausted.

"That was Hera's suggestion," Hercules said softly, "wasn't it?"

"Yes," the Oracle whispered. "Her hatred for you knows no bounds."

And then a strange clarity came over his features, and

he sat up straight again. When he spoke, it was with the roar of a lion: "*Seek out the gate to the underworld, Hercules. The god of death is also your uncle. Do not forget the power of blood or the ties of kinship . . . Favors are yours for the asking.*"

A light swelled up before him, and when he blinked, Hercules found himself plodding down the road beside Atalanta. It had been a daytime dream of some kind . . . a vision.

"*And beware the cold that burns . . .*" The words echoed in his mind, the same words the priestess of Athena had used. "*Beware the cold that burns . . .*"

After a few heartbeats, when he was certain the vision had ended, he stopped. Atalanta and Hylas paused, looking at him wearily.

"I just had a vision," he told them.

"It was the cheese, wasn't it?" Atalanta said.

Hercules regarded her with bewilderment. "What?"

"That was supposed to be a joke."

"Oh." He swallowed. "I saw the Oracle from Troy."

She swallowed. "The one we rode out to see?"*

"Yes. He came to me in a vision . . ." He let his voice trail off.

"So?" Atalanta demanded. "What happened? What did he say? Don't leave us wondering!"

"*Can* we get Jason back?" Hylas asked.

"Yes, it's possible to rescue him. According to Apollo— at least, I *think* it was Apollo—I must ask my uncle for his return as a favor."

Atalanta blanched. "Your uncle . . . you don't mean Poseidon, do you?"

He shook his head. "Hades."

"I was afraid of that. I thought we would simply sneak

*See Book I, *The Wrath of Poseidon*.

in and steal Jason away, like the time you rescued Theseus."

Hercules shook his head. "That would only be asking for trouble. I must ask for Jason's release."

"Somehow, that sounds too easy."

Hercules chuckled without humor. "First we have to get there."

CHAPTER SEVENTEEN

Hercules, Atalanta, and Hylas traveled uneventfully for two days, following the road away from Arbora and heading for the distant mountains. The countryside grew wild and desolate, and though they spotted a handful of farms—if little walled outposts that seemed more like little fortresses than anything else could be called "farms"—this seemed a largely unsettled part of the world.

"They must be defending themselves from something," Atalanta commented as they reached the third such settlement. It sat fifty yards off the road, surrounded by a ten-foot-high wall built of fieldstone.

An alarm must have gone up at their approach, for a dozen grim-faced men in leather armor suddenly appeared atop the wall. Hercules waved and called a greeting, but the men only put arrows to their bowstrings.

They did not fire, but motioned for the travelers to continue on their way. Hercules frowned. He wasn't used to being treated in such an offhand manner, and it offended his sense of hospitality deeply. The farther he got from the civilized world, he thought, the less people seemed to observe or even care about the common courtesies.

"Not the friendliest types," Atalanta said darkly. He could tell she had been looking forward to stopping long enough to rest and refill their waterskins.

"If we weren't in such a hurry," Hercules said, "I'd be tempted to teach them a lesson in manners!"

"Why wouldn't they talk to us?" Hylas said. "Don't they want news and stories of the outside world? Maybe we'd want to trade with them, too!"

"It could be any of a hundred reasons," Atalanta said. "They're afraid of something. They wouldn't have those walls without good reason. We must respect their wishes for privacy."

"Huh! It's not like three people are much of a threat."

Hercules shrugged. "We *are* well armed. For all they know, we might be scouts for an army." Then he glanced over his shoulder. The men still watched from atop the wall, though they had lowered their weapons. "But courtesy should have brought at least one of them out to talk to us."

Taking a deep breath, he lengthened his stride. They still had a long way to go, he told himself. Perhaps it was for the best that they continue without pause.

They passed several more walled farms throughout the day, and each had higher walls than the one before. None of the inhabitants would talk to them, though all showed weapons.

Hercules began to wonder what sort of threat lay ahead. Bandits? Warring neighbors? Some monster? It seemed Atalanta's assessment must be correct: clearly they feared something. But what? He vowed to keep careful watch from now on. No monster would take them unprepared!

But nothing exciting happened. The first range of mountains grew ever nearer, and then they entered low foothills covered with a dense growth of pine trees. Here the road became little more than a winding trail. The air grew still, birds and insects hushed, and for the first time Hercules began to feel uncomfortable.

"I have the strangest feeling we're being watched," Atalanta whispered.

"Me, too," Hercules said. "Tell Hylas to keep up, then get your weapons ready."

"Right."

Behind him, he heard Atalanta admonishing Hylas to pick up the pace, and when he glanced over his shoulder, he found them both just a few steps behind.

The trail entered a small pass between hills, and suddenly war cries echoed all around them. Men carrying spears and clubs burst from the underbrush on either side in a huge wave. Their faces, chests, and arms had been painted with bright red and blue patterns. They surged forward in one shrieking mass.

"Watch my back!" Hercules cried, whipping his spear up and plunging toward the closest attackers. His lightning spear thrusts caught the first two men by surprise, and the swinging haft knocked two more senseless almost before they knew what had happened. Men behind them began to trip on the bodies or backpedal furiously to escape.

Hercules pressed his attack, leaping forward. Screaming like a madman, he swung his spear. The bronze spear-tip sliced through unarmored flesh as though it were grass, and half a dozen more savages reeled back, dazed and bleeding.

"Come on!" Hercules bellowed as the attackers wavered. "You want to fight! So *fight*!"

He charged the nearest man, ripped a heavy wooden club from his grip, and backhanded him across the face with it. Hercules heard the man's neck snap like kindling. Even before the body hit the ground Hercules had moved on, bashing another man in the side with bone-crushing force, then another, then another. Wrenching a spear from another attacker, he picked the fellow up and flung him thirty feet uphill, into a thorn bush. The man's screams ended in a yelp.

"Fight me! Come on!" Hercules charged the remaining savages, but they had the sense to turn and flee. "*Come on!*"

Slowly Hercules stopped. Turning, he found Atalanta and Hylas gaping at him. And the ground was littered with bodies . . . a few groaned and stirred, but most were dead.

"Wow," Hylas said. "I want to learn how to do that."

Hercules snorted. "They annoyed me."

"You *must* be having a bad week," Atalanta said with a half-bemused look. "You actually look *happy* for the first time in days. I guess you needed to take your anger out on someone."

Hercules took a deep breath. He had to admit he felt better. "The main thing is that none of *us* got hurt," he said. He stepped over and around the savages' bodies gingerly. Hopefully their friends would return soon to care for their injured and dying. "Come on, I want to get out of here before they work up the courage to try again."

"After *this*?" Atalanta gestured at the men. "You killed twenty-two of them in the first few seconds."

"But twice that many got away!"

"Remind me to stay on your good side." She put her bow away, then headed back up the trail toward the mountains. "Come on, we still need to save Jason."

As Atalanta predicted, they had no more trouble the rest of the day. The trail wound through the foothills, as Hercules had seen in his vision, and finally it led to a narrow pass through the mountains. They began to pick their way through, climbing over small rockslides, skirting fallen trees, and generally keeping to the remains of the path as much as possible. They stopped only once to rest and eat a light supper, then pressed on.

As darkness began to fall, they finally made it to the other side. Here the ground began to open up, but Hercules found their way blocked by a high fence made of logs. Beyond it he could see farms, fields, and a few scattered buildings . . . civilization. Clearly the fence was meant to keep the savages on their own side of the mountains.

"There's a gate!" Hylas said, pointing to the left.

Hercules squinted and could just make it out . . . it seemed to be made of logs like the rest of the fence, but cleverly hinged so it could swing inward.

"Good eyes," he said, starting toward it. "Come on, if we're lucky we'll sleep with a roof over our heads and warm food in our bellies tonight!"

Fifteen minutes later, they reached the huge gate. It stood twice as tall as Hercules and seemed sturdy enough that it would have taken a battering ram to get through. Hercules studied it. There didn't seem any way through, nor any way to signal for someone to open it.

"Any ideas?" he asked.

"Try it the old-fashioned way," Atalanta said. "Knock."

Hercules pounded on the gate with one fist, shouting, "Open up for travelers!"

After ten minutes of shouting, he heard movement on the other side. Slowly the gate swung open, and a man in military uniform stepped through. His high plumed helm, polished bronze breastplate, and long sword spoke of wealth—an officer, certainly—but his eyes had a crafty look that Hercules found unsettling. *I would never trust this man with my life*, Hercules thought. But he couldn't quite say why.

"Who are you?" the man demanded. "What is your business in the Kingdom of Lyrcos?"

"I seek my uncle here," Hercules said evenly. That was certainly true. "I am Hercules, and these are my friends and companions, Atalanta and Hylas."

"Hmm." The officer studied them, then their weapons more carefully. "I am Captain Xeor, guardian of the Sherite Pass. I bid you welcome."

"Can we talk on the other side of the fence?" Atalanta asked, glancing over her shoulder.

"You're worried about the Sherites?" he gave a snort of derision. "They will not follow you here. They have had more tastes of our weapons than they like. I am surprised a group as small as yours made it through alive, though . . . or did you lose comrades along the way?"

"No, we lost no one," Hercules said. "These Sherites have no real battle discipline, and we found it easy enough to beat off their first attack. Fortunately for them, they did not try again."

"I am impressed," Captain Xeor said, nodding. "I have never heard of such a small party of travelers making it through without even a single casualty." He stood back and waved them through the gate. "Please, enter Lyrcos. There is, of course, still the matter of the toll . . . but we can take care of that later."

"Toll?" Hercules squinted. He never much liked tolls. It always felt like he was being robbed. "What toll?"

"A pittance, really," the captain said with a diffident shrug. "King Espero imposed tolls on all his borders six years ago to help pay for the soldiers who keep them safe for travelers such as yourselves. I'm sure you can see the value. The toll will be twenty commons per man and ten for your, ah, lady friend. Fifty for your whole party."

"*Ten* for me?" Atalanta stiffened a bit at the slight.

"I'm sure you are worth much more," Xeor said with a bit of a leer, "but I only collect tolls, I do not set them."

With a sigh, Hercules dipped two fingers into his money pouch and pulled out a small Athenian silver coin. "This will more than cover it . . . plus room and dinner, if you can provide them."

Captain Xeor's eyes lit up when he saw the coin. He took it with feigned casualness, bit it, and then grinned happily. "Of course, you must all be my *personal* guests tonight. You just missed our annual Feast of Apollo, but there is still food and drink aplenty."

Hercules nodded. "That will be more than suitable."

"Follow me." Xeor escorted them to a long, low building. Through the open doorway Hercules saw rows of low beds; probably the troop's bunkhouse. A scarred old veteran lounged in the doorway, but he straightened and saluted as Xeor approached.

Xeor returned the salute. "This is Klemeon," he said to Hercules. "He will escort you to the inn at Three Oaks. My cousin Dederos owns it. He will see to your every need. Klem?"

"Yes, sir!" Klemeon said. He nodded.

Xeor turned back to Hercules. "I will see Dederos tonight and settle your account. Simply mention my name and he will give you the best of everything."

"Thank you," Hercules said.

Xeor nodded absently. "I wish you success in finding your uncle," he said.

"This way," Klemeon said. He started up the road— here it had become a true road again, Hercules noted.

Atalanta cleared her throat as soon as they had left sight of Xeor's camp. Klemeon glanced back at her.

"Your captain said King Espero rules this land. What kind of a king is he?"

Hercules, too, always liked to know as much as possible about any new land he traveled. It had saved his life on more than one occasion. As he looked around them at the neat lines of fruit and olive trees, he had to admit the land looked peaceful and prosperous.

Klemeon scratched his right ear. "King Espero keeps us paid and our bellies full, so he must be a good king."

Hercules asked, "Is he just? What do people say of his taxes and tolls?"

"Oh, nobody much likes the taxes . . . but what else have they to complain about? The crops are good, the wine is sweet, and the maidens grow more beautiful each year." He grinned at Atalanta, but she pretended not to notice. "As for tolls . . . only foreigners pay them, so why should anyone care?"

"Only foreigners?" Hercules said.

"No one else leaves or comes to Lyrcos."

"Never?" Atalanta demanded.

Klemeon shrugged. "Why should they?"

"Well . . . how about adventure? Or war?"

"No . . . no one's much interested in those. Here we are!"

They rounded another grove of apple trees and a sprawling wooden building came into view. This had to be the inn . . . though it also seemed to be a farmhouse. A dozen wagons, all laden with reed baskets of figs and dates, sat parked in front. Horses gazed at them from a small corral next to the stables, while several dozen chickens strutted in various side yards. Beyond the inn, amid a scattering of smaller buildings, Hercules spotted pens of pigs and goats.

"I'll leave you here, unless you have more questions?" Klemeon said.

"Thanks, that's all," Hercules said. He dug out a coin and gave it to Klemeon, who seemed delighted with his tip—almost as though he seldom saw money. Quickly he tucked it in a pouch at his belt.

Then he cupped a hand to his mouth and called, "Dederos! Guests from over the mountain! Your cousin Xeor says to treat them well!"

A man appeared in the doorway. He was small but broad of shoulder, with short, curly black hair and a beard. He grinned happily and motioned everyone forward.

"Come in, come in!" he called. "There's always room for more!"

Atalanta ducked through the inn's doorway, blinking her eyes at the sudden dimness. She found herself in a large, clean room with a flagstone floor and plain wooden walls. Three long tables with benches stood in the middle, and a group of what looked like farmhands sat there, eating an early supper of roast pork, fresh bread, and dates, figs, apples, and other fruits and vegetables from the farm. Her mouth began to water at the smells.

"Leave your belongings by the door," Dederos said, "and then you must join us for supper."

Atalanta stowed her pack and weapons, and Hercules and Hylas did the same. Dederos was already calling, "Make room, make room!" to the farmhands, and several of the younger men slid over, leaving space at the end of the closest table. Atalanta, Hercules, and Hylas sat. Now this was the sort of service she could get used to, Atalanta thought—fast food, friendly innkeepers, and good company!

"These poor travelers must be half-starved!" Dederos called to someone in the next room. "Marna—bring plates for our guests!"

A middle-aged woman with an apron bustled in from the kitchens with her hands full of plates, wine bowls, and utensils, which she quickly set before them.

"Marna is my wife," Dederos said proudly, giving her a squeeze.

"It is poor country fare," she apologized, wiping her hands. "But it is good and hearty, and I have never had a complaint."

"It will seem like a feast after our long journey," Hercules said. Dederos, meanwhile, had already begun to fill their bowls with red wine from a small amphora.

Atalanta sighed happily. Yes, it felt good to get back to civilization, she thought. She took a deep sip of her wine and nodded approvingly: good indeed.

After a heavy meal, with second and third helpings urged on everyone by an ever-bustling Marna, everyone at last rose, groaning and stretching. The sky outside began to darken toward night, Hercules noticed, and everyone seemed in a talkative mood. As the younger farmhands pushed the tables aside and shoved the benches against the wall, everyone began to take seats around the edge of the room. There would probably be storytelling, music, and gossip next, Hercules thought.

"Join us!" Dederos said, when Hercules started for his pack.

"Ah, but your wife fed us too well!" Hercules said with a laugh, patting his full belly.

"Surely you can stay a few hours more!"

"We have a long journey ahead," he said to Dederos, "and we must be well rested."

Everyone seemed disappointed; it seemed they got few enough travelers and would have welcomed news of the outside world. Several of the farmhands had been eyeing his lion skin throughout dinner, Hercules knew. Doubtless they would have asked for its tale. Well, they would just have to wait for his return—with Jason in tow, he thought.

Dederos took their packs and led the way up a narrow flight of stairs to a suite of small but clean rooms under the eaves. Each had a comfortable-looking straw bed, but little else beyond the barest of necessities.

"Shout if you need anything," Dederos said. "We will be downstairs till after midnight." He started back down.

"Thanks," Atalanta said. "We'll see you in the morning." She nodded to Hercules and Hylas, then went into her room and closed the door.

Hercules gave Hylas a nod, then went into his own room. Shrugging off his lion skin, he sprawled on the bed in his undergarment. Straw rustled beneath him as he tossed, trying to get comfortable. *Too soft.* Closing his eyes, he took several deep breaths and tried to put their mission from his mind. He knew he needed his rest; tomorrow would be another long day. In his mind's eye, he could still see himself flying over the land, following the road to the next set of mountains—then down, down, down to Hades.

Sleep did not come easily. His mind went over their journey again and again, looking for clues and portents. The Oracle's words still troubled him. He did not wish to give up his quest for the Golden Fleece. But to save Jason . . . he would do it. And *"beware the cold that burns"*—what did *that* mean?

He turned this way and that, but found himself more

awake than ever. *Perhaps a snack*, he thought. Cold roast, some more wine—that's what he needed. It had probably been an hour, maybe more, since dinner. He could eat something light.

Rising, he stretched, relieved himself in the chamber pot, and glanced idly toward the small window.

Furtive movement caught his eye. He paused, staring. There—dark figures were slowly creeping toward the inn from the orchard. He felt his heart beginning to pound with excitement. An attack? Bandits? He hesitated. *Or something more sinister?*

CHAPTER EIGHTEEN

We need scouts," Theseus said as he looked over the sorry remains of the Argonauts. Thanks to his knowledge of healing herbs and medicines, none of these patients would die . . . but several would be badly scarred, and he suspected Tralon would never hold a sword in his right hand again.

The initial excitement over Hercules's return had long worn off, and slowly they had sunk back into their lethargy and despair. He had to set them on a task—get them up and moving—or he feared the quest for the Golden Fleece might well end here.

"I'll go," said Orestes, and Nestor seconded it.

They were the least injured of all the Argonauts and had been doing most of the work to keep the camp running. Unfortunately, Theseus didn't think he could spare them.

"I appreciate your offer, but I need someone smaller and quicker," he said. His gaze fell on Réas and Emeras, the two brothers who had joined the company on Sattis. Réas had taken a shallow gash to the chest that would soon heal, and Emeras had been knocked unconscious by a blow to the head—his left eye was swollen and purple, and he had twice complained of dizziness, but by and large they were able-bodied enough to serve as scouts. They had trained together, and he knew they would watch each other's back.

The brothers nodded and stood. "We should go ashore by night," Emeras said. "In case someone is watching for us."

"Agreed," Theseus said. "Find Koremos's camp. Report back an hour after sunset tomorrow. A boat will come for you in the cove."

"Done!" they both said at once. Rising, they began putting together small packs and checking their weapons.

Theseus noticed how the rest of the Argonauts had all taken an acute interest in everything he had said to Réas and Emeras. *We all want revenge*, he thought. *We all want Koremos dead.*

Not for the first time, he turned toward shore and wondered how Hercules, Atalanta, and Hylas—who seemed to have joined their party without permission—fared on their way to the underworld.

That night, Réas and Emeras went ashore. Theseus rode in the boat with them, and while Orestes and Panceros saw to the oars, he told the two brothers all he knew of Koremos . . . of his outlaw band near Troy, how he had tried to steal the *Argo*, and how the Argonauts had beaten him the first time they met.

"His men may be cowards, but he is not. He fights like

a demon, and he is more clever that you suspect. Do not underestimate him."

"We will be careful," Emeras said. "We may love adventure, but we love life more."

Theseus nodded, satisfied. They would not try anything rash.

At last the boat's hull scraped on sand, and Réas and Emeras eased themselves overboard, crept onto the beach, and vanished into the shadows. Theseus watched for several heartbeats, but did not spot them again. Truly, he thought, they moved like ghosts.

"Take us back out," he whispered. Orestes and Panceros began to row back toward the island.

Réas and Emeras hid their packs, scaled the cliffs silently, then prowled without a sound through the trees and bushes along the drop. Réas listened intently, but heard no sounds beyond the rustle of mice and the occasional flap of a bat. At last they reached the far end of the cliffs.

"They aren't here," Emeras said in a low voice. "No sentries."

"Agreed. They must have a camp somewhere close by, though."

"We'll find it tomorrow."

Réas nodded. "Wait here. I'll get our packs."

He slid down to the base of the cliff, making little effort to hide the sound, then retrieved their bedrolls and provisions. When he returned to the place he had left his brother, though, Emeras was gone.

He felt a prickle of alarm spread down his back. Silently he drew a knife.

Pine needles crinkled softly behind him. He whirled, knife ready, and something moved in a blur of sudden motion. A hoof-kick knocked the knife from his hand. He yelped in pain.

It was the centaur, he realized, as the shadows came to life and men surrounded him.

"Emeras!" he called.

"Your friend?" the centaur said, a hint of a sneer in his voice. "I'm afraid he can't hear you any more."

"Where is he?" Réas asked slowly, trying to keep fear from showing in his voice. One hand edged toward the sword at his side. If anything had happened to his brother—

"I'm afraid," the centaur said, "that he didn't play nicely. *Now*, please, Lorron?"

Hands like slabs of meat seized Réas from behind, and when he opened his mouth to cry out, someone stuffed a cloth into it. He gagged and choked, kicking, trying to get free, but by then half a dozen men had him. They began to bind his arms and legs with ropes. Several of them chuckled evilly.

Maybe Emeras is still alive, Réas thought. *They haven't killed me. Maybe they haven't killed him, either.*

More hands closed around him, and the black centaur's band began to drag him through the trees—toward what fate, he did not know.

CHAPTER NINETEEN

Hercules leaned forward, staring down through the window, and caught the glint of moonlight on an armored helm. *A soldier?* Something made him think of Captain Xeor. *I didn't trust him from the moment I saw him.* He recalled how Xeor's eyes lit up at the silver coin he had used to pay their border tolls. *It must be him. Greed sent him to try to take the rest of our money.*

He shrugged on his lion skin, grabbed his spear and his pack, and went to wake up Atalanta. But as he opened his door, he found her poised to knock. She had her pack in one hand and her bow in the other—once again she seemed to be one step ahead of him.

"Bandits—" she began softly.

"Soldiers," he said. "I saw them, too."

"You think it's Xeor?"

"Must be. Where is Hylas?"

"I sent him to the stables for horses. We'll meet him there."

"What! And miss the fight?"

"It's better this way. Xeor won't hurt anyone here; he's after us. If we stay and fight, we'll only end up destroying the inn, and I know innocent people will die. We'll take care of Xeor on our way back."

Hercules nodded—she was right, as usual. Turning, he headed down the staircase. He heard voices from the common room ahead and made his footfalls softer, straining to hear.

They were talking about the harvest like they hadn't a care in the world, he realized. Clearly Xeor hadn't involved anyone here in his plans. *Fewer people to share in the loot, after all.* Well, that made things a little easier—they might well be able to slip away before anyone inside the house noticed.

Nobody noticed as they padded past the commons and down a little hallway that ended in the kitchen. Marna was supervising three other women as they cleaned up from supper.

"Marna," Hercules said.

"Eh?" She turned, surprised, then made shooing motions with her apron. "What are you doing here? Back to the commons with you—I'll bring whatever you need!"

"This is for you and Dederos," Hercules said. He poured a dozen silver coins into her hands. She gasped in amazement. "Do not give it to him until tomorrow morning."

"But—"

Hercules shook his head. "Captain Xeor is going to lead an attack on the inn. Get your women to a safe place and hide. We are leaving now. This will pay for three horses."

"It's too much—"

He closed her hand around the coins. "You are good people. Take care of yourselves."

Atalanta had positioned herself by the back door. She peeked out carefully. "It's clear," she said.

Hercules patted Marna on the shoulder, then joined Atalanta. It was dark out, but he trusted her keen vision—if she hadn't spotted anyone, nobody was out there. Xeor probably expected to find them in the common room, he told himself. After all, it was early enough that few travelers would yet be in bed.

Together they dashed out toward the corral where they had seen horses that afternoon. Bending almost double, they scurried along the fence until they reached the stables. The faint yellow glow of an oil lamp spilled out. The door stood open a foot, so they slipped inside.

A small lamp hung from the rafters, and its light showed Hylas busily tying ropes around the three horses' necks. A trio of stableboys—all much bigger than Hylas—lay bound and gagged atop a pile of hay in the corner . . . two with black eyes, one with a bloody nose. All three glared with ill-concealed fury.

Hylas grinned proudly.

"I see you're learning," Hercules said. He had to admit the lad had everything in order.

"Yep." Hylas offered him a gray gelding, and Atalanta took a black mare. Hylas kept a dappled gray mare for himself.

"No chariots?" he said.

"Not on a farm—it's bareback or nothing. All the wagons are full of fruit."

Hercules nodded. Bareback it would be. He hadn't ridden in years, but he would make do.

"Is there a back door?" Atalanta asked.

"No, just this one."

"Hmm." Hercules frowned. "Put out the lamp. We'll try to slip out without being seen."

Hylas blew out the lamp's flame, and pitch blackness swallowed the stables. Hercules let his eyes grow used to the dark, straining to hear over the stamping and snorting of the horses, the muffled groans and struggles of the stableboys, and the rubbing of leather tack.

Atalanta eased open the door enough to lead out their horses. Xeor's men were stealing up to the front door of the inn now, Hercules saw. At least two dozen men were taking part in the raid . . . the captain must have turned out his whole troop.

As two men kicked open the inn's door, the squad stormed inside. This was their chance—Hercules led his horse out, then Atlanta and Hylas followed.

Voices were shouting from the house. A woman screamed. But Hercules heard no sounds of weapons—*no one is getting hurt, at least. Yet.* He promised himself a quick return to take revenge on Captain Xeor's treachery.

They soon reached the road, and Hercules swung up onto his horse's broad back, clinging precariously to mane and rope, and urged his gelding to a trot as Atalanta and Hylas did the same. At least—from what he could tell in the dark—Atalanta seemed to be having just as much trouble keeping her seat.

"Give them their heads," Hylas said urgently. "They'll run if you let them."

Trust a farmboy to know how to ride bareback, he thought. But he stopped fighting his gelding and let the horse set its own pace, and together they thundered down the road.

A few miles from the inn all three slowed their horses to a walk. They continued at this pace throughout the night, pausing only to let the horses drink when they came to a stream. Daybreak found them many miles from the inn

. . . and approaching more mountains. *The ones from my vision*, Hercules realized. *This is the way to Hades*. Strangely, the thought cheered him up.

They let their horses rest for a couple of hours, taking a break and eating wild figs for breakfast, then they set off again, this time leading their mounts. The horses made better pack animals than steeds, Hercules thought, rubbing his aching back and buttocks whenever he thought Atalanta wasn't looking.

They bought bread, cheese, and wine from a farmhouse toward lunchtime, rested another hour, then pressed on again. Toward evening, the road came to another tall stockade fence similar to the one where they had first met Xeor. This one, though, had lookouts posted in a small guard tower, who alerted the soldiers below as they neared. As Hercules approached, a captain dressed much like Xeor had been—the same plumed helm, the same leather armor—came out to meet them.

"Welcome, travelers," he said, looking at their horses and weapons. "I am Captain Varos. It looks like you've had a long, hard journey."

"That we have," Hercules said. "We want to use the pass. May we go through?"

"Of course. Once the toll is paid, you are welcome to go whichever way you want."

Grumbling, Hercules took out his coin pouch. Another fifty commons—perhaps more with horses. This mission was costing him a fortune.

Captain Varos said, "Three of you plus three horses . . . that will be six commons."

"Six!" Hercules exclaimed.

Varos shrugged apologetically. "The king sets the tolls, we just collect them. If it's too much for you, perhaps we can barter for passage."

Atalanta said, "We came through the Sherite Pass yesterday and Captain Xeor charged us fifty!"

The captain scratched his beard idly. "That does seem a little high," he admitted.

"It's robbery!" Hercules said. "But somehow, I'm not surprised."

Varos looked at him. "What do you mean?"

Atalanta hesitated. "Someone led an attack on the inn where we were staying. We suspect it was Xeor. We saw soldiers."

Varos frowned. "Those are *very* serious charges. Did you see Captain Xeor? Or recognize any of his men?"

"No . . . we left just as the attack began."

"So you *didn't* see him. All you know is that he charged a little too much for the tolls."

"Someone attacked the inn!" Atalanta said.

"You mean the one his cousin owns? Why would he attack it?"

"Because his cousin wouldn't complain about the attack after it ended—if he got our money."

Hercules added, "No one else knew we were there. It must have been Xeor."

"Perhaps." Varos shook his head. "But you have no proof. It seems to me you have only one legitimate complaint about Captain Xeor, and that's overcharging the toll. You should take such matters up with his superior, General Tsodos."

"And where would we find him?"

Captain Varos turned and pointed east. "In Spaers."

"And *that* would be . . . ?" Hercules said.

"The capitol. It's about sixty miles."

Hercules snorted. "Too far. We'll make sure we see Xeor on our way back."

Varos smiled thinly. "I would remind you that assaulting an officer is a capital offense . . . *if you're caught*." Hercules noticed how he placed the emphasis on the "if you're caught" part, as though inviting them to take care of matters themselves, then escape over the border. Clearly there was no love lost between these two officers.

Varos went on, "Now, to present business . . . I still have a toll to collect."

"Here." Hercules handed over a silver coin.

"Wait."

The captain headed for a nearby building. Hercules assumed he planned to weigh the coin and return with appropriate change. Varos certainly seemed a much more efficient, not to mention honest, soldier.

"Xeor . . . I'll wring his neck twice now!" Atalanta said.

"After I'm done with him, you'll be lucky to *find* his neck!" Hercules said, feeling the anger tighten in his chest.

With a shake of his head, Hylas began to lead his horse toward the closed gate. "I'll see if the guards know anything about the road ahead," he said. "Maybe I can learn something useful."

Atalanta snorted. "I think we've just been shown up!"

"At least he has his priorities straight," Hercules said, forcing a laugh. "He's right. Jason and the road ahead are what's important—we cannot let Xeor distract us."

"Two hundred and two copper commons," Varos announced, returning from his office. He counted out the coins, which Hercules tucked into his pouch.

"My thanks," Hercules said. "Should we run into General Tsodos, I *will* speak highly of you."

Varos nodded. "A good journey to you," he said.

He waved to the gate, which two men slowly swung open for them. Hercules lead his horse forward, and Atalanta matched him stride for stride.

From behind, Hercules heard a distant voice shout, "*Wait! Hold them!*"

Glancing over his shoulder, he spotted Captain Xeor riding toward them in a war chariot, followed by twenty-five or thirty more chariots filled with soldiers. Xeor had an angry expression and whipped his horses repeatedly.

Varos leaped forward and drew his sword. "Hold there!" he commanded loudly. Under his breath, he said, "Run!"

"Ha!" Hercules said. He leaped onto his horse's back, kicking the gelding to a gallop. To Xeor, he knew it would look like Varos had tried to stop him. Much as he wanted to settle the score with the captain, he knew this wasn't the time or the place for it; so many soldiers would have cut them all to pieces. Courage and muscle only went so far against superior forces. And though Atalanta and Hylas might be as courageous as they came, neither was a demigod like him.

"Shut the gate!" Varos called a moment later—a moment too late. "Don't let them out!"

The men at the gate began to shut it again, but before they had it half-closed Hercules galloped through after Hylas and half a length ahead of Atalanta. From behind, he heard the clatter of chariots drawing to a stop as the gate shut—too late!

"*Open!*" he heard Xeor yelling. "*Fools—open the gate! Hurry!*"

Luckily the road ahead lay clear as far as Hercules could see. Although their horses were laboring, he knew they had enough strength to make it another few miles— hopefully beyond Captain Xeor's ability or desire to chase them.

Hunching low, holding on to the mane for dear life, he urged his mount on. The gelding held his pace, though white flecks of sweat began to dot his sides and foam streamed from his mouth.

The road entered the forest. When he glanced back, he could no longer see the stockade fence. He knew Xeor had the gate open by now, though, and already would be driving hard to catch them.

He must have taken our escape as a personal insult, Hercules thought. Why else would he chase them so far? A few coins could never be worth so much effort.

Suddenly the road split, and he reigned in his mount, hesitating. The gelding shuddered beneath him. To the right, the road circled foothills at the base of the mountains. His vision had showed the passage to Hades lay deep in the mountains, however, so that meant they would have to take the other fork . . . which looked old, rocky, and seldom traveled. On the other hand, he thought, its roughness might work in their favor. Xeor's men would be hard pressed to follow them with chariots.

"This way," he said, turning left. He let his horse pick its own way through the fallen rocks and the vines and protruding roots.

Atalanta and Hylas followed him. The road rapidly grew choked and hard to follow, and by the time they rounded a curve and passed among a grove of pine trees, it had become little more than a goat trail.

Behind them, Hercules once more heard the clatter of chariots—but the noise came and went in a matter of seconds. He grinned at Atalanta. His plan had worked. Xeor went the wrong way.

"They'll be back, I think," she said. She dismounted and began to lead her horse, and he followed her example. "I'm sure it's going to be a matter of pride for Captain Xeor to catch us. We've embarrassed him in front of his cousin, his men, and now Captain Varos."

"We'll see how big a fool he is, then," said Hercules. "He can follow us all the way to Hades, for all I care. The next time we meet, I won't be running away!"

CHAPTER TWENTY

Hercules, Atalanta, and Hylas walked their horses the rest of the afternoon, following the pass deeper into the mountains. Hercules noticed how both his companions had begun to drag their feet, and their horses looked ready to drop. Time to rest, he thought, and he began looking for an easily defendable spot.

"Why is it so cold?" Hylas complained. "It's supposed to be autumn. Shouldn't it be warmer?"

Hercules noticed, then, that his breath too had begun to plume in the air. It felt like winter, suddenly, and he shivered.

"We're in the mountains," Atalanta said hesitantly. "The mountains are always cold."

"Not like this!" Hylas shivered and his teeth began to chatter.

Beware the cold that burns. The words came back to Hercules suddenly. The Oracle had been trying to warn him of something, some danger in his path. They must be getting close to it, whatever it was.

He squinted up at the sky. It would be dark soon.

"Look for a camp site," he said.

They walked in silence for another ten minutes, and as Hercules gazed at the steep, rocky cliffs to either side, his unease grew. There *wasn't* any place to make camp, he realized. They would have to keep going . . . or turn back.

And the temperature continued to drop. His fingers grew numb, and he felt ice crystals forming in his horse's coat as its sweat froze. The gelding took on a wild, panicked look, nostrils flared, eyes rolling.

"They sense something," Hylas said, stopping. "There's danger ahead." He spoke soothingly to his mare, stroking her neck, and she grew a little calmer. Hercules and Atalanta did the same with their horses.

"I don't like this cold," Atalanta said, shivering. "It's not natural."

"It *is* too cold," Hercules said, shivering a little himself. "Too cold and too quiet. Listen. You can't hear anything."

Suddenly the narrow pass opened up into a valley perhaps two hundred yards wide and a thousand yards long. Mountains rose steeply to either side, and the pass continued far ahead. But Hercules couldn't stop gaping at the land directly ahead.

Once it had been lush and green, full of towering oaks and fields of grass. But that had clearly been long ago. The bare, leafless trees looked like the skeletal remains of a forest. Their trunks and branches, black as death, were crusted with thick sheets of ice. The grass, once verdant, was yellowish white with many layers of old frost.

The cold felt strongest here. *Beware the cold that burns.*

He swallowed. Then he paused, listening. Not a sound broke the graveyard silence. No animals moved in this wood; no birds flew overhead, and no insects hummed from the grass or the drifts of leaves on the ground. It seemed a dead place, and he sensed magic in its deadness.

Hylas was blowing on numbed fingers to warm them. Hercules knew how Hylas felt. With each breath he sucked, the cold knifed his nose and chest.

"There's a fortress!" Atalanta said, pointing to the right.

Hercules turned and followed her arm. Sure enough, to their right was an old stone fortress, built right into the side of the mountain. It must have guarded the mouth of the valley in ages past, when men lived here, Hercules realized. For now, it seemed to offer their best hope of shelter for the night.

"Let's go," he said. He led his mount forward.

Just as they reached the gates, a great rushing sound like the unfolding wings of some great animal came all around them. Winds came tearing through the dead trees, sounding like a hundred weirdly fluted musical instruments.

The horses began to buck and rear, throwing off their packs and pulling their reins free. Suddenly they bolted across the grass, hooves kicking up frozen grass and turf. Hercules stared. The winds seemed to be *following* the horses, he realized.

Hylas started after them, but Hercules caught the lad's arm and pulled him back.

"No. Let them go," he said.

"Get the packs," Atalanta said, gathering up her own belongings. "Let's get inside."

Suddenly afraid, though he couldn't say why, Hercules gathered up his own belongings and trudged the last twenty feet to the gates of the fortress. They were closed.

He put his shoulder to the wood and pushed, but they seemed to have been barred from inside.

"Can't you open it?" Atalanta asked, teeth starting to chatter.

"It's barred from the other side."

"Use that legendary strength!"

Hercules gave a grunt, dropped his pack and spear, and set his shoulder to the door. Digging in his heels, he began to push as hard as he could.

Fortunately, the wooden bar on the other side had seen better days. It creaked, groaned, and finally snapped with a crack like thunder. Hercules pushed the door open and stepped inside.

Instantly something hard and sharp pricked the small of his back. He stiffened.

"Who are you?" he said loudly.

Atalanta held back, just outside, her hand dropping to the knife at her belt.

"I have a bow," a woman said in Greek with an oddly musical accent that Hercules found quite pleasing. "The arrow is against your spine. One move and you are a dead man."

"That would be very messy," Hercules said.

"*Slowly!* Raise your hands!"

Hercules swallowed. She spoke so with such ill humor that he didn't doubt her words. She really *would* shoot him in the back if he didn't do as instructed.

"Who are you?" she went on. "What do you want here?"

"Three travelers seeking shelter from the cold."

"Travelers don't come this way."

"You realize," he said after a few minutes of standing quite still, "that this is essentially an untenable position on both our parts." When she didn't answer, he went on. "My arms have already begun to ache. In fact, I shall have to at least put them on my head in a moment, or drop them to my sides. I assume that you, too, are getting tired of standing there."

"Not really."

"Do you intend to keep me here all night?"

"Stop complaining. Gannar will be here in a moment. We'll just stay the way we are until then."

"My name's Hercules, by the way," Hercules said. It was harder to kill someone you knew. "I don't believe you've introduced yourself yet."

"Isdal."

"Delighted to meet you."

Boots clattered on flagstones as another person approached. *Gannar*, Hercules assumed.

Behind him, Atalanta confirmed it: "He's a soldier of some kind. He's in uniform, but it's not like Xeor's men. He's got a bow, too."

"That's right. And he knows how to use it." The sharp pressure against his spine let up. "Turn around," Isdal said.

Hercules did so and found himself facing a man and a woman, both with bows pointed at his chest. The man was tall and gaunt, with just a touch of gray to his hair, and he wore a tattered brown uniform of a cut Hercules didn't recognize. The gold on his shoulders marked him an officer, though low-ranking, Hercules thought.

"He said his name was Hercules," the woman—Isdal—said to Gannar.

Hercules inclined his head. "Quite so," he said. He studied her in turn. She wore a dress cut from the same cloth as Gannar's uniform. Her hands intrigued him. You could learn a lot from a person's hands, and hers seemed soft and uncallused; not a soldier's hands. Even so, she held her bow like a veteran. That, and the hardness of her expression, marked her as dangerous . . . more dangerous than Gannar, probably. Hercules knew he'd have to be careful around her. Beyond her expression, there was a certain beauty to her face: the deep sea-green eyes, the high cheekbones, the finely chiseled nose and chin.

"Outlanders, eh?" Gannar said. "What are you doing around here, then? You're not kitted up for a long journey. Exiles, are you?"

"Hardly that," Hercules said. "We were on a quest to win the Golden Fleece. Unfortunately, we lost Prince Jason and are journeying to bring him back." He didn't think it necessary to go into too many details. The story sounded unlikely enough before adding a trip to the underworld to win Jason back from Hades!

"You expect us to believe a story like that?" Isdal demanded. "You're criminals, more likely. Fleeing justice!"

"It's the truth!" Hylas broke in. "Haven't you ever heard of Hercules before? He's a demigod and one of the greatest warriors in the world!"

"A demigod?" Gannar frowned. "Seems like I have heard of you, somewhere."

Hercules bristled. "I see we have gone far enough from home that all common courtesies are forgotten," he said. "Have we come to a land of rude assassins who turn on travelers, insult them, and keep them at bowpoint in the cold?"

Gannar laughed, deep and booming, and lowered his bow. "Hardly that, Hercules. Come in, come in. You have nothing to fear from us, and Isdal's bark is worse than her bite."

Isdal glared at her companion, but said nothing. She did lower her bow a little.

"Thank you," Hercules said, smiling for the first time. He stepped forward. Hylas and Atalanta joined him inside the fortress. Hercules noticed that Atalanta kept one hand on her knife and watched Isdal closely. She was right, he thought—Isdal struck him as the more dangerous of the two.

"Help me close the gates," Gannar said.

"Why? What do you fear outside?"

"We will talk about that inside, where it's warm."

Hercules smiled. "Yes, I think we all need to thaw our bones by a fire."

He pushed the gates closed. Gannar dragged out a wooden beam to replace the one Hercules had broken, and together they lifted it into place, barring the gates firmly shut for the night.

"This way," Isdal said. Turning, she led the way across the courtyard to a small building, opened the door, and went in first. Atalanta and Hylas followed.

Gannar caught Hercules's arm before he could follow. "A word, friend," he said.

"Yes?"

"How did you get to this cursed valley?"

"We walked."

"Are there more of you . . . out there?" He nodded toward the gate. "If so, speak now and we will let them in. They will not live through the night otherwise."

"Because of the cold?" Hercules asked, nodding.

"That, too . . ."

"No. We are alone." He hesitated a moment, wondering if Xeor would dare to chase them so far.

Gannar caught the pause. "There is something else. What are you not telling me?"

After a second's thought, Hercules decided to tell the whole story of Captain Xeor's treachery and pursuit. He summarized it briefly, then concluded, "If Xeor is fool enough to follow us here, we will worry about it then."

Gannar relaxed a bit. "If he is as bad as you say, I almost welcome him—he would not leave this place alive."

"What do you mean?"

"There is a creature out there." He jerked his chin toward the gate. "You were lucky."

"A monster?" He found his heart starting to beat a little faster with excitement.

"We lost fifty good men. I do not want to lose more."

"Fifty!" Hercules exclaimed. "How?"

"I do not know. I have never seen it, just heard it. And I have seen what it does to the men it catches."

Hercules remembered how the wind came rushing . . . and how it followed the horses when they bolted. Perhaps they *had* met the creature after all.

"Atalanta must hear this," Hercules said. "Save your story for telling around the fire."

"Very well. If you do not think it will panic your wife or son?"

"They are friends and traveling companions, not kin. And both fight well against monsters . . . both human and not."

"Good. We may need their skills, then, if we are to get out of this valley."

They followed the others inside, and Gannar shut the door behind them. It was much warmer here, Hercules discovered with relief—a small fire crackled at the hearth, and there were benches around a table. He smelled soup bubbling in a pot and hoped Gannar and Isdal had enough to share.

Gannar and Isdal had a simple enough story to tell: Isdal was a princess of a neighboring land, and her marriage had been arranged to the third-born son of King Espero. Rather than using the well-traveled route, which had been plagued by bandits of late, the king sent Isdae via an old trade pass through the mountains, accompanied by fifty of his best guards and half a dozen maids and matrons. All had gone well on the trip until they reached this valley. They made camp here, and as darkness fell, the screaming began.

"It was horrible," Isdal said with a shudder. "All around camp, people were being devoured by something that came out of the ground—something cold that moved with the sound of rushing wind."

"I acted quickly," Gannar said. "I gathered up the princess and ran for safety. We made it here, and here we have remained for almost a month. I hoped we could hold out until either King Espero or King Levastor sent rescuers."

"But what about food? And firewood?" Atalanta asked.

"Fortunately we found stores of wood in several buildings," Gannar said. "We are careful to use as little as possible, but still we are running out. As for food—I have had to go back to the site of the massacre twice to forage for provisions."

"The last time he barely made it back alive," Isdal said. "The monster followed him as far as the gates of this fortress."

Isdal served the soup—watered down a bit to make enough for everyone—as Hercules and Atalanta told a more detailed version of their own mission, including Captain Xeor's treachery, the attack on the inn, and their subsequent escape, thanks to Captain Varos.

As they finished, Hercules heard a familiar sound, distant but growing closer: the dull thunder of hooves and chariot wheels—it could only be Xeor. He tensed and glanced at Atalanta, who gave a slight nod—she had caught it too.

Gannar stood. "That must be your friend Xeor," he said.

"He is no friend." Hercules frowned. "He does not give up easily, though."

"Come. We will see."

Isdal picked up her bow. Gannar took his own, then led the way out, and together the five of them made their way across the courtyard, up a narrow set of stone steps, and onto the fortress's wall.

Dusk was trailing away, with only the faintest pink smearing the west. The first stars had begun to appear overhead. By night the land here looked more desolate than ever, but took on a strangely unreal beauty. The ice and frost on the dead grass and trees shimmered in the moonlight.

Squinting, Hercules could just make out twenty chariots now pulling up thirty yards from the fortress. He counted thirty-five men.

Xeor and two other men in full battle armor stalked forward. They squinted up at the walls, but clearly did not recognize Hercules, Atalanta, or Hylas in the dark.

"Hail the fortress!" Xeor called.

"Who are you?" Gannar shouted down. "What brings you here like bandits in the night?"

"I am Captain Xeor, and I seek three criminals fleeing the king's justice! Have you seen them?"

"Aye, they are here!" Isdal shouted. She glared at Hercules. "I knew it," he heard her mutter.

"We do not open the gates after dark," Gannar called down. "Come back on the morrow."

"We'll camp here, then."

"No!" Gannar called. "Go back and wait beyond the pass!"

"Why? So the prisoners can escape?"

"There is a monster—"

Xeor gave a derisive snort. "What nonsense is this? Our prisoners will escape if we leave. We are staying here!"

He waved to his men. Dismounting, they began to unhitch their horses and set up a rude camp just outside the fortress gates.

Hercules stepped back and found both Gannar and Isdal staring at him questioningly. Isdal's eyes were hard, and her voice harder.

"Criminals, like I thought! What did you steal?"

"Nothing," Hylas said. "They tried to murder and rob us!"

In a softer voice, Hercules said, "I know you are intended for the third son of their king, but you have a lot to learn about manners, Princess Isdal."

"They will be dead by morning," Gannar said flatly. "This Captain Xeor is more a fool than he knows."

"You seem certain of his fate," Atalanta said.

"As certain as I am of yours!" Isdal said.

Gannar shook his head. "This is getting us nowhere. Hercules is in our camp and under our hospitality. If Captain Xeor is still alive in the morning, we will discuss what to do then. Meantime, Princess, I suggest you sleep. I will stand first watch." He looked at Hercules. "And the second?"

"I will take it," Hercules said.

Below, horses began to scream, shrill and high. The sound iced Hercules's veins, and for an instant he just stood there, unmoving, unable to move. The world seemed to be slowing down, taking on a nightmare quality. Suddenly the cold pressed at him from all directions, so sharp it made his bones ache.

Beware the cold that burns, he thought.

"It is coming," Gannar said.

Another horse screamed, and as though a spell had been broken, Hercules rushed back to the wall. Leaning forward, he gazed down on chaos. By the light of several small cooking fires, he saw rearing horses, running men, and Captain Xeor frantically shouting orders.

A noise like rushing wind came at them, and as the campfires flickered, Hercules thought the ground was heaving and boiling like water. More horses screamed, thrashing at the ends of ropes, and the earth moved beneath them. Xeor brandished a sword, looking helplessly for some enemy to fight.

Black lines snaked across the ground. Suddenly Hercules realized the ground was opening like a giant mouth. The horses fell first. They tried to run, still screaming their fear and panic, but the ground fell away beneath them. Their cries dwindled, as though they fell a great distance.

Some of the men were running. Lines of darkness followed them. Most headed for the woods, but a handful fled for the keep, shouting to be let in.

Shuddering, Hercules looked at Isdal and Gannar. Neither of them moved to unbar the gates.

"Damn you," he said. "How can you leave them out there?" He turned and ran for it himself.

Men were pounding on the gates now. "*Open!*" they screamed. "*By all the gods, open for us!*"

"Leave them!" Gannar called.

"They're men!" Hercules said. "You can't leave them out there!"

He heard footsteps behind him, then a hand grabbed his arm and spun him around.

"No!" Gannar snarled. "The princess must be kept safe! We cannot risk letting the monster inside!"

"Coward!" Hercules roared. No man deserved to die alone in the dark at the hands of some unknown monster. He wouldn't stand for it.

He shoved Gannar back, then raced forward, pulled out the bar, and let the gates open. Six men tumbled inside.

Hercules waited half a heartbeat, hoping some of the

other soldiers might make it to the keep, but the sounds of rushing wind, screaming horses, and dying men simply faded away. They were . . . *gone*.

He swallowed. *I should have been faster*. But then he might have had twenty of Xeor's men to face instead of just six.

Before the monster could return, he shut the gates and barred them again. If any soldier somehow survived, he could always open them, he thought.

A moment later, Gannar joined him with a torch. By its flickering yellow light, he rubbed his jaw ruefully.

"I'm sorry about that," Hercules said. "I didn't mean to hurt you."

"Do not be sorry. It makes me believe your story all the more. No criminal would have let those soldiers inside."

That reminded him—Hercules turned to where the six men he had let into the fortress huddled against the wall. Xeor was shaking all over, and a light frost covered his skin and clothes.

When Xeor spotted Hercules and realized who had let them into the fortress, he blushed and looked at the flagstones.

"What do you have to say for yourself?" Hercules asked him.

"H-Hercules," Xeor managed to stammer. He dropped to his knees and laid his sword at Hercules's feet. "I am shamed before you. My life is yours."

Hercules picked up his sword. After a moment, he handed it back. "There is someone here who needs your help," he said. "Princess Isdal—"

"The princess is here?" He leaped to his feet, looking around. "She was reported killed!"

"I am here and quite alive," Isdal said from the side.

Xeor hurried to kneel before her. "Lady! We must get you back to civilization!"

"That is easier said than done," Gannar said. "We have been trapped here by that monster for almost a month."

Atalanta joined Hercules. "I still don't trust him," she said.

"Neither do I," Hercules said. "But he may be the key to getting Princess Isdal back to safety."

CHAPTER TWENTY-ONE

Réas lost consciousness several times as, whooping and hollering in triumph, Koremos's followers dragged him through the forest and underbrush. His head banged sharply on rocks; roots and sticks slashed open his back and arms; and every now and then his captors kicked him in the sides for good measure. Whenever he passed out, they paused long enough to pour cold water on his head. Then their game began anew.

At last they hauled him up before a roaring campfire and let his legs drop to the ground. Groaning, he tried to roll over, but he no longer had the strength. Every inch of his body had its own different agony. He had never hurt so much in his life.

Black hooves stepped in front of his face. Slowly he managed to raise his head.

It was Koremos, of course. The black centaur smiled

down at him almost kindly. "Welcome to our camp," he said grandly. "I want to know where Theseus took the *Argo*. Talk quickly and I may let you live through the night."

"They—sailed away—gone now—" Réas managed to spit out. "Won't—be back—"

Koremos made a tsk-tsk sound. "Kill the other one," he said to one of his men.

"No! Wait!" Réas tried to sit up. Where was his brother? He looked around the camp as best he could, but his vision blurred and swayed, and for a second two images of Koremos wavered before him. Slowly they slid together. Réas winced.

"Tell me what I need to know!" the black centaur commanded.

"Show me my brother first. I want to see him alive."

Koremos nodded to someone, and a second later they threw Emeras to the ground beside him. Réas gasped in horror—even in the dim, flickering light of the campfire, he could see the dozens of knife wounds on his brother's face. He had been tortured.

"Emeras!" he said. "Emeras!"

A low groan, little more than a breath, passed his brother's lips. His eyes didn't move.

Réas felt his stomach tightening into knots. *We're going to die here*, he thought. *We're going to die, and nothing anyone can do will save us.*

"Well?" said Koremos, still in his kind-and-gentle voice, as though trying to coax a frightened horse back into a pen.

Réas licked his lips. "They are—a day's sail west—in a small cove." Perhaps the lie would buy the others some time.

"Excellent." Koremos paced a bit. "Now, what were you two doing here?"

Emeras groaned softly again. It sounded like *No!* to Réas.

"We were sent to find your camp," Réas said. He was starting to recover his breath. "Theseus plans to attack—to kill you—as soon as the rest—of the Argonauts—are recovered enough for war."

"Excellent." Koremos paced again.

Réas heard murmuring among the centaur's band. Raising his head, he saw they had all gathered in a circle around the campfire and were watching with savage gleams in their eyes. They all held swords and knives at the ready.

"Koremos—" Réas said softly. "Let us go. We can do you no more harm."

The black centaur chuckled. "Oh, that's a mistake I never make. When I have my enemies in hand, why should I let them go? They would only attack another day."

Réas's mouth went dry. He almost missed the black centaur's next command.

"*Kill them.*"

Koremos's men leaped forward, dogs closing in on the kill, knives and swords swinging. Réas closed his eyes, felt the bright hot sting of bronze blades, and—nothingness.

The next thing he knew, Réas found himself trudging down a dirt road beside his brother.

"Emeras!" he cried. "You're—"

"Dead, like you," said his brother flatly.

Réas felt a hollowness inside. *Yes. They killed us.* He knew it more certainly than he had ever known anything else in his life. *So much for honor among thieves.* It would have been a simple matter, an easy matter, for Koremos to let them go. In their condition, it would have taken them weeks if not months to recover enough for battle.

"What now?" Emeras said.

"Well, if you don't have a better plan, we can always haunt them."

Emeras snorted. "How? Have you ever haunted someone before?"

"Not in this life!"

"Nor have I. It's the underworld for us . . . rebirth . . . new lives in the world! Hopefully we'll be brothers again. Now shut up and look for the Styx!"

"Uh, Emeras, how are we going to pay the ferryman?"

Emeras stopped short. "That's right. Koremos isn't going to bury us with proper ceremony." That included a small coin in each of their mouths, which they would then use to pay Charon to ferry them across the Styx. Emeras bit his lip thoughtfully. "We're going to be stuck here forever unless we think of something."

"Maybe we *should* look into haunting Koremos," Réas said, half joking. "At least it's something to do."

"Well, maybe Charon and his toll are just tales to frighten children," Emeras said.

"Or perhaps someone built a bridge."

"That's right. You never know!"

Side by side, they continued walking for what seemed days, although the sun never appeared. Now and then they overtook other walkers—also dead—or were themselves overtaken. *All the dead in the world come this way.* Réas thought. He felt a growing depression. The only good thing about being dead seemed to be their lack of physical sensations—he felt neither tired nor hot, neither hungry nor thirsty.

The road they traveled wound down, passed through a light mist, and finally ended at a broad plain. Hundreds if not thousands of dead people wandered or sat, talking little, doing less. At the far edge of the plain Réas spotted a ribbon of black water.

"That has to be the Styx," he said.

Emeras nodded. "Come on, let's take a look."

They pushed through the crowds to a small stone dock. A gaunt figure dressed in black stood in a small boat, accepting coins from half a dozen dead people who had lined up there. He had room for a couple more passengers, Réas saw with growing excitement.

"Maybe we can make a deal with him," Emeras said softly.

"Ha!"

"It can't hurt to try."

A woman beside them turned suddenly and said in a flat voice, "If you do not have a coin, he will not let you cross. We have been stuck here for ages."

"Still," Emeras said, "you never know."

"Do what you want." The woman turned away listlessly.

"You try first," Réas said.

Nodding, Emeras led the way to the dock. Charon raised his pole as they approached.

"Where is your payment?" he demanded in a cold, hard voice.

"We don't have coins," Emeras said.

"Then be gone! I do not have time to waste on you."

Charon began to push his boat away from the dock, but Emeras stepped forward. "A trade, then," he said. "I have information you need."

"Information?" Charon hesitated. "What do you mean?"

"You will shortly have visitors. Bring us across and I will tell you who to expect."

Réas caught his arm. "Is this wise?" he whispered. "Maybe Hercules wants to surprise them."

"You cannot surprise the gods," Emeras whispered back. "With all those Oracles and temples that Hercules and Jason keep visiting, do you really think the gods haven't noticed them?"

"Good point."

Charon said, "Visitors do not matter to me. I see everyone here, eventually."

"These particular visitors matter quite a lot. You would do well to listen."

"Tell me," Charon said flatly, "and if I like your news, I will bring you both across."

Réas exchanged a glance with his brother. "Bring us across first," he said.

"No." Charon turned and began to pole away from the dock once more.

"Wait!" Emeras said. He hesitated. "Very well. Hercules is coming with two companions."

Charon paused. "Hercules."

"That's right," Réas said, nodding. "Now bring us across."

"No." Charon returned to his poling.

Réas and Emeras just stood there. Réas felt stunned.

"Why not?" Emeras finally called.

"Because," said Charon, voice like gravel, "I do *not* like the news. I do *not* like Hercules. And I do *not* like you."

Emeras sighed. "Well. So much for that idea."

Réas gazed to the right. "We'll find another way across," he said, starting forward. "Come on."

CHAPTER TWENTY-TWO

The cold let up a little over the next hour. Hercules thought back to how Xeor had been covered with ice when they let him in. Clearly this creature—whatever it might be—used ice as a weapon. How do you combat ice and cold? *With fire*, he thought. *With heat*.

He climbed to the top of the wall and looked out across the ice-glimmering nightscape. A plan had begun to form in the back of his mind, but he could not quite figure it out yet.

Atalanta joined him. "You should have let Xeor die," she said. "He's going to turn on us. He's grateful now, but in the morning . . ." She shrugged. "You cannot trust a snake."

"Perhaps. But I *do* know he will guard Princess Isdal well on their way to Lyrcos."

She snorted. "A pampered snob."

"But still in need of help."

"True." She sighed. "Any ideas?"

"Yes. But we're going to need bait." He looked at her, and together they said, "Xeor!"

At first light, everyone except Princess Isdal crept out to see what had happened. The camp had been . . . *ravaged* was the word that came to mind, Hercules finally decided. The bodies of both soldiers and horses had been literally torn apart. Pieces lay scattered across the ground like so many flower petals.

Xeor kept glancing around nervously, hand on his sword. "We should leave here," he said. "If we can make it to the pass before it returns, we can get back to Lyrcos."

"Unless it decides to follow you," Hercules said. "Do you want to be the one who leads it to civilization?"

Xeor paled. "It wouldn't—"

"You never know."

"The bodies don't look *eaten* so much as torn apart," Atalanta said.

"It is just like what happened with our men," Gannar said, nodding. "It comes up from below, then kills and feeds."

Atalanta bent down and studied an arm, still clutching a sword. "Take a look at this, Hercules," she said.

He joined her. "What?" The arm looked a little blue, but he didn't see anything unusual.

"Two things," she said. "First, it's frozen solid."

"What!"

She nodded. "Touch it."

He reached out hesitantly and discovered the arm felt like a solid block of ice. The man had been frozen solid, then his body shattered. *That explains why there's so little blood.*

Hylas looked visibly ill, as did Xeor and most of the

soldiers. Hercules had to admit to a little queasiness himself. He had never seen a battlefield like this one before. It wasn't *right*.

"What can kill an ice monster?" Atalanta wondered.

"Xeor's men had campfires," Hercules said. "It didn't save them. But I think that's the right idea. This thing must be *huge*. Campfires felt like pinpricks. We need a sword."

"What do you mean?"

He waved at the trees, and the plan clicked into place in his mind. "Look at all the firewood. The trees have been dead so long, they're going to burn like parchment."

She looked at him, then slowly smiled.

They worked carefully all morning, planting torches from the keep in strategic places, gathering fallen wood, and pushing over trees. Slowly a large circle began to form just to the left of the massacre sight.

Gannar kept the gates open, and every time the temperature began to drop sharply, they all ran to the fortress and safety. Twice the monster passed them by. Both times they saw nothing—*But it's there as surely as I'm alive*, Hercules thought as he heard the rushing sound of wind and wings.

As afternoon edged toward night, they finished the trap: a circle of wood perhaps thirty feet across, and at its center a small platform of twelve torches tied together.

Hercules stood back and surveyed everyone's work. Crude, but hopefully effective—time would tell whether it worked.

He turned to Captain Xeor. "You said your life was mine," he said. "Did you mean that?"

Xeor bowed his head. "Yes, Hercules."

"Then I give you a chance to win it back—and redeem

yourself. You will be the one to stand in the trap and kill the monster." .

"*Me?*" Xeor gulped.

"Think of it—you can be the hero who kills the monster and brings back Princess Isdal. That would surely mean a great deal to your career."

"Unless I'm eaten!"

"It's a possibility."

He licked his lips, then looked at the trap. Slowly he nodded. "I *will* do it."

"Good."

Hercules's breath began to mist the air, and he shivered. The temperature had begun to fall again. *It's coming*.

They had kept a torch burning for just this occasion. Hercules pulled it out of the ground and handed it to Xeor. "Good luck," he said.

Turning, he ran back toward the fortress, and everyone else followed.

They did not have long to wait. As Hercules paced the wall, staring down at the now tiny-looking circle of wood, Atalanta, Gannar, and Isdal joined him.

"I just thought of something," Atalanta said. "I know he's there as bait, and that he's going to light the fire when the monster appears. But how is he going to get *out* of the trap once it's burning? Not, of course, that I necessarily *want* him to survive, of course."

"I think you've found the one flaw in my plan," Hercules admitted. "But villains have a bad habit of surviving even the most carefully laid traps. It's possible he will get out somehow."

The whistling wind began. Xeor held his ground, but the torch he held shook. The air froze in Hercules's lungs. Knives of ice seemed to cut his nose and chest.

The ground began to buckle around Xeor. Still he held

his ground. *He's waiting too long!* Hercules thought. *He'll be dead before he starts the fire if he's not careful!*

"*Light it!*" Hercules called down. "*Do it now!*"

Xeor plunged the torch into the platform upon which he stood. One by one the torch heads flared. Then the earth around him dropped ten feet and he vanished from sight—throwing the torch out at the last second. It sailed out . . . and fell two feet short of the pile of wood. The trap wasn't going to catch fire.

Hercules cursed. He hadn't counted on Xeor waiting too long and screwing up his plan. Turning, he sprinted for the gate. He had no choice—he had to get out there and set the fire himself.

"Wait!" Atalanta called. "Hercules! It's working!"

He did an abrupt about-face and hurried back.

The wood hadn't caught fire—but the dead grass had. And it burned quickly, like a wildfire, spreading out in a ring from where the torch had fallen. In seconds it reached the piled wood . . . and after a few seconds of rising smoke, he saw flames start to leap and play through the smaller branches.

Still the earth buckled and heaved in the center of the trap. An arm appeared . . . then another . . . and Xeor pulled himself out of the hole. His entire body was covered in white. *It's ice*, Hercules realized. *He's covered in ice*.

Fire ringed him. Flames danced ten feet into the air, then twenty, and their roar reached the fortress walls. Everyone began to cheer.

Xeor waved, then began to cough.

Behind him, from the hole, movement caught Hercules's eye. A huge white hand emerged, then an arm, then a second arm. A creature twenty feet tall began to pull itself out.

It was shaped like a man, but was white as a slug, with an eyeless head and roughly shaped features. Opening its mouth, it roared in what must have been fear and anger.

It reached for Xeor—but Atalanta acted first. Notching an arrow, she let fly a perfect shot, catching the monster in the center of its chest. Her arrow stuck there for a second, but the creature brushed it away like a giant swatting a fly, scattering drops of water with its hand. It roared again.

The flames leaped higher.

"It's melting!" Gannar said, almost in awe.

"Keep it busy!" Hercules said. "Hit it with arrows! Don't let it get Xeor!"

Around him, everyone leaped to obey. Atalanta fired shot after shot, as did Gannar and Isdal. Their arrows found their mark, and as the creature swatted at them, trying to save itself, the fire surrounding it burned all the brighter.

Suddenly the creature reared back, screaming in pain—and then it collapsed, its flesh turning to water. A wave a foot high swept out in all directions, quenching the fire . . . and the creature was gone. Xeor stood alone in the center of the now-smoldering trap.

Everyone began to cheer. Feebly, the captain gave a triumphant wave.

The cold let up almost immediately. Hercules felt the warmth of the sun on his face and knew the creature was dead. Grinning happily, he congratulated himself on an excellent plan. It had worked even better than he could have anticipated.

He went down to meet Xeor and found the captain just sitting in the grass with his sword across his knees, staring off at the sunset.

"I want to thank you," Xeor said. "You could have been the one to kill the monster. But you let me have the glory. And yet I wonder . . . why?"

Hercules shrugged. "I have killed more than my share of monsters. It's like pulling a bad tooth . . . the pain is gone, but it leaves a hole. Killing you would have been the same. Better to save the tooth and have it whole."

"I see, I think."

"Good." Hercules glanced toward the fortress. "You'll bring Isdal and Gannar back with you, and everyone will know you for a hero. I ask only one thing—try to live up to your new reputation."

"I . . . I *will*." Xeor straightened. Then he smiled and rose, and he grasped Hercules's arm. "Thank you. I don't think I'll ever be the same again."

They spent one more night in the fortress, then set off the next morning, each going their own way. Hercules knew it couldn't be much farther to the entrance to Hades. Then their troubles would start anew. He shivered at the thought of that long, dark descent. Atalanta and Hylas had no idea what lay ahead . . . or they wouldn't be so enthusiastic about their coming ordeal.

CHAPTER TWENTY-THREE

When Réas and Emeras failed to return from their scouting mission, Theseus knew the worst had happened: Koremos had found them and, more than likely, sent them on their way to the underworld. *Two more souls for Hercules to rescue*, he thought grimly.

The Argonauts continued to mend. Most could walk again, and at least half had returned to battle-ready condition. They worked out on the island, sprinting, practicing swordplay, readying themselves for the coming battle with Koremos. It wouldn't be much longer, Theseus knew, until they were ready to take on the black centaur . . . and kill him once and for all.

Koremos parted the branches of a bush and peered down at a small cove, frowning in growing anger. *They lied to me.* He had no doubt about it now. The two Argonauts he had captured and tortured for the location of the *Argo* had lied to him.

He had spent the last day creeping up the coast, looking for the cove where their ship lay at anchor. And he hadn't found it. He had gone three miles, then five, then ten . . . and found no trace of the *Argo*.

"Just as well you're dead," he snarled to himself. "I would have killed you myself, if you'd still been alive!"

He let the branches fall back, turned, and began to head back to his main camp. *How could they lie to me?* he wondered. *I might have spared their lives.* Then he chuckled. No, he would not lie to himself. He never spared *anyone's* life. They must have realized it and tried to steer him off course.

He frowned. So—where had the Argonauts gone?

CHAPTER TWENTY-FOUR

Hercules led the way through the valley, following a faint old trail that vanished in places—swept away by the passing of storms—before returning a hundred yards ahead. For the first time, Hercules was glad that Hylas had accompanied them. The youth spotted the trail on several occasions when he and Atalanta had all but given it up for lost.

So they proceeded throughout the day, heading higher into the mountains. They reached a high pass where the snow never melted, and here the trail ended at the mouth of a wide, deep cave. *This is it*, Hercules thought. It matched his vision exactly.

"How far is it from here?" Atalanta asked.

"I don't know," Hercules said. He paused in the mouth of the cave, listening, staring into the darkness. A faint odor reached him . . . dry, dusty as old bones, and ancient as the world itself. He swallowed. He remembered that smell from the last time he had visited the underworld.

"I found torches!" Hylas called from one side. "Torches and . . . someone!"

"Someone? Who?" Hercules said. Turning, he hurried over to where Hylas stood at the far side of the cave.

There, behind a small pile of fallen rocks, lay a skeleton. The empty eye sockets gaped at him, and the teeth smiled crookedly. Hercules let his gaze drift over what little remained of the man's clothing and armor. Most of the leather and cloth had rotted away or been eaten by rats, but the corroded green remnants of a shield and breastplate remained.

"Who was he?" Hylas asked.

"An adventurer who made it here before us," Hercules said. "Only he died of wounds or in a rockfall long before we were born."

"At least he came well equipped," Atalanta said, nodding toward the half dozen long wooden sticks with oil-soaked rags bound tightly around one end.

"I think not," Hercules said. The torches looked much more recent than the skeleton. "Someone else cached their supplies here. Those torches aren't very old."

Hercules picked one up for himself, passed one to Atalanta, and gave the rest to Hylas. They would come in quite handy, he thought.

"Good spotting," he said. "We'll need these, I think."

Atalanta took out flint and iron, and soon nursed a spark into flame. With her torch blazing, she turned to Hercules and lit his.

"Keep close behind me," Hercules cautioned as he started forward. "We don't know anything about these caves. I am certain we will have quite a few dangers yet to face before we reach Hades."

* * *

The main cave led into a series of tunnels. Whenever the path forked, Hercules paused at each branch, listening, smelling the air, feeling for an updraft of wind.

"*You may not continue!*" A faint, quavering voice cried in Greek. "Turn back!"

Hercules looked around, but saw no one.

"Who's there?" Atalanta called. Hercules heard a slight quaver in her voice.

"*A friend . . .*"

Hercules snorted. "If you're a friend, you know we must continue," he said. "Show yourself or be gone!"

"*The light hides me . . .*"

Hylas gulped. "It's a ghost!"

"They can't hurt us." Hercules raised his torch and strode forward.

"*Turn back . . .*" the voice echoed. It grew fainter and fainter as they continued walking. "*Turn back . . . turn back . . . turn back . . .*"

The air grew colder.

"Was it like this the last time you were here?" Atalanta asked, her breath pluming in the air before her. She was shivering, Hercules saw.

"No. I came a different way. It was not this cold."

"Oh."

They came to a place where the cave became a tunnel. Hercules spotted chisel marks on the walls and floor where the rock had been leveled out. Probably the work of Titans, Hercules thought, or other elder denizens of Earth.

They passed alcoves. Inside them stood the skeletal remains of almost-human-looking warriors, armed with long, curved swords of a design Hercules had never seen before. They still held round shields painted with green and gold geometric designs.

"I don't like the look of this place," Atalanta whispered.

Her voice echoed softly. "If someone wanted to ambush us, this would be the spot for it."

"They're long dead," Hercules said with an impatient shrug. "They can't hurt us."

When they reached the center of the corridor, a deep voice called, "*I smell the blood of the living!*"

The skeleton at the farthest end of the corridor stepped out from its alcove. Its eyes glowed with red pinpricks of fire. Its armor was heavier and fancier than that on the skeletons they had passed thus far. Hercules took a sudden deep breath. Had this been their king or general?

"What were you saying?" Atalanta asked almost wryly.

"I'll talk to him," he said. "He'll let us pass when he finds out I am a demigod."

He strode forward. The skeleton king drew his sword. "*No farther, human!*"

"That's demigod, actually," Hercules said. Impatiently, he motioned the skeleton out of the way. "Stand aside, undead creature. We have business with my uncle, Hades."

"*You may not pass!*"

"Why not?"

The skeleton did not answer. It was probably just doing its job, Hercules thought, and trying to keep people from wandering aimlessly into the underworld.

He took another step forward, hoping the skeleton would move aside, but instead it slashed at him. Calmly he seized its arm and twisted. A human would have had to drop his sword from pain, but the skeleton's arm simply snapped off with a dry, brittle sound like breaking deadwood.

Hercules felt ridiculous holding the arm, which still gripped the sword, so he pried the blade loose, handed the bones back to the skeleton, and said, "Stand aside, please. I really don't want to hurt you."

"Kill them!"

Hercules looked back. The other skeletons were stepping out of their alcoves, raising their shields and drawing their swords.

"Run!" he cried to Atalanta and Hylas.

He knocked the skeleton king out of the way with his shoulder, then sprinted forward. When he glanced back, he saw that Hylas and Atalanta were at his heels . . . and the skeletons were swarming behind them.

Ahead, the tunnel narrowed. This would be the place to make a stand, he thought.

"Keep running!" he called as he leaped to one side. They darted past.

When they were safely ahead of him, he turned, holding the king's sword ready. Here the skeletons could only face him one at a time, and their king was in the lead. He stopped and stared at Hercules with those burning red eyes.

"Consider well, creature!" Hercules said. "For I will kill you if you continue to pursue us! We have business with my uncle. Look to your own affairs and do not meddle in mine!"

" . . . *Go*." The word came like a raspy gust of wind. Abruptly the skeleton king turned and led the rest of his skeleton army away. In a few heartbeats they were gone.

Hercules found he had been holding his breath and let it out explosively. Sweat covered him. His bluff had worked—he could have fought off a dozen men if they faced him one at a time in this tunnel, but he wasn't so sure about skeletons.

He joined Atalanta and Hylas, who had paused to watch twenty yards up the tunnel.

"I thought we were going to be killed!" Hylas said, awe in his voice. "They were dead!"

"Undead, actually," Hercules said. He frowned. "We

will have to return to the surface another way. They will be waiting for us here, and I don't think they will let us pass in peace."

"How much farther can it be to your uncle's palace, if we're already seeing dead guards?" Atalanta asked.

"Not much farther." Hercules sniffed. That old, musty smell had grown even stronger. "We still have to find the River Styx, though."

He took the lead again, and they followed more passages downward, deeper into the Earth. The stone walls of the tunnel glistened with seeping water.

At last the tunnel opened up into a vast chamber... Hades, the dark reflection of the living world. The ceiling rose so high, Hercules could not see it, though he heard a distant moaning sound of tortured winds far, far above. Ahead, dark leafless trees broke a desolate landscape full of rocks, sand, and barren earth.

"Put out your torches," he said.

He lowered his own and ground it out in the sand. Atalanta and Hylas did the same.

Darkness surrounded them. Only then did Hercules begin to see the faintest of lights. A thin gray glow illuminated this underground chamber, like the last rays of the sun as night arrived. He blinked, letting his vision adjust to the dimness, and in a few minutes he could see passably well. Everything had a blue-black look to it here, and nothing cast a shadow.

"This is it," Atalanta breathed. "We really are in the underworld."

"Not quite, but we're close," Hercules said. "We will be there soon."

He began to walk forward, picking his way around stray rocks. The stone floor became sand, then dry dirt. Dust puffed out beneath his sandals with every step. Slowly the low hills on the horizon began to draw nearer.

They spent what seemed hours walking in silence, crossing dry gullies, skirting sandpits and stray boulders. At last they came to the hills, and these too they crossed in near silence. The oppressive atmosphere seemed to swallow sound; Hercules noticed that neither Hylas nor Atalanta—both normally chipper and talkative—said a single word. Both began to look depressed and fearful, as if they had only just begun to realize what a horrible mistake they had made in coming this far.

At last, on the other side of the hills, a stone wall fifty feet high appeared before them. It had been built aeons ago to help contain the Titans, he knew. It stretched left and right as far as Hercules could see. Half a mile to the left, he saw immense wooden gates. They were closed.

"This way." He started toward the gates. Silently, Atalanta and Hylas fell in step behind. When he glanced back, he saw their faces had become gaunt and drawn, as though the very life was being leeched out of them. *I don't like the looks of that*, he thought. *Humans were not meant to live down here. And they are not under a god's protection.* Best get it over with as quickly as possible, he thought.

He lengthened his stride and soon reached the gates. He put his shoulder to one and began to shove with all his might. Slowly, hinges groaning, it opened. From the other side came a low growl of anger, so soft that Atalanta and Hylas missed it.

He paused. "Step back," he told them.

A three-headed dog was chained just inside. Two heads snarled at him. The third looked at Hercules and whined, and then its tail began to wag faintly.

"He scents our warm blood," Hercules whispered. "He knows we do not belong here. But he also knows I mastered him once before, so he will not harm me."

"What of Atalanta and me?" Hylas asked with a gulp.

"Don't pet him."

"I won't—and that's a promise!"

"Let's get through as fast as we can," Atalanta said. Hercules heard the crackle of stress in her voice.

"You must wait here," Hercules said. "I must go on alone!"

"How can we wait with *that*!" Hylas demanded.

Hercules stepped forward and grabbed the two snarling heads by the scruff of their necks, shaking them. Cerberus began to whine. Idly, Hercules began to scratch the friendly head behind the ears and received a lick on the arm for his trouble.

"Good boy," he murmured. He glanced at Hylas. "Try giving him some food. Maybe he'll make friends."

"All right," Hylas said doubtfully.

"What about you?" Atalanta demanded.

"I'm a demigod," he pointed out. "I have a certain advantage here. And Hades is my uncle . . . he receives few enough visitors at his court that he should be glad for company. Even if it's me!"

"Good luck, then," Atalanta said. He saw her swallow. "Don't do anything stupid!"

"Thanks," Hercules said. "I think."

Then, straightening his lion skin, he walked past Cerberus, through the gates, and into the underworld. The very air itself seemed to darken and press down on him.

Behind him, the three-headed dog began to growl at Atalanta and Hylas. Its hackles rose, and ribbons of drool fell from its snarling mouths.

Turning, Hercules snapped, "Heel!"

With a faint whine, Cerberus lay down and grew silent.

CHAPTER TWENTY-FIVE

The time has come," Theseus announced in a quiet voice. Not all the Argonauts were battle ready, but surely twenty-eight of them in full battle armor would conquer Koremos's bandit rabble.

He stood on the highest point of their little island, gazing toward shore with brooding eyes. Hiding from Koremos galled him. Each day they spent here worked on his nerves, and though he never showed anything but calm before the rest of the Argonauts, part of him—a large part—wanted to rush to avenge Jason . . . to push the attack as quickly as possible . . . to free them of the black cloud that now hung over their whole party.

A strange clarity came over him. For a moment he thought it was one of those rare moments of perfect vision, when all the world lays itself open before you and you know that everything you do will be right and good.

But when he turned, he found a woman in armor standing before him. Her face glowed faintly, as though fires burned beneath her skin.

"This is not the time," she said.

He stared at her. "What—who—"

"You know me, Theseus." She chuckled. "You have made enough sacrifices in my name."

He fell to his knees, bowing before her—the goddess Athena, come to Earth. For he knew her now as surely as he knew his own name.

"What must I do?" he asked humbly.

"Bide your time," she said. Her voice trailed off as though the words were caught in the wind. "*Wait for Hercules and Jason.*"

"They're coming back?" he gasped, looking up.

He stood alone on the top of the hill. A hot wind blew, carrying the scents of wild thyme and the sea.

CHAPTER TWENTY-SIX

Hercules walked for another hour. Around him, from the corners of his eyes, he sensed movement as pale forms darted this way and that—ghosts, spirits of the underworld, men and women doomed to spend the rest of their existence trapped down here. A chill filled the air, and he heard soft moans that might have been the wind . . . or something more deadly.

At last he came to a bleak shore. A hundred yards wide, the River Styx barred his path. Dozens of pale men and women—the newly dead, still clinging to their earthly forms—congregated there. He joined their midst, waiting.

A ferry, poled by a skeletal figure, glided silently out of the mist. Softly it bumped against the riverbank, and then one by one the pale men and women stepped on board and seated themselves. Each surrendered a small coin to the ferryman.

"Hold!" Charon said, raising his hand and barring the way when Hercules tried to step aboard. "I scent the warm blood of the living!"

Hercules frowned. Had Charon forgotten their last meeting, where he had wrestled the ferryman for passage, defeating him? He knew he could do it again, if he had to.

"You know me, Charon," he said. "Give me passage across. I do not come seeking trouble."

"Hercules . . . they spoke the truth, then."

Hercules frowned. "Who?"

"Two friends . . . they said you were coming . . ."

Hercules looked up and down the banks, but saw no one he recognized. "Who?" he asked again.

"They are gone now . . . wandering spirits. But they will be back. They always come back . . ."

Hercules swallowed. If they were wandering spirits, that meant they hadn't been buried with proper ceremony and with coins in their mouths to pay for passage across the Styx. Bad news, indeed. Doubly bad—if they knew he was on his way to Hades, they must have been Argonauts . . . and they must have died after he set out to find Jason. *Trouble.* Theseus must have run up against Koremos again.

He pulled out his coin pouch. "Here," he said. He handed two coins to Charon. "Give them passage the next time you see them."

"Very well . . ."

Hercules tried to step into the boat, but Charon blocked his way. "You may not travel with me," he said firmly.

"Do you remember what happened the last time you refused me passage?" Hercules asked. "You wound up swimming back to shore. Take me across or you will find yourself overboard again. I do not have time to play your games."

"Very well . . ." Charon stepped back, and the dead souls made room.

Hercules climbed aboard and seated himself in the center of the boat. He kept a close watch on Charon, who began to pole them across the river without a word, but the ferryman ignored him. Mists slowly closed around them, cutting off the outside world. Charon moved them steadily onward.

The motion of the boat, the quiet lap of waves, and the splash of water all lulled him toward sleep. Hercules found his eyes starting to close. Forcing himself awake, he stared at the ferryman's bony hands as he worked.

Before he knew it, the boat bumped against the far shore. He stood, stretched, then hopped out.

"Thank you."

"Next time, pay your way . . ."

Hercules snorted. "The dead pay, not the gods."

"You are not a god . . ."

"A demigod is close enough in this place."

"I will tell Hades you said that." Charon chuckled, then turned to the dead souls still seated in his boat. "Out!" he commanded. "Out and find your own way!"

The dead began to disembark. Hercules gave Charon an insincere nod and a wary smile, then turned and started up a low hill toward the dark palace above.

He strode up the long walkway to the palace. Skeletons guarded the tall gates, and as he neared, they lowered their spears to block his way.

"Living flesh!" one of them said through the gaping hole where its lower jaw had once been. "Go back! You have no business here!"

"Make way for me," Hercules said. "I am the son of Zeus, and I come to see my uncle, who rules."

Hissing faintly, the skeletons raised their spears to let him inside. But as he stepped over the threshold, they fell into step behind him, the bare bones of their feet clattering on the black paving stones.

Through the gateway they entered a courtyard. Benches sat around a large dead tree in the exact middle, and on one of the benches sat another pair of skeletons.

They stared at Hercules, but made no move to block his passage.

Hercules picked the largest door and headed for it. It led to the audience chamber, he remembered.

He passed through cobwebs and had to pause to brush them out of his face and hair. Behind him, he heard one of the skeletons chuckle. The sound cut through him like fingernails on slate.

Taking a deep breath of the dusty air, he strode forward with his head high and his shoulders back. He would show them that he had no fear of this place.

The passageway turned, and then he came to the throne room. Hades sat in audience, a dark man-shaped lump all in black atop a high wooden throne. A dozen skeletal figures knelt before him.

"I smell the blood of the living," Hades said, straightening. "What blasphemy is this?"

Hercules said, "It is I, your nephew Hercules."

"Welcome to Hell, nephew." Hades turned dark eyes upon him. Hercules felt a blade of cold pass through his heart. Against his will, he swallowed.

"Hello again, Uncle," he said. "I hope you are well."

"You do well to remind me of our kinship." Hades gave a low laugh, a sound like a tomb door shutting. "And how is the land of the living?"

"As always, Uncle," Hercules said. "It is summer. Men work or fight, live or die, as the Fates decree."

"And few think of me."

Hercules bowed his head. "You are always in mortals' thoughts, Uncle."

Again Hades chuckled. "Eat, drink, and be depressed, nephew." He waved his hands and gaunt, almost skeletal servants dressed in black carried in trays laden with delicacies: succulent roast pigs, choice fruit, cheese and bread and pastries of all sorts.

Hercules shook his head. If he ate here, he might never return to the land of the living. That was how his uncle had trapped his wife: he had kidnapped her, kept her here, and when she had eaten as little as six seeds of a pomegranate, she had become trapped for all eternity. Only the intervention of the rest of the gods had given her a reprieve, and now she could return to the land of the living six months of each year to visit her mother.

"Why have you come?" the god asked. "You have freed prisoners, borrowed Cerberus, and defiled my court sufficiently already. What more can you do to me?"

"I have come," Hercules said, throwing back his shoulders, "to ask you to return my friend Jason."

"The dead are mine!" Hades declared, voice a sudden roar. The god suddenly towered over Hercules, a vast and powerful being. "You ask the impossible! No one may return to the lands of the living once they have come here!"

"They may return if you permit it!" Hercules countered. He knew Hades had the power to restore the dead to life if he wished. "What must I do to win this favor . . . Uncle?"

Hades leaned back and seemed to think. At last, when Hercules had begun to suspect the god might have forgotten him or fallen asleep, he spoke:

"I will set four great tasks for you to perform," he said. "If you complete them to my satisfaction, you will be free to carry Jason back to the lands you have left."

"Agreed," Hercules said.

"First," Hades said, "you must catch the North Wind and make it sweep through the underworld, carrying off the stench of death and decay."

"Done!" Hercules said.

"Second, you must stop the River Styx for a day and a night."

"Also done!" Hercules said again.

"Third, you must find someone willing to take Jason's place here in Hades."

Hercules paled. That would be the hardest task of all, he knew. No one would want to cut short his or her own life to take another's place in Hades. Still, Jason was not just a prince, but a great hero. Surely someone—one of his relatives, or one of his subjects—would willingly trade places with him.

"What of the fourth task?" he asked.

"I will set that one once the first three are completed. Believe me when I tell you this—it will be the most difficult of all!"

"Very well, Uncle, I will do all these tasks. And as I finish each, I shall return here for your blessing to continue."

"Where will you start?" the god asked softly.

"With the North Wind," Hercules said. "I will find him and return."

"Then I wish you luck," Hades whispered. He sank back in his throne and waved one skeletal arm, and Hercules abruptly found himself on the shores of the River Styx. Charon the Ferryman stood there patiently, leaning on his pole.

"I have been waiting for you," the ferryman said with a faint sneer. "All aboard."

"What trick is this," Hercules said warily.

Charon shrugged. "There will be no charge for *leaving*," he said. "I am eager to be rid of you."

Hercules stepped into the shallow boat and seated himself. Slowly Charon poled them away from the shore, heading toward the other side.

"I know of the tasks which our master has assigned you," Charon said slowly, when they were about halfway across.

"Oh?" Hercules said. That was quick. But then news traveled quickly among the dead.

"Yes . . . you should have started with the River Styx."

"Perhaps."

"It will be more difficult than you know. But I will assist you."

"Why?" Hercules asked suspiciously. "You have never helped me before!"

"I want you gone from here. I want you back in the lands of the living. Your earthy smells of flesh and blood offend all who dwell here. If we must assist you to be rid of you, so be it!"

"Very well," Hercules said. "How would you help me?"

"Look at the water," Charon said, still poling steadily. "It moves in two ways at once."

"Two ways?" Hercules frowned. "What does that mean?"

"See for yourself!"

Charon leaned down and picked a pair of wooden splinters from the bottom of his boat. He cast them both into the water. One began to move left and one began to move right . . . two different directions, Hercules saw, exactly as the ferryman had said.

Hercules leaned over the edge of the boat, watching the splinters, trying to see if someone or something below the surface of the water had moved them.

Then something hard hit the back of his head. Pain coursed through him, and he tumbled overboard, arms flailing. A second later icy waters closed over him.

He fought his way to the surface, gasping. The river felt so cold, it took his breath away.

Charon was rapidly poling his boat away. *He must have hit me when I wasn't looking,* Hercules realized.

"Come back here!" he shouted.

A fiendish cackle drifted toward him.

"*Charon!*"

Mists closed around the ferryman, and then he was gone. Hercules found his hands growing numb. Turning, he began to swim as fast as he could toward the far shore. He soon reached it and pulled himself up onto the bank, gasping. He lay there for several minutes as his strength slowly returned.

Boreas, the North Wind, will be first, he thought. The last time Hercules had seen Boreas, he had been spending his nights asleep on Mount Parnassus. That would be the place to start.

There were many entrances to Hades, but few exits. Parnassus was the highest mountain in the world, so it made sense that it should be reachable . . . he would simply have to climb.

So thinking, he turned and studied the horizon until he picked out the highest peak in the underworld, which disappeared among gray clouds. That seemed a likely place to start.

Taking a deep breath, he rose and struck out for it. His lion skin weighted him down, but it dripped steadily as he walked and slowly began to grow lighter. *I'll spread it out to dry when I get back home,* he thought. In the cold and dark and damp of the underworld, it would never get completely dry.

After what seemed like days of walking—yet he never

grew tired or thirsty or hungry—Hercules reached the mountain. He saw no sign of anyone or anything, living or dead, the whole way. Perhaps that was best, he thought. He moved fastest when he moved alone.

A trail wound its way up, so he followed it, turning this way and that, gradually ascending. At last he entered the clouds, and a white misty fog closed around him. Still he climbed.

Finally, the mist parted and he found himself in sunlight. A cool breeze gusted from the east, and he turned his face to it, smelling the scents of Earth—grass and trees, flowers and leaves, all a thousand times more beautiful than he remembered. After Hades, it seemed impossibly lush here.

Turning, he gazed down on fertile green lands. Here and there squares of land had been cleared for fields; neat rows of trees marked olive and apple orchards. It seemed so *alive*, so vibrant with a thousand shades of green, that it took his breath away.

Still, he had a task to do, he reminded himself. Boreas, the North Wind, awaited him.

Turning, he began to climb once more. This time he moved more quickly, and soon he reached the top of the mountain—a broad, grassy expanse dotted with little clusters of trees. A large brown rock sat to one side, so he crossed to it, stripped off his still-soggy lion skin, and spread it out to dry. The sun, almost directly overhead, told him that he had many hours of daylight left. So he stretched out to take a nap and wait, and soon he dozed off.

It was nearly dark when he came awake with a start. An inner sense had warned him of something, he realized, sitting up a little groggily and rubbing the sleep from his eyes. *What?*

He looked around, then realized a sudden stillness had come over the mountain. Not a leaf, not a blade of grass moved. A hush had fallen over the insects and birds. It was a rather eerie sensation.

Slowly he reached up to the rock and caught the tail of his lion skin, pulling it down and shrugging it on. It felt warm and completely dry now.

Suddenly, with a roar, a blast of wind struck him as Boreas arrived. The grass flattened; the trees bent almost double. Hercules grabbed a rock to keep from being blown away.

Then the wind eased, and a low snoring sound filled the air. It seemed to be coming from a small copse of trees.

Hercules crept forward cautiously. As he approached, small blasts of air pushed at him, each in time to a snore. He pulled back a branch and peeked in.

Boreas—in human form now, looking like a man of middling years with a long brown beard, wild hair, and bushy eyebrows—lay asleep inside. He snored loudly, shaking branches and leaves.

Hercules smiled. The wind was exhausted from a day's labor, sweeping the clouds across the heavens. Hopefully he would sleep all the way to the underworld.

Carefully, moving slowly and deliberately, Hercules eased into the circle of trees, bent, and lifted Boreas as easily as a man might lift a child. The wind stirred, but did not wake. Holding his burden gently, Hercules crept out and, by the light of the moon and stars, began to make his way back down the mountain.

He passed into the clouds again, and without the light of the heavens to guide him, he had to tread carefully, feeling his way inch by inch. At last, though, he passed through the bottom of the clouds, and sure enough he found he had followed the same path: once more he was in the underworld. A wan yellow light surrounded him. The air tasted dry and dead. Dust puffed out with each step he took.

Boreas began to stir and cry out, and then his eyes opened. When he saw Hercules holding him, he roared—and a wind with the force of a hurricane blasted at Hercules.

"No you don't!" Hercules called, keeping his grip on Boreas. The wind struggled to free himself. "I need your help!"

At last the gale lessened, and as he had hoped, Boreas took on his human shape once more.

"What do you want?" the wind demanded. "Why have you seized me?"

"I need you to sweep through the underworld, carrying off the smells of death and decay," Hercules said. "It is a labor that Hades has set for me—and I cannot accomplish it without your help."

"Huh!" Boreas sneered. "This is the land of death. The smell will only return again in a day or two!"

"I know. But it is Hades's will that it be gone for now."

Boreas bowed his head. "Very well, Hercules. I know you are stronger than me—release me and I will do what you ask. If you do something for *me*."

"What?"

"You must promise never to seek me or any of my brothers again. Leave us to our work, and we will leave you to yours."

"Agreed!" Hercules cried. He released Boreas. "Now—do as you have promised!"

Boreas stood silently for a long time, gazing across the desolate landscape. He seemed to be trying to decide where to start, Hercules thought—it *was* a huge task.

At last the wind leaped into the air, his body vanishing, and as a gale he swept across the land. Dust rose and joined him in the force of his passing; small rocks and dead brush tumbled across the ground. And then he was gone, heading across the underworld, scouring it free of smells.

Hercules sniffed. The air almost tasted fresh, he decided. It still had a chill dampness to it—nothing could take that away—but he no longer smelled the sickly sweet odors of decay. Hades would be pleased.

Turning, he set out for the River Styx. As he reached its misty shore, he found Charon waiting for him.

He made as if to grab the ferryman, but Charon raised his bony hands in surrender.

"Peace, Hercules. Hades has reprimanded me for hurling you into the waters. As punishment, I must carry you anywhere you wish to go, anytime you wish me to take you."

Hercules snorted. "A fitting punishment. Take me across the river. I have finished my first task and must speak to your master again."

Charon bowed his head, and Hercules stepped carefully into the boat and seated himself. Without another word, the ferryman poled him across. Hercules watched for tricks, but Charon kept to his best behavior. *We'll see how long it lasts*, Hercules thought.

He leaped ashore and without a backward glance set out for his uncle's palace. The trek seemed even longer than the last time, but at last Hercules strode into the throne room.

Hades still sat there. He gazed down and Hercules actually saw a smile upon his face.

"I am pleased," the god said. "The air is fresh again."

Hercules nodded. "Uncle," he said, "since you are satisfied with the first of my tasks, I will halt the Styx next."

"Do so."

Bowing, Hercules turned and left. He headed for the river again.

Stopping the Styx would be much harder than trapping Boreas, he knew. The Styx, unlike its Earthly counterparts, was a dead body of water. It did not take human form; it did not have one. It was merely cold, dark water, flowing endlessly around the underworld.

"Charon!" he shouted. "I have need of you!"

A few seconds later, he heard light splashing. Then the ferryman's boat glided out of the mist and bumped against the shore by Hercules's feet. Without hesitation, Hercules hopped on board.

"Where do you want to go now?" Charon intoned.

"Take me to the head of the Styx."

"Impossible."

Hercules snorted. *I knew his cooperation wouldn't last.* "I thought you said you would take me wherever I need to go," he said scornfully. "That's my destination."

"Impossible," Charon said again.

"Why?"

"The river has no head. It flows in a circle, with neither a beginning nor an end."

"But surely there must be some way to stop it!"

Charon hesitated. "No," he finally said.

But did that mean there wasn't a way . . . or merely that Charon refused to help him? Hercules could be quite stubborn when he wanted to be, and this seemed to him like a good time to dig in his heels.

"Tell the truth," he said. "Remember, Hades ordered you to help me. Is there a way to stop this river or not?"

Still Charon hesitated. "I do not think Hades meant for me to reveal the secrets of the underworld," he said. "I think he meant for me to take you where you need to go. Tell me your destination or get out of my boat. I have work to do."

"Very well." Hercules folded his arms stubbornly. "Take me to the place where I can best stop the River Styx for a day and a night!"

"Very well," Charon said. He began to pole the little boat out toward the center of the river, then he turned to the left and continued poling until they reached a place even with the palace. Here he paused.

Hercules peeked over the side of the boat, but only saw gently drifting black water. Nothing *seemed* different here.

"This is it," Charon announced, leaning upon his pole. "Get out."

Hercules glared at him. "This is the middle of the river! Do you take me for a fool?" he demanded.

"Yes."

Hercules half rose. "I have a mind to cast you overboard!" he snarled.

Charon merely stared at him. "Then you truly *are* a fool. I have done what you asked. You must find the answer yourself."

Hercules hesitated. "Very well," he finally said. "Wait here for me."

"As you wish."

Taking a deep breath, Hercules jumped overboard. The icy water of the Styx closed around his feet and legs and waist—and then he hit bottom. The water here only came up to his belly, he realized—but it was still numbingly cold.

Experimentally he stomped with his foot. Hard stone lay underfoot . . . not the mud or sand he had expected. Something clearly was wrong here.

He glanced at Charon, but the skeletal ferryman had seated himself with his back to Hercules, offering no help whatsoever. *I'll have to do it myself*, Hercules thought. For a moment he wished Theseus were here; he was clever enough to figure it out. *Well, there's no one else. I have to do it myself.*

He began to feel around with his feet and finally began to suspect he now stood on the top part of a huge boulder. The sides sloped gently down all around him.

Why a boulder? Could it be blocking something . . . perhaps some sort of exit for the river Styx? Hercules found his excitement growing. An exit would give the river an end . . . and he could stop it for a day and a night if it had one!

But how to move the stone? How could he get sufficient grip on it to move it?

Well, he could only try. Taking a deep breath, he leaned forward and began touching the surface of the boulder, feeling for anything that might offer a good grip. And then he found the huge iron ring set into the boulder's side. It was nearly as wide across as his arm was long. It would more than do.

Feeling a growing excitement, Hercules grabbed the side of the boat and searched the bottom. "Do you have a rope?" he demanded.

"Yes."

"Give it to me."

Silently Charon reached behind himself, picked up a small coil of rope, and passed one end to Hercules. Hercules took another deep breath, turned, and ducked under the water again. His hands fumbled a little in the icy water, but finally he had tied a secure knot.

Then he climbed back into the ferry, dripping wet and panting for breath. The cold had sapped even his great strength. At last he forced himself to sit up.

"Take me to shore," he said.

Silently, Charon began to pole the little boat toward shore. When the bottom scraped against rock, Hercules took the other end of the rope and jumped out.

Turning, the rope across his broad shoulders, he began to pull with all his strength. He felt the rope begin to stretch; the boulder didn't budge—until suddenly, and with a great sucking sound, it pulled free.

Instantly a whirlpool began to form in the center of the Styx. Water swirled downward faster and faster, and Charon and his boat began to drift toward it. The ferryman poled frantically toward shore and barely made it to safety.

The Styx was draining rapidly into the hole he had opened, Hercules saw. It fell a foot, then another foot, then another as he sat and watched. Finally the boulder began to appear; it was easily twenty feet in diameter. *I can't believe I moved it*, Hercules thought.

Still the water drained.

Throughout the day Hercules remained there, seated on the riverbank, watching the Styx drain away. It took hours, but at last the rush of water slowed to a dribble and the whirlpool vanished, replaced by a gaping hole perhaps fifteen feet across. The whole river was nothing more than a vast mud puddle now. Charon stood on the bank beside him, gazing passionlessly at his stranded boat.

"Well," Hercules said, rising and dusting himself off. "That's one more task done."

"Put the boulder back," Charon said.

"Ha! I was told to stop the Styx, not fill it back up. I'll leave that to you."

Turning, he strolled toward the palace, whistling happily. *Only two more tasks to go and Jason will be free.*

Hades was waiting for him at the gates. The god seemed unperturbed by his second success. He merely gave a nod, then said,

"For your next task, I again ask the nearly impossible:

You must find someone willing to take Jason's place here."

"How shall I do this?" Hercules asked. "Must I travel the world above searching until I find someone?"

"You know Jason's closest friends. You will visit them in their dreams tonight, and one of them must agree to give up his or her life in exchange for Jason's."

Hercules swallowed. This would be nearly impossible, he knew. Everyone loved life. Who would willingly give up his own, even to save a leader as great and good as Jason?

But neither could he give up without a fight. "Very well," he said. "I will find someone."

Hades smiled thinly. "Then come, nephew. A bed awaits you in the palace. As you dream, you will visit each of your friends in turn."

CHAPTER TWENTY-SEVEN

Theseus slept fitfully. Visions of dead men haunted him, Jason mostly, but also all the others whom he had known through his long life.

"*Theseus, old friend,*" a familiar voice whispered.

"Hercules?" he heard himself say.

"*I am in Hades, and I must now find someone to die in Jason's stead. Will you trade places with Jason, so he may live to find the Golden Fleece?*"

Theseus shuddered. He remembered his first trip to Hades, when he had been captured and chained to a rock outside the palace gates. When Hercules had rescued him, he had vowed never to make that mistake again . . . to cheat death as often as possible . . . to live a long and happy life in the world of the living. He couldn't give up that life, not even to save Jason.

"No . . ." he whispered. "I love life too much, Hercules. There must be another way . . ."

And then Hercules was gone, swept away like a whisper in a tempest, and once more Theseus faced dreams of the dead he had known . . .

Atalanta sat patiently waiting for Hercules to return, and as she waited she let her eyes close—*Just for a moment*, she thought.

Instantly she found herself dreaming of skeletons in armor chasing her down endless winding tunnels. She felt herself start to whimper in terror.

Then Hercules's voice broke into her panicked thoughts. "*I need you, Atalanta*," he seemed to be saying. "*You can save Jason . . .*"

"How?" she whispered.

"*Trade places with him. If you stay behind, Hades will set him free.*"

"No!" she cried. "I'm too young!"

"*Jason is younger still—*"

"It's not my time! I'm not ready!"

She blinked and found herself waiting beside Hylas, who slept. *Just a dream*, she told herself with a shudder. *I won't sleep again until Hercules gets back.*

Hylas dreamed of the *Argo*, of the glorious journey to find the Golden Fleece. *I can't believe I'm part of the crew*, he thought. *I wish my parents had lived to see me now.*

He heard a soft voice in the back of his mind say, "*You can still tell them, Hylas.*"

"Hercules?"

"*Listen well, young friend: I must find someone to take Jason's place in Hades for him to live again. Will you join me at the dark god's palace? Will you made this sacrifice, so Jason can live?*"

Hylas gulped. "You're talking about killing me?"

"It will be painless . . ."

"No—no!"

Gasping, Hylas sat up, suddenly awake. He shuddered. *I'm not ready to die!* he thought. *I like Jason, and I'll fight for him, and I'll follow him to the very gates of Hades, but I won't lie down and give up my life without a struggle.*

"Bad dream?" Atalanta asked.

He shuddered again, then gave a nod. "Yes."

"We're too close to the underworld," Atalanta said. "That must be the cause. I had a nightmare, too."

One by one Hercules visited the various Argonauts in their sleep, whispering of his mission. As he expected, not a single man would give up his life in exchange for Jason's. *It isn't fair,* he realized. *It's one thing to die in combat, fighting for a cause you believe in. It's another thing entirely to lie down and die so someone else can live.*

Despairing, Hercules rose from the bed Hades's servants had provided for him. The small sleeping chamber reminded him of a prison cell more than anything else. He took a deep breath, then went out to find his uncle.

Servants directed him to the gardens in the center of the palace. He found his way there, but it seemed an even gloomier place than he had ever dreamed possible: leafless trees, flowerbeds filled with brittle, thorny stems, dusty soil. Hades sat on a bench in the center of the dead garden, staring into a small dry fountain.

"This place was beautiful, once," Hades said softly. "I had my servants bring growing things from the world above to cheer me up."

"What happened?"

"They died. Everything here dies." Hades glanced over at him. "Did you find someone to take Jason's place?"

"Not among his friends and comrades above."

Hades smiled thinly. "Then you have failed. Return to

the mortal world, Hercules. Do not trouble me again."

"Not so fast!" Hercules found his heart pounding wildly in his chest. He swallowed and took a step forward. "You said I must find someone willing to take Jason's place. *I* will do it."

"You!" Hades looked surprised. Then he laughed. "How can a demigod die? No, Hercules, you will not do."

"You did not say someone had to die." Hercules took a step forward. "You said someone had to stay in Jason's place. Alive or dead, it matters not. I *will* stay. And you *will* honor our bargain."

Hades folded his arms and glared. "Very well. And *you* will honor our bargain as well."

The god of death stood, and suddenly he towered over Hercules like a man over an ant. The walls of the palace swept back, and the two of them stood at the edge of a vast plain. Yellow grass, tall and ripe for mowing, rippled faintly at an unseen breeze. It stretched as far as the eyes could see in all directions.

"Behold the Elysian Fields," Hades proclaimed. "I want to see them mowed within one day—that is your fourth and final labor!"

Hercules gaped. "Impossible!" he said. "They are too vast to *ever* be mowed!"

CHAPTER TWENTY-EIGHT

As Hercules raised his scythe and prepared to start cutting the grass in the Elysian Fields, a huge roar filled the air overhead. Hercules gaped up as the roof of Hades began to split. Brilliant white light poured through. At its heart sat a machine of some kind . . . a golden chariot without horses, he finally realized. It began to descend from the heavens.

And riding in that chariot—

"Father!" Hercules cried.

Zeus beamed proudly down on him. His eyes, his blinding white robes, his long curled beard and rich mane of hair—there could be no mistaking the king of the gods.

"Why are you in Hades?" Zeus demanded of him, voice rolling like thunder. "You are living. No son of mine should be here, in this dark and dismal place!"

"I have come to save a man who did not deserve to

die," Hercules said, holding his head up. "He perished because I abandoned him when he needed me most. For him to be restored, I must take his place here."

"I will intercede on your behalf," Zeus said.

"No, Father, I made a bargain with Uncle Hades. The Elysian Fields must be cut by this hour tomorrow for Jason to be free."

"Hmm." Zeus turned his dark eyes toward the king of the underworld. "Tell me, son, did this bargain prohibit you from getting help?"

"No . . ." Hercules said.

"Then I shall use my thunderbolts. They will make short work of the grass . . . *and everything else!*"

"No, no," Hades said quickly, stepping forward. "Brother—please, just take Hercules back to the lands of the living with you! As far as I am concerned, our deal is done."

Hercules set his feet stubbornly. "We made a bargain and I will stick to it," he said. He saw the tide had turned in his favor. The last thing Hades wanted was thunderbolts blasting through his dark realm. "Give me the first one, Father. Perhaps we can be done by supper!"

Zeus chuckled and reached down into his chariot.

"Wait!" Hades cried. "Let us make a *new* agreement, then!"

Hercules feigned puzzlement. "A new agreement, Uncle?"

"Yes . . . go, and you can have all the Argonauts who have been lost!"

Zeus smiled and nodded. "That sounds better," he said.

Hercules said, "And Atalanta and Hylas, who wait for me now by the gates to Hades? You will see them returned safely as well?"

"Yes—anything—just go!"

"Very well, I agree to your bargain!" Hercules cried. He threw down his scythe and grasped his uncle's cold hand to seal their agreement, grinning proudly.

"Come, Hercules," Zeus said.

Hercules ran to his father's chariot-machine and climbed inside. "Send all my friends back to the *Argo*, Uncle. I will meet them there!"

Grumbling, Hades turned his back on them and stalked away.

"Well done!" Zeus threw back his head and laughed boisterously.

"Thank you, Father."

Then the machine began to rise up into the air again, making huge creaking and grinding sounds, and the ceiling of the underworld approached. It peeled back before them, parting like water before a ship, and soon they burst out into daylight, heading up—up—up—into the heavens and across the land.

Hercules leaned out and stared at the land far below. Lush green forests, patchwork farms, and strange seas rushed past. He saw unfamiliar lands, towns and cities and seaports bustling with activity, valleys and mountains and all in between.

At last they began to circle downward. With a clatter, the chariot-machine landed atop a small island. Hercules could see the *Argo*'s masts sticking up over the crest—he had returned to the place where Theseus and his other friends waited.

"Thank you again, Father," he said softly. "I will make a great sacrifice to you when this quest is done."

Zeus laughed mightily, then his machine rose once more into the air and vanished into the heavens as quickly as it had come. Feeling a little dazed, Hercules stared up at the heavens after him for a long time. Everything had moved so quickly. And it had turned out better than he ever could have hoped.

"*So,*" a familiar man's voice said behind him, "You couldn't get along without me, huh?"

Hercules whirled. "Jason—"

Prince Jason stood there, dressed in the armor in which he had been buried, looking none the worse for having died. He stepped forward and slapped Hercules on the back.

"Thank you, friend," Jason said. "Now, let's get to camp and see what Theseus has been up to during our absence."

There was mad celebration in camp when Jason and Hercules strolled in. Theseus ran up to them, crying in happiness, and embraced them both. He wept with joy.

"I wondered if I would ever see you again!" he kept saying to them both.

"It was difficult," Hercules said, "but I couldn't have done it without help."

Theseus's expression changed to one of deep mourning. "We will remember those you lost along the way," he promised.

"Do you mean Atalanta and Hylas?"

"Yes—aren't they dead?"

"No. At least, I don't think so. They should be here soon."

Theseus's grin returned and grew even larger. "A feast, then!" he shouted. "A feast in honor of Hercules, the greatest warrior the world has ever seen! And Prince Jason, returned from the land of the dead!"

Everyone took up the shout for a feast, and half a dozen men hurried to unload extra provisions from the ship. Wine, dried fruits and meats, and plenty more—Hercules knew it would be a night to remember.

In all, eleven Argonauts had died thus far on the voyage, seven of them at the hands of the black centaur and his band. As the day wore on, first one then another then another strolled into camp. Some looked dazed. Some looked elated. Some looked merely confused, as though they had awakened from a bad dream to find the world set right once more.

When Atalanta and Hylas arrived, though, the feast had well begun. Atalanta folded her hands and stared at the laughing, shouting, eating, dancing, singing, and general wild reverie around her.

"Isn't that just like him," she muttered. "Figures he'd start the victory celebration without us!"

"Don't be silly!" Hercules said from behind her. "Of course I waited for you."

She turned to find him standing behind her with a bowl of wine in each hand. She took one and drained it immediately. Her stay in Hades—or just outside—had left her quite parched, she found.

"It just wouldn't be the same without you," Hercules went on. "You know I couldn't start our victory celebration without you. Come on, it's time for dancing!"

He linked his arm with hers and led her forward, to where lines of dancers pranced up and back to the beat of drums and lyres and voices raised in song.

Atalanta grinned happily. Yes, she thought, this was their celebration. To have ventured to the edge of Hades and returned—this was an adventure which bards would long tell.

CHAPTER TWENTY-NINE

Réas and Emeras—who had returned to life with the rest of the formerly dead Argonauts—protested most strongly of all when Jason announced his plans to continue the quest for the Golden Fleece without tracking down Koremos.

"You cannot let that evil continue!" Emeras said. "He will seek us out again, and next time he might well succeed in taking the *Argo*!"

Jason looked at each man's face around him. He saw anger, outrage, and determination as strong as stone in each man's eyes.

"Very well," he said. It seemed the decision had already been made. And, truth to tell, he felt the same way in his heart. "We will seek Koremos first, and only once his blood has darkened the Earth shall we continue."

Everyone began to cheer.

"Bring out your weapons," Jason commanded. "We will go ashore at once!"

The crew moved with the speed of the North Wind, loading the *Argo*, and soon they had the oars unshipped and began to row. They went around the little island, anchored twenty yards out, and began to break out the small boats.

Hercules found himself on oar duty again, thanks to his great strength, but he did not mind. If anything, he looked forward to the coming battle with even more anticipation than usual. *We have old scores to settle, Koremos*, he thought. *This will be the final reckoning*.

They landed their boats on the broad, sandy beach. Fifty-eight men in full battle armor, with weapons ready, with shields held high, marched up the steep cliffs to where Koremos had launched his attack.

Réas remembered the way they had dragged him, and he led the way straight to their camp. Unfortunately, they found it deserted.

Hercules crossed to the campfire and bent to touch the ashes. Cold—the centaur had not been here for at least a day.

Atalanta joined him as the others began to mill about, searching for clues. "Maybe Jason was right," she said. "Perhaps we should let Keremos go and get on with the quest. We have wasted a lot of time on him."

Hercules shook his head. "A second chance like the one we gave Captain Xeor is one thing. But Koremos has had more chances than he deserved. He grows bolder by the day."

"Still—"

An arrow whizzed past, catching her arm and spinning her around. More arrows flew—coming from all sides at once—and the Argonauts began to take cover, shouting warnings and drawing their weapons.

Hercules pulled Atalanta to the ground and shielded her body while he checked her wound. It didn't look serious—the arrow had grazed her, drawing blood and catching in her clothing. He snapped it in half and disentangled it.

"Just a scratch," he announced with a laugh.

"Don't sound so disappointed! I'm not out of this fight yet, Hercules—and I'm going to kill twice as many of them as you!"

"In your dreams!"

Hercules leaped to his feet, grabbed his spear, and turned in time to face the first wave of attackers. Men in mismatched armor and carrying every sort of weapon imaginable, from spears to swords to clubs, sprang from the underbrush. Roaring a battle cry, Hercules leaped forward, spear thrusting, and caught the nearest attacker in the chest. He died before he hit the ground.

Grimacing, Atalanta climbed to her feet. "Where's my bow?" she demanded. Then: "You stepped on it! That's cheating, Hercules!"

"Sorry!" Hercules shrugged apologetically. "If you want to back out and let me protect you . . ."

"Ha!" She pried the sword from the bandit's hand. "Watch your back!"

Hercules wheeled in time to see a huge man—nearly a head taller than himself—lumbering toward him.

"Lorron crush!" the giant announced.

"Oh?" Hercules jeered back. He cast his own spear aside and leaped forward, hands out.

They locked arms. Hercules's feet slid on loose stones for a second and he tumbled backward, with Lorron on top. The giant closed meaty hands around Hercules's throat.

Hercules found his air suddenly cut off and ground his teeth together. This fellow was strong—but not strong enough. Gripping Lorron's wrists, he pushed them back inch by inch. Suddenly he could breathe again and he took a couple of deep breaths.

Lorron's face purpled. He strained with all his might, but could not break free of Hercules's grasp.

"Now," Hercules growled, "*Hercules* crush!"

He suddenly released his opponent. As Lorron fell on top of him with an unexpected gasp, Hercules wrapped his arms around the man's back, locked his hands around his own wrists, and squeezed with all his might.

Something snapped in Lorron's spine. His face went red, then white, and his eyes rolled back. Drooling, he went limp.

Hercules pushed the body aside and rolled to his feet.

The battle was nearly over, he saw. This time, without surprise on their side, the bandits had been cut to pieces. Most of them lay dead or dying. To the left, a ring of ten men and Atalanta had surrounded Koremos. The black centaur bled from dozens of spear cuts on his back and haunches. He kept rearing back and striking out with his front hooves, trying to knock a hole in their circle to escape. But Theseus, Jason, Orestes, Atalanta, and the others held him at bay.

Hercules found his own spear, grabbed it, and hurried over. This was what he had been waiting for.

"Hold there!" he called, joining them. "I have an old score to settle with Koremos."

Koremos sneered. "Of course, a demigod has to protect the poor weak men. I should have known they couldn't fight their own battles. Why else would they have you along."

Hercules bristled.

Jason stepped forward. "My score with Koremos may

not be as old as yours, but surely my death takes precedence."

Koremos laughed at him. "Run and hide behind Hercules, little man. You need his protection."

Hercules said, "He's trying to goad you into fighting him. You are no match for a centaur."

"Nonsense." Jason hefted his spear. "I'm as good a thrower as anyone here."

As if to prove his point, in one swift and unexpected motion, he threw his spear at Koremos. The bronze tip struck the centaur dead center in the chest, burying itself deep in bone and flesh.

Koremos had been taken completely by surprise. It was a cold, unexpected move, and it shocked Hercules.

"You are not a man, to be given the honors due a warrior," Jason announced to the stunned centaur.

Koremos sank to his four knees. Blood poured from his chest wound, and when he opened his mouth to speak, more blood poured from his lips.

"You are a criminal. A murderer. A thief." Jason drew his sword and stepped forward. "I sentence you to die as I myself died—with a sudden, swift, unexpected blow. The dishonor is yours."

He raised his sword and, in one swing, decapitated the centaur. Tangling his fingers in Koremos's hair, he raised the head high and shouted, "No more will Koremos plague this land!"

The few remaining bandits threw down their weapons and fled. A few Argonauts gave halfhearted chase, but soon returned.

"What shall we do with them?" Hercules asked, looking around at the bodies.

"Bury them," Theseus announced. "Bury them with all due ceremony. They will be reborn, and perhaps their next lives will be better."

Jason nodded. "Do it," he said. "One large grave will suffice."

They spent the rest of the day burying Koremos and his men. Theseus went to each body in turn, placing a coin in each mouth so they would be able to pay Charon to ferry them across the Styx. Grimly the Argonauts worked, but at last the task was done.

Silently they headed back toward the Argo. Hercules realized Hylas was beside him and looked at the lad.

"Yes?"

Hylas licked his lips. "I don't understand," he said. "Why didn't Jason face Koremos in single combat? Wouldn't that have been the honorable thing to do?"

"Jason would have died," Hercules said flatly.

"But—"

"No. Koremos knew it. Jason knew it." He shrugged. "Perhaps it wasn't the best path, but in the end Jason was right. Koremos had no honor. He deserved to die by whatever means necessary. We have a quest to finish . . . and Jason must win his throne to save his own people. That's why he's a prince. He will always have hard decisions to make."

"Oh." Hylas looked away, and Hercules could tell it still troubled him.

Hercules grinned. "Look at it this way. We won. Now it's time to celebrate, right?"

Hylas grinned. "Right!"

They reached the beach in time to hear Jason proclaiming a day of feasting and games in honor of their victory. Everyone cheered, especially when Jason promised a pound of gold to the winner of the wrestling competition.

"Hmm." Hercules scratched his chin. "I could use that gold. What do you think my odds are this time?"

"Slim to none," Atalanta said, joining him. "I saw how

easily Jason beat you last time. He wouldn't put up such a sum unless he planned to win it back himself!"

"We'll see about that!" Hercules said, striding forward confidently. "I challenge all comers! That gold will be mine! You won't trick me out of it this time!"

Everyone began to laugh, and Hercules joined in. It felt good to have their company whole again, he thought. With Koremos gone, with the gods on their side, what more could possibly stand between them and the Golden Fleece?

"Form a circle," Jason called. He began to strip off his armor, grinning. "I will wrestle Hercules first!"

"I told you!" Atalanta whispered to him. "Watch yourself, Hercules! He's tricky!"

"Not this time. I'm ready for him!"

He threw off his lion skin and strode confidently into the ring. And ten seconds later found himself landing flat on his back, as Jason did an unexpected backflip that sent him flying out of the circle. Hercules groaned. "Not again!"

Laughing, Jason dusted the sand from his arms and back. "Charon taught me that," he said.

Grumbling good-naturedly, Hercules climbed to his feet.

"All right," he said. "You beat me this time. But I'm going to be ready for you the next time!"

Everyone began to laugh, and Orestes stepped forward to have a go at winning Jason's gold.